'A brilliant, thought-provoking, well-crafted tale that
deserves the widest possible circulation.'
Rev Canon J John

'An intriguing and chilling premise makes *The Key Of All
Unknown* a page-turner with a highly original protagonist.'
Howard Linskey, author of No Name Lane *and*
Behind Dead Eyes *(Penguin)*

For Gemma

Every blessing,

The key *of*
all unknown

K A Hitchins

K A Hitchins

instant
ap☐stle

First published in Great Britain by Instant Apostle, 2016.

Instant Apostle

The Barn
1 Watford House Lane
Watford
Herts
WD17 1BJ

British Library Cataloguing-in-Publication Data

A catalogue record for this book is available from the British Library

This book and all other Instant Apostle books are available from Instant Apostle:

Website: www.instantapostle.com
Email: info@instantapostle.com

ISBN 978-1-909728-56-1

Printed in Great Britain by Clays Ltd, St Ives plc

For Elizabeth and Harrison
Don't leave without the Key

Thou met'st with things dying, I with things new-born.
(Shepherd, Act 3, Scene 3, lines 106-107, *The Winter's Tale*,
William Shakespeare)

Acknowledgements

With thanks to my family, for their continued love, support and encouragement, and to Instant Apostle for taking the risk and offering me a contract before I was a quarter way through the first draft. I'm especially grateful to my editors, Sheila Jacobs and Nicki Copeland, for their help in knocking my manuscript into shape.

I am indebted to my beta readers for their invaluable feedback: Doug Hewitt, Elizabeth Rutt, Anne Shearer, Chris Short, Graham Weller and Elizabeth Weller. I believe this is a better book for their input. Thanks also to members of THE Bookclub Facebook group who checked the medical information contained in this story, in particular Shushmita Chakrabati who really went the extra mile.

I am grateful to the BeauSandVer Writers' group, who gave vital critical feedback during the writing process.

Tribute must also be paid to the medical staff at Watford General Hospital who cared for me when I was ill, and without whom this book would not have been finished.

Prologue

We lie next to each other on the grass, holding hands. The late afternoon – plump and golden as a pear – is thick with pollen. I watch the shadow of the sycamore tree as it lengthens over the grass. Long blades prickle the back of my legs. Diaphanous creatures dance above our heads in a wild frenzy, unaware of the frosts that will descend like Armageddon in a few months' time. I know I'll be covered with unsightly bites tomorrow, but I'm willing to pay the price.

'So... do you feel like an accident of the universe today?' he asks.

'Not an accident. An outcome, perhaps.'

'That can't explain what we're feeling. What I'm feeling. Tilda...'

'It's a biochemical process.'

'No higher meaning?'

'It means something to me. Isn't that enough?'

Our picnic plates are crawling with ants. Michael waves away a drowsy wasp and packs the remains of the food and the rubbish into his rucksack. I lie completely still to calm the trembling under my skin, caught between magic and logic. It's just the ticking of my biological clock.

The heat is leaching from the day, the happiest of my life, and for the first time I sense autumn in the air. The shadow from the tree is creeping over me like a bruise, a dark longing, slow, inexorable. I can't bear to leave this place, can't bear to stay. I watch as he cleans his sunglasses on the bottom of his T-shirt. His face is strangely naked without them; he has two red pinch-marks at the top of his nose.

'Let's go,' he says.

'Go where?'

'Back to my place, of course.'

He pulls me up when he sees me shiver, but I'm not cold. He throws his arm across my shoulders as we walk down the hill towards the descending sun. I squint up at him, dazzled by the intensity of his gaze. We are drenched in liquid light. My eyes are watering. I close them against the brilliance, and when I open them I'm plunged into darkness.

Chapter 1

The darkness is absolute. It must be the middle of the night. My heart lurches with disappointment. I've been dreaming, dreaming of Michael. I lie quite still on smooth sheets, resisting the resurrection of consciousness like a diver surfacing, careful of the pain that's waiting if I rise too fast.

It was so real. Realer than real. How did the sunlight glow so brightly in my sleeping mind? A warm, fetid smell still lingers in my nostrils. The scrape of a grasshopper synchronises with the pulse of blood in my ears. If I concentrate, perhaps I can fall back into that warm evening where Michael swings his hand in mine and we buy a bottle of wine at the off-licence on the way to his flat. He will tell me he loves me and we will kiss on his sofa. I try to close my eyes and spirit myself back to sleep, but I've forgotten the knack, forgotten how to make my eyelids shut, forgotten if they are even open. Perhaps I'm still asleep.

Relax. Breathe deep. Ignore the pressure in my head. I see myself in his bedroom mirror, my hair tangled and full of grass. He laughs at his forehead, red and shiny from the sun. Have I crossed the border back into a dream or am I remembering something real? My head throbs. I don't think I can be asleep. Such pain belongs to the physical world.

Did I have too much to drink last night? I can't remember, but this is worse than any hangover I've had before. My mouth is dry and tastes of salt. A rasping pain prevents me from swallowing. Maybe I'm suffering from sunstroke, the curse of the pale-skinned. I reach for the water on my bedside table, but my arm won't respond. I'm paralysed with sleep.

Usually a chink of moonlight creeps between my bedroom curtains. Usually I hear a distant drone from the dual carriageway. My heart lurches upwards; a spasm of pain ripples down my ribs. This is not my room. These are not my sheets. They're too smooth and cool. I always sleep on brushed cotton. I strain to hear the sound of breathing at my side. Am I with him at last? Is he here beside me? A heartbeat. Silence. A silence more absolute than the darkness. The world wobbles. There is nobody with me and I don't know where I am. Something is very wrong.

Think! I must think. I need to work out where I am and what has happened. Was I with Michael last night, or was that a memory from an earlier time – or perhaps no memory at all, but a wish so strong that I dreamed we were together?

Dread has me by the throat. I want to go home but my arms and legs are not responding. Perhaps I've had some kind of stroke. Is that why the blood's pounding in my temples? Thoughts scatter in panic. It's ludicrous. I'm slim, fit, and relatively young. *Stay calm. Focus on the last thing I remember.* I retrace my steps, scrolling backwards. I reach a gap. A wall. A black hole. Frustration rises, hot like lava beneath the crust, searching for an escape. I need an expletive to release the pressure, but can't remember the expression. I'm lost in the spaces between the words, lying on a bed in the darkness.

Perhaps I've been drugged. That would explain the hyper-reality of my hallucination. I remember a newspaper article about Rohypnol, but I don't go to pubs on my own, and I'm inconspicuous in a crowd; I've never been the type to receive unwanted attention from strangers. So why can't I remember what happened last night? Panic sweeps through my body, faltering my heart. Pain oozes from my head, down my neck and into my chest, constricting my ribs so tightly I feel as though I'm being crushed in a vice. The grasshopper calls faster, more of a bleep than a chirrup, and I'm trapped in the key – high pitched and impersonal – and lost in the pain.

Footsteps. Someone's coming. A rectangle of light suddenly dazzles. From the corner of my half-open eyes, I see the silhouette of a man.

Who's there? Who are you?

The words resound in my mind; no sound comes from my lips. He approaches the bed, leans over, pulls open my eye and shines a torch directly into the pupil.

Where am I? What am I doing here? How did I get here? Don't hurt me! Please don't hurt me!

He fiddles with something behind my head. A tapping sound. More bleeps, lower in tone. Something warm and heavy stealing up my hand and inside my arm. My head is full of static.

Help me! Somebody help me! Please!

Small pricks of light sparkle before my eyes like stars on the night sky. No! No! I must fight this overwhelming terror… this suffocating blanket of darkness… I must stay awake… I will not let him… I need… I need… to know…

When I next wake, the room is lighter. Voices. Distant footsteps on hard flooring. I'm reassured that several people are nearby rather than the lone figure in the dark. My eyes are already half-open. Everything's blurry, but through my lashes I make out pale walls and a garish curtain half-drawn across the room. I'm in hospital.

An antiseptic smell mingles with the aftertaste of a succession of powerful dreams. Not dreams exactly, but muddled and arbitrary images which float through my mind like homesick ghosts. In the last one my flatmate, Kiki, is screaming. I don't understand what she's saying. She seems so close that I'm surprised she isn't here.

Hello? Can anybody hear me? Is anybody there? Again my thoughts are trapped inside.

A tube has been forced up my nose and down my oesophagus. This accounts for the dry soreness of my throat. I want to cough, but I can't. I want to gag, but can't gag either. Fear and claustrophobia swell like a swallowed scream, and for a few minutes I think I'm going to choke. I would pull the tube out if I could, but my arm won't respond to my command.

My head is hurting. I want to touch it where the pain is biting through my skull. I try to shift to ease the agony, but I can't move at all. My right leg, grossly fat, is raised in a hoist with a blue blanket tossed on top. Wires and bags and tubes dangle and entwine my bed like bindweed. A monitor emits a persistent beep. I feel the sting of an insect bite on the back of my hand.

A door pushes open with a suck of air. The curtain swishes aside. From the corner of my eye I glimpse a man with a stethoscope round his neck, followed by a man in a dark suit.

'As you can see, there's no improvement in her condition. In fact, the longer she remains like this, the worse the prognosis.' When he speaks the room turns cold and blue.

'Why are her arms strapped to her sides?'

'It's to stop her pulling at the tubes.'

'She's moving, then?'

'No. Not yet, at any rate. She's out of the medically induced coma, but so far there's been little change.'

'But her eyes are open, doctor.'

'We can't read too much into that at this stage. Unfortunately, she's not responding to outside stimuli.' Their words are distorted as though I am hearing them from under water.

The man in the dark suit steps nearer, bends, and stares into my eyes. His face is lined and sallow. Yesterday's stubble clings to his jaw. I try to pull back.

Excuse me. I can hear you. I am here, you know. They take no notice.

'People come out of comas,' he says, abruptly.

'She was in a coma last week because we put her in one. She's out of that now. We hoped to be able to decrease the intracranial pressure until the swelling came down. It's a way of lessening potential brain damage. If she were still in a coma, her eyes would be closed. She seems to be experiencing a sleep-wake cycle. It's called unresponsive wakefulness syndrome.'

'But she's looking right at me.' The sallow man gazes deeply into my eyes, searching. There are small flecks of gold around his pupils. They are kind eyes. I try to smile.

'Yes, but what you're seeing is partial arousal rather than true awareness. We used to call it a vegetative state.'

'A vegetable!' The man straightens up.

Please… please don't look away. I'm here. I'm struggling to breathe in, breathe out, do anything. I'm trying to remember how to speak.

'That's why I prefer the term "unresponsive wakefulness". There are less negative connotations.'

Help me! If you look at me again, you'll see I'm here. I strain to escape the prison I'm in, but my body is as stiff as iron bars.

'Her brainstem is uninjured,' the doctor continues. 'That's why she can breathe unaided. The lower, vegetative functions such as respiration and digestion are working normally. If she remains like this for a couple more weeks, however, the condition will be termed "persistent". After a year with no improvement, it will be classified as a permanent vegetative state.'

'I see.'

What's the matter with you? Why aren't you listening to me? Where's Michael?

'Do you know what happened? Her notes are sketchy,' the doctor enquires.

'I'll ask the questions, if you don't mind, sir.' The other man's tone is muscular, taut. 'And the blood tests? Was there any alcohol in her blood?'

There's movement at the bottom of the bed, the sound of pages turning. I assume the doctor has picked up my notes.

'A small amount. One glass of wine, perhaps.'

'Drugs?'

'No.'

'And in your medical opinion, have you seen anything inconsistent with an accidental fall? Anything to suggest something else?'

'Attempted suicide, you mean?'

Suicide? Why would I try to kill myself? Hasn't Michael told you? We love each other.

'Or murder.'

'You need a body for that, inspector.'

I want to scream at them to stop talking about me as if I'm not here. Their words are rising like bubbles, each one bursting upon my understanding with a sharp shock.

'Yes. You're right. I'm pre-empting the situation. Hypothetically speaking.'

I sense, rather than see, the doctor lean over the bed. I can't turn my head to see what he's doing, but his hands rest with a shriek on the side of my head.

'Difficult to say. She's received a traumatic brain injury consistent with a fall. Whether it was intentional or an accident is up to you to decide. She's had neurosurgery to dig some skull fragments out of her brain, so everything we're seeing here – the bruising and swelling around her face – is probably a result of the patch-up job.' His words fly like starlings round the room, scattering black feathers, squawking in the corners.

'So we've lost any forensics?'

'Probably. There have been a lot of people working on her. '

'So if a blunt instrument was involved...'

A blunt instrument! Rage and panic rise within me. I gag in terror.

'She's coughing,' the inspector says.

'Just an involuntary reaction to the feeding tube.'

Imbecile! When I can talk, I'll have you struck off. Have you even bothered to give me an MRI scan?

'The wound is healing. There might be microscopic particles in the skull but they'll be absorbed into her body. Would you like me to speak to the staff in A&E who treated her on arrival? They might have noticed something.'

'We'll do that, thank you, sir,' the inspector says, asserting his authority. He begins to pace back and forth across the room. He crosses my line of vision intermittently. 'As things stand, I'm unable to order a post-mortem or hold an inquest. You told me last week you didn't think she would survive. What do you make of her chances now?'

'Difficult to say. She may wake spontaneously within a few days or weeks. Her heart rate quickened unexpectedly last night, and my colleague sedated her lightly to prevent the risk of cardiac arrest. Chances of recovery depend on the extent of the injury and the patient's age. Younger patients do better. At 35, she has an average chance, but the longer she's in this state the more severe the resulting disabilities are likely to be. It's not something I'd say to her friends and relatives, of course, but between you and me, to all intents and purposes, Dr Matilda Moss is dead.'

Chapter 2

I'm dying! A lurch of gut-wrenching nausea. Cold, black fear like I've never experienced before crawls from the pit of my stomach and up the back of my neck like an infestation of lice. My lungs are being pressed like two overripe grapes. The edges of the room are sharp as razors, but the ceiling is shimmering overhead and making my head swim. I'm sure my heart's going to give out. I'm losing my mind. I'm going to black out again…

I'm not sure when the men left. Was it a few minutes ago, or hours, or days? Time and space no longer operate as distinct categories. I'm here, and I'm somewhere else as well. Sleep takes me by surprise. In a blink I'm adrift, dreaming of a siren wailing, reliving the rattle of steel on steel. A glint of metal, the smell of rubber. A band tightening on my arm. Then I'm awake; faces flick in and out of focus, noses too big, too close, their cheekbones receding into the distance. Voices echo loudly and then recede into a hiss of static, incomprehensible and elusively malign. Something very bad has happened. By the sounds of it, I've been in hospital for a while.

It's impossible to comprehend what the doctors are saying. Accident! Murder! Attempted suicide? Persistent vegetative state. Brainstem injury. Things like this are not supposed to happen. Images of broccoli sprouts and cauliflower brains hover over my bed. The crunch of white cabbage. A knife slicing through an onion, the delicate membranes slippery between pungent layers. But if my brainstem is my only functioning mental apparatus, how am I thinking? What are these images that scurry through the room, accompanied by arbitrary sensations – the random taste of asparagus, the smell of white spirit, the sound of Michael's throaty chuckle echoing along the hospital corridor, making my heart leap with anticipation, only to be flattened by despair when a couple of junior doctors walk past my door, laughing.

The drone of the hospital air conditioning scratches my eyes. The white tiles on the ceiling dance in a strange optical illusion. I endlessly count the bolts that hold them in place, unable to look away, until something in my brain suddenly decides to shut down with a small audible click of my eyelids, and I'm plunged into a dark monotony more tedious than the ceiling.

I'm waiting for something to happen, listening for my door to open, hearing the distant phone endlessly calling, but not calling for me. *Someone pick up the phone! I'm trying to think!*

Then someone comes. I'm washed and turned like a chicken in the oven, without ceremony.

What are you doing? You're hurting me. Please stop. Stop it now!

I realise in horror that I'm wearing incontinence pants. She changes my nappy and wipes my behind. I'm beyond mortification. Then my elbows are briskly basted with cream, each circular movement increasing the agonising constriction in my ribs until I think my heart will be crushed.

We're going to have a falling-out if you don't listen to me! I scream wordlessly at the nurse. *What did I ever do to you? I'm a human being. If I'm going to die, then let me die. Anything but this torture!*

Then, without a word, I'm abandoned again to a headache of white noise and the smell of antiseptic handwash.

I didn't mean it. I'm sorry. I don't want to die. Please come back.

My father comes and sits by my bed, stroking my hand. I can't move my eyes, which are fixed on the paisley curtain, but I sense the bulk of his body on the periphery. My brain is trying to compensate; the edge of the room appears fluid and translucent, as though I am looking through goggles.

He brings the smell of leather and mahogany. He tells me I have to fight. He says he loves me. I want him to kiss away my pain and make everything better again, but he doesn't have that power, and never had. He comes with music, his favourites. Mozart, which tastes of lemons, and Chopin, which tinges everything with gold. 'Mozart for the mind and Chopin for the soul,' he used to say when I was a child. I know what he's doing now. He's trying to unlock my prison, but he needs a different key.

A younger man with a square head arrives in a red mist. At first I can't recall his name, and then I realise he's my little brother.

'All right?' he mutters. 'Any news?'

He pulls up a chair next to Dad, who adjusts his own in the small space between the bed and the wall. The scrape of the legs on the floor releases a smell of bleach. Now I can see them both. Dad looks older and smaller than I remember. Oscar is wearing a two-day stubble.

'No... but I saw the doctor earlier.'

'What did he say?'

'Nothing good.'

My heart sinks. The room contracts. Suddenly I'm seeing them from far away, as though from the end of a dark tunnel.

'They've removed the straps. That's a good sign, isn't it?'

'I don't know, son. I think it means they're not expecting her to move.'

'What about the police? Have they been in touch?'

I strain to hear Dad's reply.

'Inspector Lake phoned yesterday, asking more questions. I told him again she would never try to kill herself. She had no reason. She was happy.'

'Was she? Pushing 40 with no man, no kiddies, just a cat and a mad flatmate?'

Is that how you see me, Oscar?

'She had a career. She was earning good money,' Dad replies.

Stop talking about me in the past tense!

'There's no need to rub it in.' Oscar's tone is petulant.

'I didn't mean that. You're completely different people. She enjoyed working hard.'

'And me?'

'You play hard instead... I'm not comparing you –'

'No. Just judging me.'

'Stop it, Oscar.' The room falls silent.

'Did you know she refused to back my nightclub idea?'

Because you hadn't costed it properly or researched the legal position of setting up a nightclub in the middle of a retail park.

'For once, can everything *not* be about you? Your sister's lying here with a fractured skull, five broken ribs, internal injuries and a smashed-up leg. I don't want to argue with you. She might be able to hear us.'

Quick footsteps cross the floor. The atmosphere changes.

'How's she doing, nurse?' Dad asks.

'As well as can be expected. She's comfortable.' I recognise the woman's voice, though I can't remember having heard her speak before. She's probably been in my room many times when I've been sleeping, leaving a trail in my subconscious.

'Comfortable!' Oscar cries.

'As far as we can tell.'

'And how far is that? Nobody seems to be able to give us any idea when she might wake up.'

'These things take time. There are no guarantees.'

'We know that, don't we, Oscar? It's just so hard, nurse.' I think my father is crying.

'We're doing everything we can, Mr Moss.'

'Any chance of a coffee?' Oscar asks.

'The café's on the ground floor. Just take the lift down and turn right.'

He swears and flounces out of the room in a crackle of electricity. The red haze instantly vanishes.

'I'm sorry… Take no notice of him. He's very upset about his sister.'

'That's understandable.'

'Do you think she knows I'm here?'

'I'm afraid I couldn't say.'

'Do you think she can hear us?'

Of course I can hear you.

'You never know. I had one last year who smiled when her hair was brushed.'

'Perhaps I should try that. Can I?'

'Maybe when her wound has healed some more.'

'Yes… when it's healed. I'll do that. I'll bring a brush.'

A buzz of static and the scene changes, as if I've flicked channels on the remote control. Although I can't see out of the window, I sense night is falling. The electric lights send out a high-pitched hum which grazes my spine. Kiki is sitting next to me, her chair close. She smells of milk.

'Hello, Tilda. It's me. Kiki. Just stopped by to see how you are. I hope you can hear me. You look a bit better. Better than when… you know…'

No! I don't know. Tell me!

'This is awkward, Tills. I feel a bit silly, but the doctors said we should talk to you. Pretend as if you can hear… so… Everyone's been asking after you at work. Oh! I brought you some get-well cards. This one's from the accounts department. Everyone's signed it. Colin said, "Congratulations! You're officially sick. Enjoy the break." He's an idiot. He writes that in all the cards. I don't think he knows what happened...'

I don't know what happened.

'This one's from Mrs Squires, next door.' She thrusts a cardboard rectangle in front of my face. It's too close for me to focus, but there's a blur of colour in the centre of the white. Probably a picture of flowers. 'She says, "You are in my prayers, dear Tilda. Come back to us soon. Lots of love, Doreen." Samantha sends her love, but there's no card. Mean cow.'

She stands up and reaches past my head to place the cards on my bedside table, out of my eyeline. I hear her moving them about. I imagine she's arranging them in height order. That's the kind of thing Kiki does.

'I brought you some grapes. I don't know what I was thinking, really. You've still got that thing up your nose.' Plastic crackles. 'You don't mind me eating a few, do you? The police have been round. I'm glad I did that spring clean the other week, otherwise I'd have been mortified when they poked around the bathroom. They've been going through your things. I put it all back for you, your clothes and toiletries and stuff. It's horrible, thinking strangers have been touching your knickety-knacks. They were asking questions about your friends. The places you like to go. Whether you were worried about anything. I don't think they've got a clue about what happened... You weren't depressed, were you? I wish I hadn't gone out that night. Perhaps if I'd come straight home from work, we could have talked things through. You wouldn't have been alone. It wasn't anything I did, was it? What did happen, Tills?'

And then she's sobbing, begging me to wake up. She says she's fed the cat and tells me I'm a little fighter. And still Michael doesn't come.

I know I'm mortal – in theory, at least. I've spent enough of my time studying the processes of life and death to understand the realities. The heat from my heart is finite. Like the sun it will eventually run out of energy and will cool to the temperature of surrounding space in an irreversible thermodynamic process: hot to cold, living past to dead future. I've borne this knowledge calmly. I've had lots of distractions – work, friends, music, love – to blind me to the inevitability of death. Now I'm panicked. It's the difference between knowing it will happen in some unimaginably distant future and knowing it could happen today.

Why me? Stupid to ask when there's no one to answer. It's part of the random unfairness of life. I know in many ways I've been born into privilege – living in a European democracy, receiving a good education, free healthcare, having food on the table, a roof over my head, a career. When most of the population of the world live a more difficult life, why *not* me?

But to leave now is unthinkable. My frozen heart has only just awoken. I've waited 35 years for love, and I'm not going to have it snatched away from me now. I must survive. For him. For us. I *will* come out of this intact. I can't leave with nothing to show for my life – no child or husband to grieve for me, no important scientific breakthrough to immortalise my name.

I'm worried about Michael. Does he know I'm in hospital? Would anyone have told him? No one knows about us or how we feel about each other, this sacred thing so terrible and yet so beautiful. We kept the outside world at bay – for professional reasons, he said. And I for one didn't want my private life to be a curiosity or the object of crude office innuendo.

He would want to be with me now. I know it. Surely he can sense that I'm hurt and alone. The connection between us is so powerful that a sense of alarm *must* be agitating at his heart. My thoughts stutter to a stop. What if we were in an accident together? What if he's lying injured in another part of the hospital, wondering why I haven't come to him? What if? What if? But I can't go there. If anything ever happened to him, I couldn't go on... there would be no point... no meaning. I must fix a memory of him as a talisman, his solidity, his riotous stories, his hand in mine.

The pain in my body is overwhelming, but the mental anguish is worse. I can't even cry. Without tears, how can I cleanse myself of despair? It sits like a boulder on my chest, pushing me under. I know I'm in deep water. Surely I'm the victim of some horrible practical joke. But no one's laughing. Nobody's jumping out from behind the curtain with a video camera, shouting, 'Gotcha!'

I watch the medical staff. The consultant with his entourage of students. *Pompous quack!* I scream silently, furious at his misdiagnosis. The nurses, the healthcare assistants. Why can't they see I'm still here, trapped inside my body? I'm just a lump of meat to them. Washed briskly, turned regularly, talked over, ignored. I glower between the slits my eyelids make, willing someone to look my way, urging my thoughts to somehow jump the synapse between my crushed head and their incompetent, self-important skulls.

There's a man who visits my room to sweep the floor and clean the washbasin. His presence touches my thoughts with the green of the sea. He's with me now, in the corner of my eye, wiping the small sink in the corner of the room. His movements are slow and casual. He hums a tune I've heard before, an old-fashioned hymn from my childhood. When he's finished, he approaches the bed.

'It's me again. Just Claude come to clean up, innit.' His teeth are white as fresh tombstones. 'Yah quite a celebrity, Doctar Matilda Moss. First the local papers. Now you in the big news. "Top scientist mysteriously injured." Says you was gonna give a big speech somewheres or other. That policeman came back askin' who's been visitin'. The nurses are keepin' a list now. Those that come and those that don't.'

He leans closer. I realise with a lurch of fear and disgust that I can do nothing to stop him touching me. He lifts my fingers to his lips. I see a cannula in the back of my hand. Not an insect bite after all.

'*You* know what happened, don'tcha? Keeping quiet until you're ready to wake up just to keep them all guessin', is that it?'

I don't know anything!

'Hee hee. Tell your Uncle Claude.' He bends close so his ear is by my mouth. 'What's that you say?' His tight grey curls brush my nose and upper lip. 'Cat got your tongue? Don't be like that. You're stuck in there for a reason, girlie. I know it! You know it! The Big Cheese ain't lettin' you go so easily.'

The Big Cheese. I ask you!

'Why's that, do ya think? There must be somethin' for you still to do! God can see you, even tho' there's just a little flicker left. I betcha wished you'd paid Him more mind when you could've. That's the trouble with peoples. They just carry on with them busyness, not looking right nor left. God has a big chuckle when He hears the plans we be making 'cos He knows the truth of it. Yeah! He knowed all along this bed was waiting for you. You better start talkin' to Him. He knows more than these doctars. Ain't that the truth! Them doctars and nurses knows nothink!'

Religious crackpot!

He turns my hand over, strokes my fingers. His lips are dry on my palm. I can't believe he's kissing my skin. I'm at his mercy. I no longer own the body I'm in. I can't move. I can't scream for help. Where's the key to unlock my mouth? It must be here somewhere in the handbag of my mind. I rummage through the pockets and dark corners, where I stumble across the face of my mother, unaccountably young, laughing. Then Betsy, stretching out her claws. Oscar with his head in his hands, crying. My father begging me to wake up, it's time for school. I try to grasp another fleeting image, but it's just out of reach. Like a word on the tip of my tongue, it dances away, teasing, elusive.

The door swings open with a thud.

'What are you doing?' a woman asks sharply. Claude drops my hand and turns to face her.

'Just checkin' she's still here, innit.'

'She's hardly likely to go anywhere.'

'I'm talking about her spirit. I'm guessin' she's bored, stuck here all day. I was fillin' her in on the news in the papers.'

'She can't hear you.'

'I talks to aaallll the patients, whether they're awake or asleep. I talk to my plants. I talk to my vegetables. I talk to myself. Don'tcha know talkin' is good for the soul?'

'You're wasting your breath with this one. If I had my way, I'd switch her off. There's not enough money for kiddies with cancer, let alone keeping alive someone who's brain-dead and wanted to end it all anyway. Get on with your work. A patient's been sick in the corridor outside the third-floor toilets. Mop it up and don't let me catch you wasting time again.'

'She's here. I can feel it. She's restless.'

Hope and terror grip my heart. He knows I'm still alive, trapped inside a body as unyielding and still as a sarcophagus. Surely that's good? But who will believe him? He's just a cleaner; the doctors and nurses are supposed to be the experts. And I'm helpless to scream or push him away if he chooses to touch me again.

He shuffles to the door. 'See you later, procrastinator,' he calls from a distance in a sing-song voice. I'm not sure if he is talking to me or the nurse.

31

I hope he stays away. I don't need to hear any of his rubbish. People die and stay dead. There's nothing else. And yet... and yet... where am I now? How am I conscious of my surroundings? My head is smashed and my cognitive functions have apparently been destroyed. Am I in hell? Alive but cut off from everyone, cut off from Michael? Is Claude right? Am I still here for a purpose? Is there something I must do?

The absurdity of the question brings me back to my senses. There is no purpose to any of this. I refuse to compromise my rationality at the first superstitious nonsense thrown my way. He's a cleaner, for goodness' sake!

I've always used my intellect to work my way out of difficulties. My brilliant mind, as Michael likes to call it, isn't working as it should. I can't remember how I came to be lying on this bed like a squashed insect. I'm struggling to differentiate the real from the unreal, sights from sounds, smells from feelings. Everything is a muddle. But I must know the truth. It's buried deep within. I need to find the key that will unlock the door. All I have to work with are my thoughts, my memories and my beliefs. Although they're dissolving like reactants in a test tube, I have to try. There's no other option. I will lay out the pieces methodically. The edges, the corners, the large undifferentiated slabs of colour. Put them together until the picture becomes clearer and the puzzle is complete. I need to know what happened. I want to know who's to blame.

Chapter 3

I concentrate. My brain is running simultaneous programs. Memories and dreams are flowing through me in one undifferentiated stream; it's difficult to tell what's real and what's a fantasy. Some images emerge vivid as jewels, precision-cut, minute and glittering. Some are flat and colourless as a shadow, or a mist, or a murmur of voices.

I have too many windows open. I close them down, one by one, until the screen is blank. I need to remember what happened. That's the key to my recovery and the key to my sanity. I enter his name and roll it round my mind, an invocation: *Michael, Michael, Michael.* I conjure his face and summon the incense of his body and the feel of his fingers on my skin. I press enter. I step into the past.

I met him at a conference a year ago. I was the keynote speaker. He was a delegate. He waylaid me in the lobby.

'Tell me, Dr Moss, I'm fascinated. What makes you the woman you are today?'

I was taken aback. He was a wide-shouldered, bear-like man, with dark eyes, a beard and grizzled, receding hair. If he had been slimmer, better-looking, clean-shaven, I would have put him in his place immediately. I was in the habit of shunning the handsome ones, fearing the comparison and the pity, afraid for my heart. Best to get my rejection in first.

'Ambition. Hard work... Luck.'

'And a brilliant mind.'

'I'm sorry. Do I know you?'

He introduced himself as the new marketing manager for the company that supplied my lab with scientific compounds and instruments. We shook hands. I felt it immediately. A charge. A connection. It didn't matter that he was overweight and a decade older than me. I was unexpectedly self-conscious in my dark trouser suit, knowing my legs were a little too short and my chest a little too flat to be attractive.

I can't remember how he managed to persuade me to have dinner with him that evening, but he has a knack of getting his own way while making other people believe they're getting theirs. He limped slightly as he escorted me to my chair. He told me he had wrenched his knee playing squash at the weekend. His suit was expensive, but he avoided the pervasive slickness of the marketing professional by teaming it with a flamboyant tie. A crumpled handkerchief waved from his top pocket.

We talked about his recent move from London. He was divorced, which I suppose was to be expected of a single man his age. I guessed he had been fleeced in the settlement because he was renting a small apartment in a dingy part of Newcastle – just until he got settled into the area. He had no children.

'It wasn't meant to be.'

'Meant by who? Your ex-wife?' He shook his head slightly, as though dismissing an annoying thought.

'No. Destiny... the Fates. Whatever it is that decides these things.'

'Reproductive systems determine these things.'

'Or not, in our case.'

'Sorry. I didn't mean to pry.'

He sighed. 'Water under the bridge.'

I ordered the chicken. He ordered steak. I was too jittery to appreciate the food, and chewed mechanically. He was going to a rock festival at the weekend, sleeping under canvas. He dabbled with philosophy and played the saxophone. He had travelled widely in his younger days, and told me I should visit India and experience the spiritualities of the East. He talked about advertising and the media, until it was obvious I had nothing to say.

I was disappointed. The wine had made him garrulous. I didn't want to listen to New Age gibberish or comment on his conspiracy theories about the previous government. I wasn't interested in the people he had met down the pub the previous night and the stories they had told.

'I'm enjoying my midlife crisis, Tilda. I know it's a bit of a cliché, but maybe these things become clichés because they're true. I've come to the conclusion that life's a game. There may be rules and strategies, but most importantly it has to be fun, because whether you win or lose, the end result's the same. The pieces are tidied away. They're swept back into the box. The lid goes down. Ashes to ashes. Dust to dust. And then perhaps the big kids in the sky will get me out again at a later date for a rematch.'

'Games in our family were more about bad temper and cheating, especially at Christmas.'

'There is that too. But you get to a certain age and suddenly you're no longer immortal. You realise you haven't done much with your life, and you want to grab what's left before it's too late. I still have a few years of career left in me. I need to build up my pension pot, sort my head out, enjoy the moment. But I'm also taking time to look at the instructions for this great game we call life. I want to know what it's all about. I want to play it well. I want to be on the winning side. What about you?'

'Me?' I glanced away, unable to meet the intensity of his gaze. 'My work is very absorbing. I suppose I haven't really thought about much else. I'm not religious. I woke up from that particular nightmare years ago. I now walk by the light of science.' I paused to let him comment.

'Go on.'

'I didn't go travelling after graduating. I just wanted to get the bit between my teeth. My life has been fairly tedious in comparison to yours.' I cut a small piece of chicken and stabbed it with my fork.

'Not at all. You chose the path of excellence. I chose the path of being not very good at a lot of different things. Now I'm reduced to selling the clever stuff other people have invented to clever people who know how to use it.' There was a catch of regret in his voice. 'I used to take pride in my third-class degree, telling myself it showed I had a wide range of interests. Now I've concluded I'm just a bit thick. All the same, you should get away from your microscope once in a while, Tilda. Experience different cultures. I find people absolutely fascinating. The rich variety of human life and all that.' He waved his fork in the air to emphasise the point. 'I'm a bit of a connoisseur. There's nowt as strange as folk, as they say. You never know what they might be thinking or what they're going to do next. That's the joy of it. Digging a bit deeper. I never fail to be surprised. You, for instance. What are you thinking now?'

I blushed and swallowed awkwardly, hoping he hadn't picked up on my boredom. His eyes narrowed slightly.

'Tell me about your family.'

'There's just me and my brother, Oscar. And Dad. Mum died when I was seven.'

'That must have been tough.'

'Yes.'

'And what's the age gap between you and your brother?'

I smoothed the napkin on my lap. 'He's seven years younger than me.'

'Ahhh… I see… And does that make your relationship with him… difficult? Sorry. That was very nosy.'

'I had to be like a mother to him from a very young age. He can be a bit needy. Sometimes he likes to annoy me just for the sake of it – like a teenager rebelling against an authority figure.'

I didn't want to spend the evening analysing the psychology of my childhood, so I asked about his upbringing. I learned he had been brought up a Catholic, which went some way to explaining his love of mysticism, intrigues and atavistic stories. Even before my loss of faith, my plain Protestant background wouldn't allow for such nonsense. As if sensing my disapproval, he suddenly changed the subject.

'You intrigue me, Tilda.' He stroked his beard. 'So self-assured up on that podium, and yet you've lived such a cloistered life. You're one of life's luminaries, and yet –'

'I'm what?'

'A luminary! Yes! Don't think I don't know all about you. You're one to watch. You're getting a reputation for yourself among the scientific community. Name on papers. Groundbreaking research.' He picked up my hand. 'Such delicate fingers to be exploring the secrets of the universe.' His mouth twitched with a hint of a smile.

It was as though a solar flare flashed before my eyes, blinding me momentarily. The warmth of his expression flooded my body, flooded the restaurant with heat. My throat tensed. I didn't trust my voice to respond. He continued speaking, but his words were drowned out by the heaviness of his hand lying on top of mine. A waiter coughed. I pulled my fingers away and scrunched the napkin on my lap into a ball. More wine was poured and we were left alone again. Michael seemed to be talking about my research project with Keith.

'… and I hear the Japanese have found a way of making stem cells by dripping blood into acid.'

I was surprised out of my confusion.

'With mice, yes, but skin cells can also be reprogrammed. In the future we'll be able to create healthy tissue from a patient's own stem cells, avoiding the problem of rejection.'

'Perhaps the controversy over using foetal matter will now blow over.'

'It's early days. The technique hasn't been trialled on humans yet. I never understood the brouhaha over using embryonic cells, in any case. They're collected about four days after fertilisation. It's not a baby. There's no heartbeat, no heart, or any other structure for that matter.' My own heart began to steady.

'So you don't believe life begins at conception?' He tapped his fingers on the tablecloth as I formulated my reply.

'Life begins. It's not a person. It's a bundle of cells waiting for instructions. I call them the immortality cells.'

'Immortality! Give me an injection of that.' He raised his glass and gulped down a mouthful of wine.

'You wouldn't like it if I did. It's a double-edged sword. Undifferentiated master cells have the potential to become any cell type in our bodies, but they also share properties of immortality with some cancer cells. They continually replenish rather than wearing away, creating the possibility of tumour-genesis. Sorry… I'm probably boring you.'

'Not at all. I find you completely fascinating.' He was staring at me with an odd expression on his face.

'Cell death is a natural process,' I gabbled, ignoring the compliment. 'Older cells are more likely to suffer genetic damage, so they need to be eliminated before they harm surrounding tissues.'

'Now you're saying death is good.'

'For the rest of the body, yes. Not perhaps for the individual cell. Call it a sacrifice for the general good. Does that sound heartless?'

'Not at all. You sound pragmatic. What's the answer?'

'I'm looking at ways of transforming embryonic stem cells into specific cells before they're given to people. There's a ten-day window after fertilisation before they receive any signals. You have to catch them while they still have the potential to turn into anything, while their fate is undecided. By manipulating the process, you can turn them into whatever you want.'

'Cloning people? Growing noses on rats' bottoms?'

'The technology has enormous power. We're a long way away from being able to grow a new liver or a new leg in a lab, but it's an area that could have massive consequences for future generations.'

'It sounds perilously close to eugenics.'

'I like to think of it as improving the quality of genes in the human population.'

He wiped his lips with his napkin. 'That was a great steak. Fat and bloody, just how it should be.'

The waiter cleared our plates. Neither of us wanted dessert. I was feeling queasy with the effort of appearing unaffected by his presence, but secretly pleased he had wanted to discuss my work, even at the most basic level. He slapped his stomach and told me he needed to lose weight. He insisted on paying the bill. I tried to object, unsure how these things worked in a post-feminist age, but then he joked about his expense account. Disappointed, I realised I'd been attending a business meeting. He was schmoozing a client. Nothing more.

'So what were you thinking about earlier? I saw you blush. I'm curious to know what could embarrass a dispassionate rationalist.' His eyes were the darkest brown, almost black, his pupils fully dilated. Two black holes, pulling me into their depth.

39

A gravitational tug so great as to make escape impossible. A point of no return. My event horizon.

'Oh! I don't know. Did I blush? I don't remember.'

'You don't look like the kind of person who wouldn't remember.'

'The wine...'

I may have been mistaken but I think he winked. I tried to tell myself that the parts of the brain activated when a person sees the one they desire are unspeakably primitive, present in reptiles and birds, but it was no use. When we shook hands and parted the charge was still there. My voice trembled when I whispered goodbye. My nervous system was fizzing with electrical energy, my skin was clammy, my insides melting to warm slush.

I changed that day. Something bubbled in the crucible of my emotions – the amygdala, perhaps, or is it the hippocampus? I can't quite remember, which is strange, because I've always had the kind of brain that recalls scientific information in the minutest detail. The limbic system? Is that it? It hurts when I think too hard. The memory is slipping. I don't want to lose the warm glow of that first meeting, the recollection of his touch when something broke apart and reformed within me. It was an elemental reaction beyond my control. It was chemistry. It was biology. It was love.

The kind of person who wouldn't remember. I didn't look like it then but I must look like it now. A battered body on a hospital bed. I try to recall what happened next. My mind circles like the little blue wheel on a computer screen. The program is loading. I wait. Nothing comes. I've lost network connection. My brain has crashed.

Chapter 4

Days come. Days go. An endless cycle crushing me into a smaller and smaller space until one day I think I'll be extinguished with a small pop. Sometimes when I wake I'm filled with joy to be alive. Sometimes I'm overwhelmed by fear that I'll live and be encumbered with the kind of calamitous disabilities that constitute a living death: dribbling, catheters, wheelchairs and hoists. No work, no friends, a burden to my family. Sometimes I'm detached, serene, fatalistic. And then the nurse comes and turns out the lights and I'm stuck in the dark, furious, determined to get better and prove the idiots wrong. I indulge myself in power fantasies, leaping from the bed, demanding sackings and apologies, and landing a six-figure book deal as I retell my journey to the dark side of consciousness, the dead side of the moon. Then, exhausted, I wait for sleep, hoping my brain will give me a happy dream, hoping I will live to see another day.

One day I awake somewhere different. My eyes are closed, but the room doesn't smell like my room. I have a sharp pain on the left of my torso, just under my stomach. I'm drifting in and out of consciousness. Someone's groaning in the darkness. Then a nurse leans over me. I feel her breath on my face as she mindlessly repeats the reassurances she uses every day.

'You're going to be fine… This isn't going to hurt… You're doing very well.'

With a sharp tug she pulls my feeding tube away. It scorches up the back of my throat and down my nostril with a burning trail of pain. Once it's gone I feel light-headed and strangely empty. It had become an extension of my body. Without it, cold air floods my nasal passages and I'm drowning in space. A moment of panic when I think they're withdrawing nourishment and allowing me to die, before realising I've been fitted with a gastrostomy tube direct to my stomach. It's been decided I need long-term artificial feeding. Relieved, I succumb once more to oblivion.

I've been having a recurrent nightmare. There's a person in the shadows. I can't see their face but I feel as though I've known them all my life. Is it my mother? Oscar? Michael? The person waits but I'm scared to approach, not understanding the implications. I wake restless and empty. It's worse when I stir at night and realise I've slept through an entire day and missed what little of interest passes through my room. I lie in the dark, alone and bored, unable to move my aching limbs or distract myself from the mental treadmill of anguish and despair.

But tonight I've been dreaming of Oscar when he was little. I search for the memory. We're on holiday in Devon, digging in the sand. Oscar is whip-thin in his bathing trunks; his ribs ripple beneath his skin like a musical scale. The blue wind blows his hair across his eyes, garnishing him with sand and freckles. A golden boy.

'What a beautiful child,' a middle-aged lady in a deckchair exclaims as he runs down to the water's edge with his bucket, shrieking in excitement. I know she isn't talking about me, short and sunburned in my orange frilly swimming costume, the first hints of puberty bulging against the fabric and causing the armholes to cut into my skin.

'Do you remember coming here with Mummy when you were little?' Daddy asks.

'I think so. Did I find a crab?' I reply.

'Yes. It was quite a big crab. In a rock pool near the cliffs.'

'Where's a crab?' Oscar cries, staggering back and slopping water from the bucket into his newly dug moat, where it soaks away immediately.

'We were remembering when we came here last. Tilda found a crab.'

'Yes. I remember. We found a tiny, weeny, baby crab.'

'You shouldn't tell fibs, Oscar,' I chide.

'I'm not fibbing.'

'Yes, you are. You weren't here when we came to Sidmouth before.'

'Where was I?'

'It was before you were born,' Daddy says.

'But where was I?'

'You were nowhere, Oscar. You were nothing,' I reply.

'Nothing! I was nothing! Daddy, is that true? Did I used to be nothing?' His lip wobbles and tears begin to form in his eyes.

'Of course not, my darling heart. You've always been something. Before you were born, you were a wonderful idea. You were a twinkle in my eye, and a blush on your mummy's cheek.'

'See, Tilda! I was a twinkle. I was a twinkle when we found the crab.'

The room has turned to grey. It's very early in the morning. I hear birdsong outside, distant traffic. All these years later, the memory has made me hot and cross. He always had to be the centre of attention, even pushing himself into the time when our mother was alive, where he doesn't belong. 'Such a tragedy,' people said, 'that he never knew his mummy. She would have been so proud of the little chap.' But that was no reason to indulge him. I had lost her too.

The hospital is coming to life. I hear the first steps of the nurses. Soon there'll be the bustle of the breakfast trolley that always passes my room. Last night I was shifted on to my left side, the bed slightly raised so I'm propped on my pillows with a good view of the door. Through the vertical glass strip in the wood, I see people moving – the flick of a blue tunic, the white of a doctor's coat. They remind me of ships, distant and businesslike, with me stranded on a desert island trying to signal as they sail past, longing to be rescued. But nobody bothers to look through the glass.

I worry about my appearance, wishing I could brush my teeth and smooth my hair. What if today is the day he comes? I'm wearing a strange nightie, sensible and bland. I don't know where it's come from. I hate the thought that my father might have rummaged through my underwear drawers, looking for pyjamas and finding nothing suitable among the ratty collection of T-shirts and the new silk negligee with the label still attached. I hope the nightie belongs to the hospital, and Dad and I have both been spared the embarrassment.

A large woman gives me a wipe with a sponge. She does what she wants with me. I complain and curse at the indignity of her brisk ministrations, thrashing about within the cramped confines of my existence, while still as a statue on the outside. She doesn't hear, and the fustiness of my body is never completely eradicated. There's no mirror for me to check out the damage to my head. I can't remember my hair being washed since I've been here.

I have a vision of myself, very young, sitting at my mother's dressing table with lipstick smeared across my lips. I liked to line up her perfume bottles and lotions in order of size. To my childish mind they were magic mixtures, holding within their fragile exteriors the power of beauty, the secret of transformation. My mother – fragrant and inscrutably exquisite

44

– held these secrets close. But they couldn't protect her. 'What does it matter what I look like?' I concluded after her death. 'We all end up as food for worms. They don't discriminate between beauty and ugliness.' That's why I never worried much about my appearance before I met Michael.

How did my mind flit from the state of my hair to an image of maggots feasting their way out of my decaying body? A visceral lurch of disgust tugs at my belly. I've spent my whole life studying the laws of science, finding comfort in a sanitised rationality, reducing the entrails of existence to a specimen on a microscopic slide. Energy cannot be destroyed. It lasts for ever, transforming from one thing to another. I'm matter and energy working under the constraints of physical laws, the product of a predictable process. But I can't avoid the truth. My white lab coat always covered a skin full of stinking decay.

I must accept that I'm mortal, probably dying… but I fear it, fear the metamorphosis, fear this chrysalis state where there's no hope of turning into a butterfly, but only the prospect of a hardening and cooling of my blood. What will happen? Where am I going? What will I be?

This is nonsense! I've dumped the mythological baggage of the superstitiously ignorant, so why am I baulking now? Because this is me. *Me!* Death happens to other people. I can accept my mortality on a theoretical level, but not this minute by minute annihilation of everything I am.

Panic rises in the back of my throat. I can't bear it any longer. I must claw my way out. There's no escape from the suffocating sensation, like damp earth filling my eyes, my ears, my mouth. I hear a sound very close, a strangled gurgle. Pain from my cracked ribs shudders through my torso. The beep of the monitor tumbles over itself. I'm lost in the electronic sound of my heart racing, an unrelenting musical note that slices through my body like a knife. Darkness is falling over my eyes. A showering of stars blurs my vision, pushing me back to unconsciousness.

With a Herculean effort, I put on the brakes. I will *not* be overcome! My scattered thoughts pull together with a snap, like iron filings to a magnet. They are all I have. I must keep them safe. I must compartmentalise, lock all thoughts of death away. Embrace the pain, then dismiss it. I want to be sane when the doctors discover their mistake and dig me out of this pit. I have a story to tell. I will be proof that thought can exist beyond the usual physical structures.

A nurse arrives and checks the monitor. She picks up my wrist and feels my pulse. Her hand is cool and real. I wish she would squeeze my shoulder or stroke my arm, but I'm a medical condition to be analysed, not a person to be comforted. My heartbeat slows. The pain in my side begins to subside. My body remembers its necessary functions. Pulse, breathe. Pulse, breathe. The nurse leaves.

And now the penny drops. A delayed reaction. Before my monitor beeped into the stratosphere, my body made a sound! A gasp had jolted my broken ribs. The panic in my mind had manifested a physical reaction.

Before I can analyse the process, Claude arrives with a bang and clatter. I know it's him because the room is streaked with green. He wheels a bucket and mop across the floor. I try to locate the muscles in my throat, hoping I can duplicate the effect and cry out if he touches me.

'It's only me, missy. Just Claude, come to wash your floor.'

I hear a splosh, a soft kneading sound and a trickle of water. Then a slap as the mop hits the tiles. He sways into my line of vision, pushing the handle in a wide arc.

'That brother of yours. He's a wild one. Keeps shoutin' at the doctars, sayin' as how he's gonna get a lawyer. Says they're not doin' enough to help you. Says he wants another scan.'

My heart leaps in gratitude. For all our differences, Oscar is fighting my corner.

He moves nearer and the green darkens around me. He leans close. I feel his breath on my cheek as a briny shiver.

'Whatcha think they're gonna find? Do you think that machine can see into your soul?'

I strain against the weight blocking my voice. I rattle at the handle, pushing the door. But it's jammed tight shut. Concentrate! Concentrate! Just a small noise. Something. Anything.

He moves away and starts to hum. He recedes into the distance. The effort of trying to speak has made me light-headed. Blood pounds in my ears. A tide is coming... a roaring of waves... I'm sinking down... Suddenly everything is emerald. Everything is the colour of Claude.

It's the afternoon. I know this because the sun has moved round the building and is staring at me through the window. Also, it must be visiting hours, because Oscar is fidgeting in the chair by my bed. He's on edge. He takes a cigarette packet out of his pocket, realises where he is, shoves it back in his jacket, jumps from the seat and prowls to the window. A garish sunset fills the sky like an old bruise – purple, yellow, green. He looks at his watch, kicking his foot against the skirting board.

Even as a child he was always on the edge. On the edge of his seat at the dinner table. On the edge of tears. On the edge of trouble. Highly strung, Mrs Hedges used to call him. Sensitive. If we didn't limit his sugar intake, I might find him sitting on his bedroom windowsill, bare legs dangling outside in the cold air, singing to the night.

He never had many friends. He tried too hard to please. Too restless when the other kids were sitting quietly, too belligerent on the football field, too loud during hide-and-seek. The eagerness of desperation. One day he came home from school, boasting of an invitation to a popular boy's party.

'Are you sure?' I asked. 'Let me see it.'

He pulled a face. 'Liam promised I could come.'

'You should have a proper written invitation. It's so the mums know the date and time.'

'Maybe he thinks I don't need one because I don't have a mum.'

'When did he invite you?'

'At lunchtime. He and Andrew Ferguson said I could go to Liam's party if I went and sat next to Jessica Woods to eat my dinner.'

'Were you sitting with them?'

'I was going to. But I went and sat next to Jessica because I really want to go to the party. It's a football party. All the boys are going.'

I had to explain to him that he wasn't being invited. Liam and Andrew hadn't wanted him to sit with them and had used the party invitation as a ruse to get him to go and sit somewhere else. As I talked, his eyes filled with tears. It was a rotten trick. I told him I would get Dad to telephone the teacher.

'Will he tell her to make Liam invite me?' he asked.

'No. You can't make someone invite you to their party. But you can make them feel bad about it.'

'What's the point of that?'

'It will make me feel better.'

Even now, he's far too anxious about what people think. His friends are a bunch of heartless fakes, but he's easily fooled. His mobile rings. He snaps it to his ear.

'Hello? Yes. I'll get it, I promise… Yes… Soon… I told you, I've got it in hand.'

He tosses the phone onto the bottom of my bed. It hits the blankets with a soft thump. He flings himself back in the chair and rests his chin upon a clenched fist, hiding his eyes with his other hand. His shoulders shake. He's weeping. After a moment, he sniffs and wipes his nose on his sleeve.

'Sorry, Tilly. It's not easy for me, this whole thing. I shouldn't have said… you know… what I did. I didn't mean it. Everything was just… piling up. My head wasn't in a good place. You can't know what it's like… being me. Everything always goes wrong. It's like I'm cursed or something. I think it goes back to knowing you killed your own mother just by being born. It does things to your mind.'

I smell alcohol on his breath. It rises like a crimson fog, blurring my vision. It's an effort to focus. I long to sink back into the soft cushiony darkness. He seems so distant, a wavering outline. I want to be a good sister and attend to his problems. A listening ear is all I have to give. But he's been a heavy burden to carry. I'm tired of always looking out for him, having the responsibility, taking the blame. As a child, he didn't appreciate it. I doubt he appreciates it now.

'Make your bed, Oscar. I'm not doing it for you again.' Voices from the past, high-pitched, exasperated.

'No! You do it. That's what mummies are for.'

'I'm not your mummy. I don't want you pretending that I am.'

'You can't stop me.'

'I don't want to play your silly games. Mummy's dead.'

'No, she isn't. She's in heaven. That's what Mrs Hedges says.'

'There's no such place as heaven. Don't you know anything?' I mocked.

'There is too.'

He pushed me hard and I fell against the door, hitting my head on the round brass knob. Another bump to my brilliant mind.

'You must look after your brother, Tilda. He's younger than you,' Dad chided.

'I hate him!'

'No, you don't. Deep down you don't.'

I think about this. I don't want to dig deeper. I don't know what else I might find down there. Love and hate and heartache and anger. Too much for a 14-year-old to bear. Too much for a 35-year-old to bear.

Oscar speaks again. 'If it wasn't for me, things would have been different. I know that. But I can't help it. I've tried so hard, but everything's been falling apart. I can't tell Dad. He wouldn't understand. I need you, Tilly. I need your help. I'm in trouble. Big trouble. Please wake up. Please come back to me. You can't die now. Oh, Tilda! You can't die now.'

Chapter 5

Voices echo from inside a cobalt cave. Today, I'm nearly blind. I squint and grope forward, trying to grasp what my father is saying.

'I've been on the internet. It says that almost half of patients with PVS might have been misdiagnosed. Some of them suddenly regain consciousness even after several months have passed. They're in a – what was it called? – a minimally conscious state. Yes, some of them are minimally conscious. That means they're aware some of the time.'

A buzz of hope crackles around the room, ricocheting off the walls.

'I know what it means, Mr Moss. However, if that were the case, there would be some cognitively mediated behaviour. In layman's terms, we would be seeing something… anything… a blink, an eye movement or a finger twitch, for example, in response to something we said. Her eyes may be open but this shouldn't be mistaken for consciousness.'

I'm trying to understand what this means, how a thought, a fragile wisp, can move something as heavy as an eyelid, as solid as a finger. I'm searching for the magic word that will conjure the visible from the invisible, bring something out of nothing with a flourish, a rabbit from a hat, but the road to meaning is blocked. How did my mind, or whatever it is I'm thinking with, control my body before my injury?

'What about locked-in syndrome? Have you thought of that?'

'You can rest assured we've thought about everything. With locked-in syndrome, there's no damage to the upper portions of the brain but specific portions of the lower brain and brainstem are injured. In other words, the complete opposite of what we have here. Your daughter's brainstem is intact but it's the upper portions of the brain that have been damaged.'

'Sometimes she grunts,' Dad pleads. 'Sister said she was moaning the other day.'

'We would need more than that before diagnosing minimal consciousness. It needs to be consistent and sustained long enough to be differentiated from reflexive behaviour. I'm sorry this is not what you want to hear, but it's better to have all the facts.' His words fly away in dark circles, searching for somewhere to roost.

When they've gone, I concentrate on each part of my body in turn. If I can move a finger or blink an eye, there's the possibility someone will notice. My father is already sceptical of the diagnosis and looking for a sign. Stephen Hawking can communicate by activating a sensor using a muscle in his cheek. He still has his work. He still has a life and a voice. I must take my cue from him and claw my way back.

I move around the circuit in a methodical way, testing the connection. *Right hand little finger. Right hand ring finger. Right hand middle finger. Right hand index finger. Right hand thumb.* Then on to the left hand piggies, then each toe piggy in turn. My nose, my mouth, my eyes, my cheeks. Nothing. I'm exhausted with the effort. I resolve to practise every day in the hope I can build up my strength and construct a neural pathway out of the darkness and run wee wee wee all the way home.

'Tilda, my dear. It's Professor MacMahon. Can you hear me? I thought I'd just better check in and see how you're doing. Not so good, by the looks of you… Umm… Missing you dreadfully back at the ranch. We've got our fingers crossed and everything else we can, that goes without saying. I was only remarking to Charles Rainsworth how quiet it is without you and Keith chattering away together about your research. Keith, of course, is doing a simply marvellous job, keeping all the balls in the air while you're… how shall I say it… convalescing?

'You're not to worry about anything. He's had a look at your emails and is letting everyone know the situation. He can't find the memory stick with your latest notes on it, and the blasted police have confiscated your laptop. I was hoping you might be feeling a bit better today so I could ask you where you put it. The USB flash drive, that is.

'There's been some talk up on the fifth floor that they might not continue with your grant. It would be good if we could publish your paper. It would remind them of the groundbreaking research you're actually doing. Keith says you've nearly finished it. He would be willing to edit it for you… once we find it. It would raise the department's profile, so to speak…

'Thought maybe the sound of my voice might set off a little spark somewhere… But no, I see that's not going to be possible. Perhaps another time. I'll be taking it upon myself to step into your distinguished shoes and give the presentation to NESCI on your behalf next week.

'What a lot of lovely cards you've got! The bursar sends his best regards. Of course, the college is still paying your full salary. But if – and I'm sure this won't be the case – your recovery drags on, at some point in the future… a long way off, I'm sure… you'll be put on to statutory sick pay. Your job is always here for you when you're ready to come back, which we are all looking forward to very much… very much… yes, indeed!'

Dad's back. His voice is flat. The unbearable intensity of his hope has been reigned in. A young man in a crumpled suit is leaning against the wall, taking notes.

'I don't know very much about her work, I'm afraid, sergeant. She's a lecturer and scientist at the Institute of Genetic Medicine at Newcastle University. She only talked about her research in the most general way. She knew I wouldn't understand. I stopped being able to understand her experiments when she was about 15.'

'I gather from her boss…' he flicks through a notebook, 'Professor MacMahon, that she's working in a controversial area. Have there been any threats?'

'Threats!'

'From animal rights activists, for example.'

'I think that goes with the territory. Anyone who uses lab rats is open to abuse, particularly on the internet. She was used to it. She knew how to look after herself. Where's Inspector Lake?'

'He's working on another enquiry at the moment.'

'But he's still trying to find out what happened to my daughter?'

'Of course… What about the pro-life lobby?' the sergeant asks.

'Why would they be interested?'

'She was experimenting with embryos, as far as I understand it.'

'Not embryos. Embryonic stem cells.'

'Isn't that the same thing?'

'I'm not sure.' Dad pinches the top of his nose between his fingers. 'As I said, I don't really understand her work. I don't think you should worry about the pro-life lobby. She's not a medical doctor. She's not doing abortions. This isn't America! In any case, I think the animal rights lobby is more vociferous than the God squad. A couple of years back she did some work with chimera embryos – mixing animal and human DNA to see if it would be possible to grow organs for transplant. She had more objections from the animal rights movement than from human rights or religious groups. Besides, there are plenty of more high-profile figures to go after. She was very discreet. Low key. Absolutely wedded to secrecy.'

'So we've discovered. She's a difficult nut to crack... Sorry. That was an unfortunate metaphor, in the circumstances. What about her personal life? Boyfriends?'

'I don't think so. We tended to chat about family stuff when she did manage to find a moment to ring me. I know she's been working very long hours recently. Perhaps you should ask her flatmate.'

'How much do you know about Catherine Halliday?'

'Who?'

'Catherine... Kiki Halliday.'

'Not much. She seems like a nice girl. We've only met a couple of times. Why? Do you know something I should know?'

'Not at all, sir. This is all purely routine.'

'Routine? How routine is it to find your daughter lying in a coma with her head smashed in? It's not routine for me.'

I think about the time I spent with Michael, what he said and what I said, how he looked and what I wore. I wonder if he's thinking about me now. Perhaps he dreams of me when I'm dreaming of him. Perhaps he visits when I'm asleep. I wonder if I snore at night, or lie open-mouthed, drooling on my pillow. Maybe the grief is too much to bear and he stays away, unable to look at the one he loves in this twisted body. I swerve sharply to avoid the sting of betrayal. I must be positive. Positive thoughts have an impact on physical health. He loves me. He wants me. We have planned a life together. I must think my way out of this labyrinth, follow the thread through sheer force of will until I'm back in his arms. I won't give up hope. I can be a detective too, searching for clues, examining fingerprints, interrogating witnesses, questioning suspects.

I Googled him, of course. His LinkedIn account told me he graduated from Lancaster University more than 30 years ago, having studied marketing with psychology. His Facebook page had the highest privacy settings, so there was nothing to see except a smiling face with a receding hairline and a grey goatee. I couldn't send him a friend request. I wasn't a teenager. He didn't appear to tweet.

I carried his business card around for days, taking it out of my pocket and stroking his name, trying to pluck up the courage to ring him. In the end he contacted me first, calling my office number.

'Hello?'

'Dr Moss. Tilda. It's Michael Cameron.'

'Michael!'

'I just wanted to say how much I enjoyed meeting you the other week –'

'Likewise.'

'And I was wondering if there's anything more BioExpertise Systems can do to help the university in its drive for excellence. I'm introducing a new scheme for educational establishments, linking them with local STEM industries.'

'Uh-huh…' I shut my office door and faced the window, one arm tight around my waist, holding in the rush of excitement.

'I have several organisations that are willing to contribute towards the cost of the university's biotechnology supplies if they're allowed to brand the packaging and equipment with their logos. It's a kind of partnership. They pay to put their logo on our products. This means we can offer them to you at extremely competitive prices. They get their name known by the scientists of tomorrow, the ones they'll want to do business with or employ after graduation. You get to stretch your budget further. I just wondered whether a scheme of that kind might be of interest.'

'If you like, I can get our purchasing officer to give you a call.'

'That would be great... but I just wanted to ask... No. I know you're very busy...'

'What?'

'I was wondering if you're able to come to an Expo we're holding next week. Our entire executive team will be there, together with industry chiefs and folk from other universities. Perhaps your finance colleague would like to come too, but I think someone of your calibre, someone who's able to recognise the quality of our equipment and explain to others how you would use it in your laboratories, would help enormously. It's a lot to ask, I know... and at short notice.'

'No. That's fine. What day did you say it was?'

'Monday the 25th. From 10.30am onwards you can view the exhibition we're putting together. Then there'll be presentations – one from yours truly – followed by a buffet lunch at 12.30 for mingling. Hopefully you'll be able to stay and chat. Networking stuff.'

I struck a line through a lecture in my diary, deciding to delegate it to Keith.

'I've put it in the book. Send me the details and how to get there.' I reeled off my email address.

'That's terrific. I'm sending through the programme now... and a map. Parking shouldn't be a problem. And perhaps we can have a glass of wine together over lunch. I'd be interested to hear more about your research.'

'That would be lovely. I'll see you then.' My hand was shaking when I replaced the receiver.

'How did you get on at the university, Stevenson?'

'Not great. None of the staff can think of a reason why Dr Moss would want to harm herself. She had no enemies, as far as they knew. It's all the same stuff as before. She's brilliant, completely focused on her work, fairly conservative in her tastes.'

My eyes are closed but I'm listening.

'I thought some hint of scandal might have begun to rise to the surface.' The inspector sounds disappointed.

'Oh! There is one thing, sir. A PhD student told me he thought Dr Moss had become more approachable, more human, in the weeks running up to her hospitalisation.'

I've always been approachable and human, haven't I?

'In what way?'

'She seemed fairly relaxed when he missed a deadline.'

'Perhaps she had the hots for him.'

I wish they could hear me laugh at the absurdity of the suggestion.

'Unlikely, sir.'

'Why?'

'He's probably a decade younger than her…'

'That's no obstacle.'

'… about 15 stone heavier than her…'

'Ahhh.'

'… and the way he was flirting with me suggests he's not interested in the ladies, if you get my drift.'

'I see.'

'She'd also moved a couple of tutorials with him at the last minute, which was uncharacteristic.'

'That's interesting.'

Footsteps approach my bed. Although I can't see, I feel a presence gazing down at me.

'How's she doing today?' the younger policeman asks.

'The same.'

'Do you think she'll recover?'

'I'm not a doctor.' The inspector's tone is terse.

'My gut says it's curtains, sir.'

'My gut tells me something's not right.'

'Is that why you're here?'

'I came to collect the visitor list from the nurses.'

'They could have faxed it to the station.'

'I wanted to get their opinion of her family and friends.'

'Anything?'

'Not really. I've been sitting here reviewing the situation in my mind. She had no reason that I can see to try to kill herself. There's no note. The flat was unnaturally clean when we searched it, as if someone didn't want us to find anything. There's nothing on her laptop. We've found a small notebook of what looks like randomised passwords, but we can't find the internet accounts or documents they relate to. As far as her friends and family are concerned, there's no man in her life, but it looks as though she's recently bought some new underwear; a different kind of underwear than most of the stuff in her drawers, black lace rather than white cotton. It's brand new. What's that about?'

'I've always found it best not to question a woman's shopping choices. What does her flatmate think?'

'The flatmate said Dr Moss had been working long hours and was hardly ever at home in the evenings running up to the incident. But her colleague, Keith Gadson, said she'd been cutting back her hours. Neglecting her work, even, which is very uncharacteristic. If she was not at the office, and not at home, she must have been going somewhere. Let's go over the events of that evening again... Don't look at me like that! Humour me.'

'Yes, sir.'

'The lady next door hears a cat crying on her balcony and goes out to shoo it away. She looks down and sees Dr Moss lying flat on her back on a patio area below. Why do you think that bothers me, sergeant?'

'If she jumped, you would expect her to land on her front or side.'

'Exactly. And if she'd been hit on the back of the head by an intruder and then thrown over, you would expect to see additional injuries to her face and forehead.' I feel their eyes on me.

'She could have been pushed backwards, sir.'

'Not an easy manoeuvre. The balustrade would be behind her buttocks and thighs. An intruder would need to lift her over, making it more likely she would fall awkwardly through the air and land on her front or side.'

'Could she have bounced against something on her way down? The wall? A tree? Perhaps she rolled over before losing consciousness. There are a few surface scratches to her neck.'

'The pattern of the bruising doesn't indicate that. There are no shrubs nearby. And if you're going to kill yourself, why would you jump from a first-floor balcony with the chance you might not do the job properly? Pills and alcohol are usually the first choice of the fairer sex. And then there's the overturned table on the balcony, the broken cat bowl, indicating some kind of struggle.'

'There was no blood in the flat. Nothing to suggest a break-in.'

'Just a lot of bleach. But what's the question we always ask ourselves in these kind of situations, sergeant?'

'Who benefits, sir?'

'Exactly. Who benefits? Every death benefits someone.'

'She's not dead yet.'

'No. That leads me to my second question… Is it enough?

'Is what enough?'

'Having her in a coma.'

An ominous silence hovers between them. The inspector clears his throat. 'We have to consider the possibility that someone might come back to finish what they started.'

Chapter 6

My body has been demoted to an unsavoury exhibit. Colleagues from the university drop by in groups of two or three. People I hardly nod to in the mornings come to see the spectacle, the freak show, wanting to be part of the drama, wanting a story to tell. At first they speak in awkward whispers, self-conscious under my steady gaze, until I become like a video recorder at a wedding, forgotten, unseen, and they relax and regale each other with the latest office gossip. Mrs Squires sits and knits and tells me about her sister's gout.

Visitors are already telling lies about how wonderful I was. I've become something different, an idea of me, unaging and fixed, a dream that is misremembered in the harsh morning light. They comfort themselves with platitudes and lies, not wanting to see what I'm becoming. I wonder if any of them are responsible, if any of them are to blame. A shaft of fear pierces my heart. What if the inspector's right, and someone hasn't finished with me yet?

The stale odours of my body hang heavy and bloated in the air like thunder – the sweat and the fear and the fetid clamour of warm incontinence pants. I catch the white noise of bacteria swarming in my inner ear, waiting for my blood to clot so they can begin the great feast of consummation. I taste the bitterness of a reckoning, but don't know what I've done to deserve this punishment. I feel the colour of pain on my skin, crackling red and blistering black, and hear the deep ache of unused muscles and seizing joints.

A refuse truck reverses outside my window with a repeating beep. Take away the rubbish. Take away the broken stuff and the empty packets, the slop at the bottom of the cartons. Does someone want to do away with me, throw me on the dump, bury me forever under a mountain of waste? Is it you… or you… or you? Or is it me?

Kiki sits next to me, painting my toenails red. The sheets have been pushed back, and for the first time I see my leg in a cast. My naked foot is an interesting shade of bluey green. I don't know how long she's been here. I've been drifting in and out of beautiful dreams, and am cross to have been roused by the ringing of her phone.

'Hi. Yes, I'm still here, waiting for her dad… Worse than ever… she looks like a corpse. No. You mustn't think like that. It's best this way… I don't know how long I'll be. He comes most afternoons.' She stands and adjusts the curtain, running her thumb and fingers between the pleats so they're evenly spaced. 'I've told you, you mustn't. There's nothing to feel guilty about. I know you do… Of course. I'll see you in a tickle. Bye.'

Once she's happy with the hang of the cheap cotton, she turns her attention to the bed. She's finished with my feet, and smooths the sheet and thin blue blanket tightly across my legs. She sits and takes a packet of wet wipes from her bag and cleans her hands. She waves them in the air to dry and begins to file her fingernails. The scratch of the emery board marks off the seconds. Not a word is spoken.

The door swings open. Footsteps shuffle across the tiles.

'Kiki!'

'Mr Moss.' She gets up from her chair as though surprised to see him.

'Call me Peter, please. And sit down. I'll just bring this chair over. How is she today?'

Kiki ignores his request to sit, and hovers by the bed. 'Looking a bit better, I think.'

'Yes. I think so too.'

'I've been telling her all the news from Mrs Squires. And about Betsy.'

I don't remember this. Perhaps I've been asleep. Perhaps she's exaggerating her chattiness to please Dad.

'Thank you for coming. I know she appreciates it, even if she can't say.' He places his chair in position.

'It's no trouble at all. I wanted to come. I've painted her nails. Toes as well as fingers. Please don't, Mr... Peter... I didn't mean to upset you.'

'No, no. I mustn't... You're perfectly right, of course. We must stay cheerful for our dear Tilda's sake.'

'Come here, you.' She envelops him in her arms. 'How have you been keeping, *really*?'

'I'm surviving. How about you?'

'Worried, obviously. It's very hard. Coming back to an empty flat every night... Perhaps I could ask you about that.' They both sit down. 'Maybe I've been taking things for granted. It's the shock of everything. I should have asked before if you're happy for me to carry on living there.'

'Of course, my dear. Thank you for keeping an eye on things for her. The cat and whatnot.'

'Yes. Betsy... So I just wondered what's going to happen if...'

'If?'

'If Tilda can't come home,' she says in a rush.

'I see. I think that will be for Tilda to decide. Are you thinking she might need some adaptations to the flat? If that's the case, she might make up her mind she needs something... different... but that's up to her, of course.'

I wonder if Dad is being deliberately obtuse, or if he really does believe I'll recover.

'Yes, of course. And you're happy for me to stay in the meantime?'

'Certainly. Oscar and I are very grateful. You can stay as long as you like. It's what Tilda would want, I'm sure.'

'Yes. It's what Tilda would want.'

'Tell me a story, Tilly,' Oscar demands.

'You're too old for stories. You can read for yourself.'

'I want you to read one. You read them best.' He opens the book on his lap. 'I want this one.'

'*Hansel and Gretel*! You're definitely too old for fairy tales.'

'It's not about fairies. It's about a brother and sister –'

'I know what it's about. Shove over, then, and let me in.' I squeeze next to him in the single bed. We huddle under the duvet. I turn the pages of the large illustrated book Mum read to me when I was little.

'Once upon a time there were two young children called Hansel and Gretel. Sadly, their mother died when they were very young. Their father, a woodcutter, married again to provide them with another mother. All was well until a terrible famine settled on the land.

'"The children are too greedy," the stepmother complained. "We shall all die. We must take them into the wood and leave them there to fend for themselves."

'At first their father opposed the idea, but eventually he gave in to his nagging wife. They planned to take Hansel and Gretel into the woods the next day, but unbeknown to them the children had overheard the scheme.

65

'"Don't worry, Gretel," Hansel comforted his sister. "God will not abandon us." After the parents had gone to bed, he crept out of the house and gathered a pocketful of white pebbles.

'The following day, the family walked into the wood. Hansel lingered behind and laid a trail of stones behind them. When they reached the deepest part of the forest, the woodcutter and his wife told the children to sit down and rest while they looked for a good tree to cut down.'

'Tilly?'

'Yes?'

'Do you think Daddy will get us a stepmother?'

'No. Why should he? I look after you, don't I?'

'Then why does Mrs Hedges keep coming in from over the road?'

'I don't know. Because she likes us. Now be quiet.' I turned the page. 'Hansel and Gretel waited and waited but their parents did not return. Darkness fell over the land, but as the moon rose the white pebbles glimmered on the path. The children followed the trail and returned home safely, much to the horror of their stepmother.'

'I saw Daddy hugging Mrs Hedges.'

'When?'

'Last week. When he gave her that bunch of flowers.'

'Stupid! It was her birthday.'

'Don't call me stupid!' He folded his arms across his football pyjamas and scowled.

'The famine continued and once again food became scarce. The stepmother ordered her husband to take the children into the woods and leave them there to die.'

'Mrs Hedges is a widow.'

'I know.'

'That means she must be bad.'

'No, it doesn't. It means her husband has died. She brought us a rhubarb crumble last week, don't you remember? Bad people don't make crumbles.'

'Why do they call the most poisonous spider in the world the black widow, then? Widows must be worse than stepmothers. If a widow becomes our stepmother, it will be twice as bad.'

'Don't be silly. It's not going to happen. I won't let it. Daddy belongs to us.'

Oscar settled back on the pillow.

'Now, where was I? Oh, yes. Hansel tried to leave the house to collect more pebbles, but the wicked stepmother had locked the children in their bedroom.'

'I don't like rhubarb.'

'Quiet, Oscar!' I returned to the story. 'The sun rose the following day. Feeling guilty about what he was about to do, the woodcutter secretly gave Hansel two slices of bread before they left the house. As they trekked into the woods, the boy crumbled up the bread in his pocket and dropped a trail of crumbs behind him.'

Oscar put his thumb in his mouth, a habit that was proving impossible to break. He would soon be asleep.

'Once again, the children were abandoned in the deepest part of the forest. They waited until nightfall. The moon rose above the treetops but they could not see the trail of bread. The birds had eaten every crumb. Hansel and Gretel were utterly lost.'

'If he did get us a wicked stepmother, we'd stick together, wouldn't we, Tilly?' He yawned and closed his eyes. 'Like Hansel and Gretel.'

'Of course. I'll never leave you, Oscar. You know that. Never!'

I wake up with a bang. It's dark. Something in my head is rumbling. I'm very scared; more scared than normal. Electricity crackles around the room. There are goosebumps on my body. I feel a presence and I want to leap up and cry, 'Who's there?' but my lips are stuck together, my hands and feet tied fast.

I remember the picture in my childhood book, two figures walking hand in hand down a dark path into the wood, birds circling overhead. I realise that I lied to Oscar. We haven't stuck together. I'm in the darkest place without him, and he's in a dangerous place without me. I can't find my way back and Michael can't find me. The last crumbs of hope are being devoured.

And then a flash of brilliant silver lights up the room like a photograph. I see the shadows of the empty chairs, the curtain limp and grey. The sky explodes. Thunder rolls around my head, vicious and unconstrained. Bullets of water ricochet against the window in a cold rattle. My heart is fluttering in my chest, frantic to escape the terror of the wind dashing against the building and the rain hurling itself at the glass and the presence in the night that is coming to bear me away in its dark arms. There's nowhere to hide. I'm a scrap of wood sailing down the river of no return.

The lightning cuts open the sky again, cuts open my heart. The thunder fills my ears. The clouds weep the tears of the damned, droplets falling to their doom, and smashing on the pavement below in pools of transparent blood.

Chapter 7

I've been awake since the storm. The nurses have washed me, checked my mouth and brushed my teeth. They've changed my feeding bag and checked my drip. They've tutted at finding Kiki's nail polish on my fingers and toes. Apparently it's not allowed. One of them goes to get nail varnish remover. I feel like I'm the naughty girl in school. I'm fed up with them all, sick of them checking me every morning. I don't want to eavesdrop on their conversations. I'd rather not hear their witticisms and their complaints, saying things about me they wouldn't say if they knew I could hear.

Go away! Don't you have better things to do, patients to cure? Why bother with me? Can't you leave me in peace?

And now Claude comes, singing. His voice is cracked and tuneless. I remember the song. It comes from a faraway place. 'He got the whole world in His hand. He got the whole wide world in His hand. He got the whole world in His hand. The whole world in His hand.'

He stops sweeping and approaches the bed. I shrink back into myself, curling inside to become a small hard dot, impervious, invisible.

'Hello, Tilda. It's me again.' His breath smells of seaweed, sour and free. 'It's a cold one today, innit? Cold and wet. I thinks of you when I'm walkin' the streets, all muffled up in me coat and cap. I thinks of you here in this hot room, wrapped up like a baby. Yes, you be nice and cosy here. That's for sure.'

I realise it's no longer summer. When did the weather change? When did the days suddenly shorten? How long have I been deep-frozen… and when will this body of ice ever begin to thaw?

'I just seen your daddy arrivin'. He's down in the cafeteria gettin' his breakfast. Sure do love you, that man. He wants you to wake up, like Sleepin' Beauty. Wake up! Come on, wake up…! No? Not today, then?'

His words plunge like shoals of fish through deep water, suddenly turning, darting in unexpected directions, avoiding the vast presence that has been swimming in my room since the storm, just out of sight in the gloom.

'What you waitin' for? Oh yes! You need a prince for that. Have you got a prince, girlie? Someone to give you a big smackin' kiss and jolt your heart back to life? I'd do it myself, but nurse would sure give me a mouthful. I'll just kiss your hand, princess.'

Go away! Go away! You disgusting little man. I hate you!

He moves from the bed. He starts to sing, just out of my line of vision. 'He got you and me, sister, in His hand. He got you and me, sister, in His hand. He got you and me, sister, in His hand. He got the whole world in His hand.'

I surface from the seas of a deep sleep. A woman is sitting by my bed, reading a letter. I don't recognise her and she doesn't look like a member of the medical staff. She wears a leather jacket with a lace blouse underneath. Her hair is short and very blonde. Ornate mother-of-pearl earrings swing by her neck. Small silver studs line her outer ear like bullets near a bullseye. Her lips are the brightest red. Lines run between her nose and mouth, and between her mouth and chin, giving her the appearance of a ventriloquist's dummy. She's at least a decade older than me, though she dresses a decade younger. She sits in silence. I wonder how long she's been here. The door opens.

'Oh! Hello. I'm Peter Moss. The patient's father.' Dad shrugs out of his coat.

The woman jumps to her feet, stuffing the letter in her jacket pocket. 'Allegra. I'm a friend of Matilda's.'

Her voice is a needle. It pricks my heart, which sinks like a deflated tyre. I can't understand my reaction to her words. They shake hands.

'It's funny, you calling her "Matilda". She was only ever called that by her teachers. Perhaps Tilda's outgrown her childhood nickname at last.'

'No! Not at all. I don't know why I called her that. She still likes to be called Tilda. It's probably because I asked for her room number at the reception desk, and the nurse called her Matilda.'

'Have you been here long?'

'Five… ten minutes, maybe.'

It seems longer than that to me.

'Has she been like this all the time? With her eyes open?' Dad asks.

'Yes.'

'She looks as though she's listening, doesn't she?'

'Yes. She does.'

'But she can't respond. Not yet, anyway. It's very kind of you to visit. I'm sure she appreciates it. How did you two meet? Are you a work colleague?'

'No… I live round the corner. We're neighbours.' She answers with the seductive rasp of an ex-smoker. 'I would have come sooner. But I've only just heard.'

I'm struggling to place her. I'm not sure I know any of my neighbours, apart from Mrs Squires and the family directly opposite who I wave to when I'm reversing my car out of the drive. But her voice resonates like an echo in a cave.

'You probably know Kiki, her flatmate.'

'Oh, yes. Kiki. I didn't know that was her name. We're just on nodding terms.'

'She hasn't lived with Tilda long.'

'No.'

'A few months.'

'That's right.'

'And what do you do for a living, Allegra?'

'I'm a homeopath.'

I'm sure I would have remembered that!

'That's interesting.'

'Yes.'

'I expect you and Tilda have had some interesting discussions.'

'Yes.'

'She's a scientist.'

Exactly! Someone who believes in empirical evidence, not mumbo jumbo peddled by fraudsters and gullible idiots.

'I know. What are the doctors saying?'

'She's very poorly. They're calling it a persistent vegetative state. But time's a great healer, don't you think? The doctors will do another scan in a few days. That should give us some answers.'

'It must be difficult. How are you externalising the pain?' Her words curl around him like smoke, comforting, insidious.

'Umm… It's not easy.'

'Remind me, Peter, where is it you come from?'

'Durham. It's fortunate I retired last year. When I heard about the – her accident – I just dropped everything and came. It only takes about 30 minutes from home, but sometimes I stay overnight at a small hotel. I need to be near her. Just in case…'

'It must have been a terrible shock. What happened?'

'It's not very clear. The police are looking into it. It's difficult to imagine…'

'I understand. Look, I'd better leave you two in peace.'

'No! No need to rush off on my account.'

'I've got an appointment fairly soon. But I'll come back another day.'

'Will you? Would I be able to have your telephone number? To let you know if there's any change. And maybe if you can think of anything Tilda might have said to you, anything at all, to help us understand…'

'Of course. I'll write my number down. I've got a pen somewhere.' She rummages in a large, brightly coloured patchwork bag, unearths a pen and scribbles rapidly on the bottom of the letter from her pocket. She tears off the corner and hands it to Dad. 'I don't think I can shed any light on what happened. But I can tell you her aura is *very* peaceful.'

I swear so loudly I'm surprised they don't hear.

'Is it?'

'Yes. She's in a curative space. Her body needs time to reinstate itself. I could try some Thought Field Therapy next time I come.'

'Force Field Therapy?'

'*Thought* Field Therapy. It releases a blockage of energy by tapping specific acupuncture points. Sometimes the brain responds to trauma and pain by releasing stress hormones which paralyse the patient with fear and impedes recovery.'

'I don't think…'

'We need to mobilise her body's healing mechanisms.' She stands and combs the back of her hair with her fingers, pushing the choppy strands into the nape of her neck. Her earrings swing and clink like wind chimes.

'I'll mention it to her consultant.'

'You know what they're like!' she shrugs dismissively.

'Yes… I'm beginning to think they don't know everything. Maybe some tapping or whatnot would be good. I'll ask Oscar. Her brother. I don't think it can't hurt, can it?' Desperation rolls through his words like a bad smell.

'Absolutely not… and next time I'll bring some lavender essence for her pillow. Ring me if you'd like to try the Thought Field Therapy. I charge very reasonable rates for friends.'

'Thank you. I'll keep you in touch… if there are any developments.'

'It's been nice to meet you, even if the circumstances could have been better.'

Dad holds out his hand but she has already bowed her head and pressed her palms together, her fingers pointing upwards, her thumbs touching the small dip between her neck and her chest.

'*Namaste*, Peter.'

'Pardon?'

'*Namaste*. I'm bowing to the divine in you.'

'Oh! I see… right. Thank you. And thanks for coming. It's so important for Tilda to have visitors.'

'Yes, it is. And you can be sure I'll call in again… very soon.'

Chapter 8

I'm having another MRI scan today. I can't remember the first one, so perhaps it's more accurate to say, 'I'm having an MRI scan.' No one told me, of course. No one tells me anything. I picked it up from the nurses this morning when they were changing my nappy.

'The family have insisted. They don't want to make any decisions about future care until they're absolutely sure. Of course, she can't stay here indefinitely. She's blocking the bed. Pass me the drip bag and I'll plug it in.'

'Doctor Arnold told me he's going to try something new. He's read in a journal of a patient diagnosed with PVS who was able to activate specific areas of his brain when asked a question. His scan results couldn't be distinguished from healthy patients who were asked the same things.'

'That's interesting. I wonder what he's going to ask her.'

'Do you come here often?' They both laugh.

'Going anywhere nice at the weekend?'

'Seen any good movies recently?'

'I thought he was planning to stick a pin in her to see if he can stimulate the sensory cortices.'

'He'll enjoy that, the cold-hearted sadist!'

My bed is being wheeled at speed down a long corridor. Overhead lights flash past. The people in the corridor are a blur of arms and shoulders. My head is lying sideways and I can't see their heads or legs. I've lain still for such a long time that the movement makes me dizzy. I wish I could close my eyes and shut out the world rushing past in a torrent of colour, and the footsteps and the chatter and the smell of coffee and disinfectant. I think of my quiet room with a pang.

Drivers never experience car sickness. Their bodies subconsciously predict the motion of the vehicle. A passenger cannot anticipate the twists and turns ahead in the same way. Perhaps it's not motion sickness I'm suffering from at all, but life sickness. I can't predict the swerves that are coming. I don't know what the future holds.

We clatter into a lift. The porter presses a button and we descend with a lurch. There's another patient on a bed. I gaze into her pale eyes. She looks sad, hopeless like me. One side of her head is covered with short, mousy hair; on the other, her hair hangs lank and greasy. The lift lands with a thump. It's not until the doors open that I realise I've been staring at a reflection of myself in the mirrored wall.

A radiographer is waiting to usher us into a white room. Against the pull of gravity, the porters heave my body from the trolley and plop me down with an agonising jolt to my head and side. The radiographer straps me to the patient table and puts blocks on either side of my face to stop me moving. Am I the only one to recognise the irony? She places a pair of headphones on my ears. Without any preamble, the table moves forward like a coffin rolling towards the incinerator doors. I wish I could shut my eyes and block out the primitive terror that comes with watching the white cocoon gradually cover my face. I can't see out of either end of the tube. My nose is almost touching the ceiling. My inner ear is still registering the rotation as I was rolled off the bed and onto the MRI table. A surge of claustrophobia wells into my throat. I know from friends who have had this experience that patients are usually given a button to press if they feel panicky. They haven't bothered with a button for me, and I couldn't squeeze it if I had one.

The slow movement of the table continues until I'm completely absorbed into the belly of the machine. The creature begins to moan. At first a loud buzz, then a hammering like a pneumatic drill. I'm glad of the ear protectors and wish they would play some music to distract me from the contraption encircling my body. The earphones crackle with static.

'Dr Moss. This is Dr Arnold speaking. I would like you to imagine yourself walking through the rooms of your home. Take your time.' The scanner bangs like a sledgehammer. 'Start at the front door. Move slowly through each room looking at the furniture and gazing out of the windows. Imagine the colours of the walls and the smells in the kitchen...'

I turn the key in the latch and step into the hall. There's a pile of letters on the mat. I pick them up and place them on the console table next to the aspidistra. To my right is the lounge, light and airy, opening on to my balcony. Betsy jumps from the sofa and winds herself around my legs. I unlock the French doors and step outside. A small wrought-iron table stands between two chairs, my refuge on summer evenings with a glass of wine and my scientific journals. Pots of petunias and lobelia cluster in the corners. A fatsia japonica, cool and glossy in a terracotta planter. A lush hydrangea. Ascetic bamboo. My haven.

Betsy is calling for her dinner. I return to the lounge and walk left through an arch into the open-plan kitchen-diner. I open a tin of fish and spoon it into her china bowl. Next, the bathroom to wash my hands and splash my face. Everywhere is very tidy and smells of lemon cleanser. The pedal bin has been emptied. The toilet lid is down. Kiki has been busy.

I glide through to my bedroom. The lipstick-stained tissue left on my dressing table that morning has been whisked away, the cover on my bed smoothed down. I hang up my jacket and slip on my comfy cardigan with its deep pockets for my mobile phone, tissues and sweets. A business card. A memory stick.

I turn to go back into the hall. Opposite is the door to Kiki's room. I hover outside. I think I hear a noise. I raise my hand slowly and grasp the cool metal of the handle...

'Thank you, Dr Moss. I'd now like you to think of a happy memory involving a physical activity, playing a sport, dancing, swimming. Something that requires physical exertion. I want you to imagine exactly what your arms and legs are doing.'

My mind is blank, left dangling on the brink of opening a door, unable to continue. I don't do team games. I hate swimming. I don't dance. The only exercise I take is a twice-weekly session at the staff gym at the university.

Pulling myself away from my flat I imagine myself on a cross trainer, my feet pushing down on the pedals while my arms move back and forth as I pull on the handlebars. I count the repetitions. One, two. One, two. The rhythm is relaxing. For half an hour at a time I can blot out the stress of my work, feeling my muscles stretch and my T-shirt dampen as a trickle of sweat rolls between my breasts. One, two. One, two. Someone is on the cross trainer next to me. One, two. One, two. Her movements synchronise perfectly with mine. We stop at the same time and turn and smile at each other. She is plump and tidy. Her smile wavers uncertainly. I wipe my face on my towel.

'I needed that,' I say.

'Yes. It makes me feel a bit better about the bacon butty I'm planning for breakfast.'

'Oh! Don't talk about bacon. You're making me hungry.'

We both walk towards the exercise bikes. It's early, and apart from a couple of young men lifting weights, we are the only ones here. We sit on adjoining bikes.

'How far do you ride?' she asks.

'I don't measure the miles. I pedal until I'm whacked. That's usually about five minutes!'

'I won't feel too bad when I conk out in two, then. This is only my second time in the gym. I haven't built up any endurance yet.'

'I've been coming for over a year and I still haven't built up any stamina!' I joke. 'But then, I don't really take it seriously enough. Not like those two over there.' I nod at the weightlifters.

'Poseurs!' she whispers.

'Exactly! My name's Tilda, by the way.'

'Kiki. I work in Finance.'

'I'm from the Institute of Genetics.'

'Lecturer?'

'Occasionally. Research, mostly. And supervising PhD students.'

'One of the aristocrats, then.'

'I wouldn't say that,' I say defensively.

'I didn't mean to be funny. You learn pretty quickly that there's a hierarchy here. Anyone in admin is a bit of a pleb. You're the talent.'

'There's no hierarchy in the gym. We're all just breathless blobs of sweat.'

That was the first time I met Kiki. I imagine my legs turning the pedals. Round and round. Round and round. How many times had we met up to exercise, grabbing breakfast afterwards in the refectory together? Dozens of times, before she told me tearfully of her break-up from Warwick.

Round and round. Round and round. And I agreed to let her move in with me until she found herself a new place. But that first day, when we went to buy our breakfast, I ordered a bacon roll and turned to ask what she was having, only to find she had picked up a yoghurt and a banana.

'I thought you were having something cooked.'

She shrugged. 'I have wicked thoughts. But when it comes to it, I just can't follow through.'

A sharp pain stabs my big toe. I want to scream, but no sound comes. I can't pull away. I can't even gasp to breathe out the agony. Fury floods my mind. I want to kick out at whoever has driven something sharp into my flesh. Then a lessening. The implement is pulled away and I'm left with a burning sting. The hammering in my ears suddenly stops.

'Thank you, Dr Moss. Take her out now, please.'

I gradually emerge from my prison. The porter rolls me onto my bed and we plunge back into the torrent. I'm borne away, spitting fire, my little raft tossed in a flood of movement and noise, through the corridors, back into the lift where I stare in horrified fascination at my gaunt reflection, until I reach the silence of my room, my resting place, my tomb.

A healthcare assistant supervises my return. She complains about the blood on the sheets. There's the cold sting of wet cotton wool, the stink of antiseptic, the sticky sound of the backing being removed from a plaster, and then my toe is briskly wrapped.

'What was that butcher thinking?' she mutters to a nurse who enters to check my monitors. 'A small pinprick would have sufficed. He should have used a neurotip, not a scalpel.'

'He used some kind of plastic cutter,' the nurse replies. 'The radiographer said he couldn't use anything metal near the scanner.'

'That's as maybe. But what was he trying to do? Bleed her to death?'

Chapter 9

I arrived early at BioExpertise Systems, parked and waited in the car until five minutes after the exhibition opened. A small stream of men in tweed jackets and corduroy trousers was heading from the car park to the main entrance – an atrium of aluminium and glass. I recognised several of my contacts from NESCI – the North East England Stem Cell Institute – a collaboration between Newcastle and Durham universities, the Newcastle Hospitals NHS Foundation Trust and the Centre for Life in Newcastle. I followed them into the building, self-conscious in my new skirt.

A piece of metal artwork hung from the ceiling in the middle of the foyer like an enormous piece of fusilli pasta, though I imagine it was meant to represent the DNA double helix. I saw Michael immediately. He was laughing, head back, mouth open, releasing a great roar of amusement. The men in suits who surrounded him were laughing too, slapping each other on the back and extending their hands as introductions were made to those just arriving. Taller and wider than the rest, Michael opened his arms to welcome his guests as though drawing a congregation into a place of worship. I hung back, feeling like an outsider. He hadn't seen me yet.

A girl in high heels handed me a brochure. I orbited Michael's constellation of admirers and slipped into a conference room full of scientific exhibits: immersion circulators and coolers, microbiological incubators and environmental chambers, nucleic acid purification systems, centrifuges, safety cabinets, clean benches and flow meters. Sales staff in white coats stood behind the tables, pulling up specifications on laptops and running upbeat demonstration DVDs for those who lingered too long by their stands. I shuffled round, smiling perfunctorily, wishing I was back in my office. A hand squeezed my elbow.

'Tilda! You came.'

I swung round. 'Yes. I said I would.'

He continued to grasp my arm and steered me to a quiet corner. His fingers were hot through my silk blouse. He stood blocking my exit, gazing down intently.

'I must introduce you to my team in a moment. They'll be thrilled, absolutely thrilled to meet you. Are you here alone, or did you bring a colleague?'

'Alone, I'm afraid. Diaries… you know how it is.'

'Quite so. Busy, busy people. I'm delighted you spared the time away from your vital research…'

I waved away his flattery.

'… and I hope we'll be able to partner with you in some small way.' He lowered his voice and leaned closer. 'It was a lucky day when fate put you in my path.'

'You introduced yourself, remember?'

'Yes. That's right. It's just that sometimes you meet a person and there's that sense of serendipity. Karma, perhaps. I believe things happen for a reason. Don't you?'

A little spurt of irritation mixed with an unsettling melting sensation in my stomach, and I answered more coldly than I intended. 'Things happen because they happen. The chain of cause and effect stretches back to the origin of the universe, but I wouldn't go so far as to call that karma.'

'Wonderfully put, Tilda. Quite so. Destined since the dawn of time…'

'And how are you settling into the area?' I asked. 'Are you liking what Newcastle has to offer, or are you missing London?'

'Of course I miss it. Great city! Insane! Inane! But never the same. Always something new going on. But life can't always be about terrible commuting and outrageous parties. It was time to swap all that for great commuting and no parties at all.'

'We have parties –'

'Perhaps I'm just not being invited to them, then.'

'Actually, thinking about it, they're probably not worth going to.'

'I'm liking the local ales, though. And I've discovered a smoky little jazz club on Pink Lane, just near the station.'

I nodded as if I knew all about the local music scene. 'And how was your rock festival?'

'Fun while it lasted. Over too soon. Like life, really. Music, food, friends, dancing till dawn. I paid for it afterwards, of course.' He patted his stomach. 'I don't bounce back like the old days, but that's no excuse for not giving the ball a good kickabout. The ticker's just about robust enough for a few more years of delight and gusto. That's the great thing about living today. You don't have to grow up. I can still haul a pair of jeans on to this sagging frame and get down with the kids.'

'Eat, drink and be merry?'

'That's about the size of it. Seize life, Tilda! Don't skimp. Grab your chances. Every day's precarious. Make the most of each one. That's my philosophy.'

'I don't have time for philosophy, I'm afraid. I'm too busy with the nuts and bolts of the universe.'

'Of course you are. Talking of which, you must have a good look at our products. Top-of-the-range stuff. But I've been hogging you. Greedy me. I'm sure there are others who would like to speak to you. Colleagues from other universities. But perhaps I could have you all to myself over lunch. I'd like to hear more about the potential of your research… and walk you through our new educational sponsorship programme in detail.'

I nodded, my heart jumping so hard at the base of my throat that I couldn't trust my voice. He guided me back into the throng, his hand heavy on the small of my back, and introduced me to a number of boring windbags.

'You must excuse me now,' he said, interrupting the small talk. 'I'm giving a presentation in ten minutes.' He turned and bent his head to my ear. His breath was warm on my neck. 'Get yourself a coffee. I must powder my nose and get my box of tricks ready for show time. I'll look for you afterwards at lunch.'

I smiled politely, breathing deeply, and wondering how I would survive another intimate conversation with him while attempting to eat a buffet of canapes and vegetable dips.

'Hello Oscar… It's Kiki. We met at Tilda's birthday party.'

'Kiki?'

'Tilda's flatmate.'

'Oh, yes. Of course.'

'We talked about your quad bike hire company.' The scrape of a chair. The sound of a wrapper tearing open.

'Did we? I've moved on from that now. I'm in the music business. Been DJing for fun for years.'

'That sounds exciting. Would you like a crisp?' The acidic smell of prawn cocktail stings the air.

'No, thanks. Don't want to get greasy crumbs on the cashmere sweater.'

'You don't mind if I –'

'I've been offered the opportunity to be part of a consortium owning a nightclub in the centre of Manchester.'

'Cool!' Crunching followed by a sucking sound as if a finger's being licked.

'It's where the money is.'

'You and Tilda are completely different. You wouldn't guess you're brother and sister.'

'She got the brains. I got the looks!'

Kiki giggles.

'I'm joking, of course. I've got some brains too. Street smarts. That's me. You can only get those in the University of Life. As for my sister, well, you could never get her head out of a book. I told her, "All work and no play makes Tilda a dead bore."'

'Shhhhh! She might hear you.'

'She can't hear dicky… and I'm not saying anything I haven't told her before. You know I'm right. She was never going to find a man looking under a microscope. She needed to get out and live a little. It's tragic. She was just coming round to my way of thinking when this happened.'

'Really?'

'Yes. She was going to invest in the nightclub scheme with me.'

'She never mentioned that.'

'The negotiations were at a delicate stage. We were keeping schtum until the deal was done in case other interested parties got wind of it and stole our thunder.'

'It sounds as though you're doing well for yourself. Did I see you parking a Porsche in the hospital car park?'

'Yes. Lovely, isn't she?'

'Certainly beats the bus.'

After a pause, Oscar says, 'You must let me give you a lift home, Kitty. It's pouring with rain.'

I recognise the tone of voice immediately. It's the one he usually reserves for women who are slimmer and blonder than my flatmate.

'It's Kiki. Thank you, kind sir. That would be greatly appreciated.'

'Sorry, Kiki. I never did have a head for names. And those blue eyes of yours are mighty distracting... I've been meaning to pop round to see you, in any case.'

'Have you?' A scrunching noise. A shuffling of feet. The clang of the pedal and the lid on the tall waste bin as the rubbish is discarded.

'It's awkward with Dad at the moment. This is hard for both of us, but he's not able to contemplate what might be ahead. There are things we can't say to each other, but I think it's important for one of us to check out Tilda's affairs.'

'He did pop round the other –'

'He's gone into a kind of protective bubble. Someone has to be realistic. I'm not saying she's going to die, but we ought to know if she's made a will, for example. Also, I need to know if she signed the paperwork for the nightclub... left a cheque...'

'Of course. I understand. I can show you where she keeps her personal papers. I can cook you a little supper while you go through them.'

'Great. Watching you tackle those crisps has suddenly made me quite peckish.'

'You've probably not been looking after yourself properly, which is quite understandable in the circumstances. Those who are closest to Tilda should support each other at this time, don't you think? Nobody else can really understand what we're going through.'

'Absolutely! It's been hell.'

I watched from the back of the room as Michael paced back and forth across the stage, microphone in hand. He gave a quick rundown of the fire procedures, mimicking the gestures of an air hostess presenting the emergency exits to passengers.

'Don't worry. We haven't had any incidents since the accident!' There was a ripple of amusement. A slick PowerPoint presentation followed, interspersed with a repertoire of ingenious jokes. I remember the smile aching across my cheeks. He filled the stage with his presence. I was mesmerised.

'What a pseud!' someone whispered. I turned and saw the girl who had given me the brochure. She was standing next to a young man in a white coat.

'He certainly loves himself,' he murmured.

I was puzzled. Was I the only one to feel the magnetism? His New Age jargon was irritating, certainly, but I was willing to put that down to *joie de vivre*. He was a big beast in an exotic jungle; I was a dowdy moth fluttering nervously towards a dazzling light, defenceless and amazed. A couple of tepid relationships. Eating dinner on a tray in front of the television. Long hours in a laboratory. Nothing in my past had prepared me for the heat and pull of Michael Cameron.

The policeman is back. He stands over me.

'She's lost weight.'

'Yes.' It's my father's voice. He is brushing my hair, the side where it still falls to my shoulder.

'I'm glad I've caught you, Mr Moss. I have a few more questions.'

'I've told you everything I know. And that's nothing, really…'

'Did your daughter have any financial worries that you're aware of?' He walks away from the bed and gazes out of the window.

'No. She was always good with money, even as a little girl. Careful. A saver rather than a spender. She lives a very quiet life. Not the extravagant type.'

'She started renting out her spare room a few months back.'

'Yes. Not because she needed the money. She was helping out a friend.'

87

'Why was that?' The policeman speaks with subdued intensity, each word as heavy as a stone.

'Her friend – Kiki – had a bust-up with her boyfriend. She needed somewhere to stay. They work at the same university. It was just temporary at first. But it turns out it suits them both.'

'How so?'

'Tilda works long hours. She doesn't always look after herself properly. And she has a cat, Betsy, who doesn't like being left on her own –'

'I'm not sure cats suffer from separation anxiety,' he interrupts sharply.

'No? Well, this one does. It's a house cat. Won't go out of the flat into the garden. Kiki is around in the evenings to feed it when my daughter works late. They also share the cooking, so Tilda has been eating better. She was beginning to put on a bit of weight before …' His voice tails off. I feel their eyes on my emaciated body.

'So Kiki and your daughter… they're not…'

'Gracious, no! Nothing like that. Why are you asking all these questions, inspector? Have you got a new lead?'

'Perhaps. I had a phone call from your daughter's boss, Professor MacMahon, this morning. The university has just finished an audit. Much to their dismay they found half a million pounds missing from college funds. And guess who was the key signatory for that area of the budget?'

'Who?' My father asks, his voice weak. He stops brushing my hair.

'Your daughter.'

Chapter 10

I really need a drink. I miss that feeling when the alcohol hits your bloodstream and your worries slip away. I need something to medicate the pain and dull the shock. I don't understand what the inspector is saying. It isn't possible for college funds to disappear. The systems are too tight.

I think of the people who have access to the server. Professor MacMahon, of course, and Keith, and the Finance Department. Every invoice is linked to a budget head. Every invoice needs authorisation before it's paid. Payments are made online direct to our suppliers' bank accounts. It's near-impossible to get petty cash for a box of mince pies on Christmas Eve, let alone filch half a million pounds!

I'm furious at the implication that I'm somehow involved. They're looking for a fall guy and conveniently I'm in no position to defend myself. Surely no one can seriously think I would steal from the university. They only have to look at my bank statements – comfortably in the black but certainly not to that extent! And if I *had* stolen that amount of money, surely I'd be somewhere more exotic than flat on my back in a hospital cot with a drip stand for company.

My father sits with his head in his hands while the inspector paces the floor. 'I don't care about any of that. I just want her back and better.'

'That's what we all want. I'm merely looking for a possible motive.'

'She didn't try to kill herself over money, if that's what you're suggesting. She never cared about being rich. She was dedicated to her work. She's as straight as a die. Ask anyone.'

'We will.'

'Perhaps it's nothing to do with her. Perhaps that's why she's here. She discovered someone else has been cooking the books and they decided to shut her up.'

'We'll be looking at every angle. You can be assured of that, sir.'

'Will you? She's been here over two months now, and you're no further forward in discovering what happened.'

Two months!

'We're taking this matter very seriously. I have several active lines of enquiry. It doesn't help that we've been unable to find your daughter's budget spreadsheet.'

'Her laptop –'

'… contains nothing of interest. It seems she was in the habit of saving her research and work files to a memory stick and keeping it with her following a hacking incident last year. We've searched her office and flat and been unable to find it.'

'I know nothing about any of this. You're making it look as though she has something to hide.'

'All of us have something to hide, Mr Moss. The question is what? And why?'

Keith didn't like the arrangement with BioExpertise Systems. He talked about the university prostituting itself to big business.

'We're getting into bed with Satan.'

'BioExpertise isn't the devil.'

'No. It's the pimp that's getting us to hook up with Havering Rieche Pharmaceuticals for a pile of filthy lucre.'

'Don't be so dramatic! It's a business deal.' We were sitting on high stools in the lab, eating our sandwiches. 'Our funding's already been cut and there are further cuts down the line. This is a way of getting the equipment our students need at a price we can afford.' I bit into a cardboard-and-cheese sandwich from the canteen.

'With their logo on everything from microscopes to latex gloves, it'll look as though we're giving them our seal of approval.'

'Havering Rieche is a reputable organisation developing vital new cancer drugs and antibiotics. What's the problem? Why shouldn't we partner with them in this small way?'

'They're a ruthless multinational developing medicines that are too expensive for anybody but the rich to afford. That's why we're here, isn't it, Tilda, rather than in the private sector? We want to share our research for the benefit of humanity, not slave our lives away for the benefit of wealthy shareholders. I don't feel comfortable about it.' He brushed muffin crumbs from his trousers and took a swig of coffee.

'You don't feel comfortable about anything. Our students are intelligent enough not to be influenced by a bit of basic branding. Give them some credit. Havering Rieche sponsorship won't affect our work in any way.'

'It's the slippery slope. They'll be branding us next!' A flush spread across his nose, emphasising the open pores and the hairs that sprouted from each one.

'Why do you have to think the worst of everyone?'

'Why do you have to be so naïve?'

'I'm not naïve. Personally, I think it was a canny move and I was glad to help set up the meetings.'

'You'd better be sure everything's above board.' He looked away, as though ashamed of his words.

'Of course it is! What are you saying? Are you accusing me of something?'

'Not at all. I know your code of ethics. Others don't. If they suspect you've received a backhander from BioExpertise Systems, there'll be hell to pay.'

'I can't believe I'm hearing this.' Tears burned my eyes but I refused to let them fall. Instead I jumped from my stool and walked towards the kettle by the sink in the corner. My hand shook with anger as I filled it with water.

'I'm only thinking of you.' Keith had followed and was standing behind me. 'We're at a crucial point in the project. It's not your job to go swanning off for meetings with the boys upstairs.'

'It's everybody's job to make the best use of scarce resources.' I chucked a teabag in a mug.

'If *I* can't understand why you're getting yourself involved with this deal, it's bound to raise other people's eyebrows. You know what the college is like. Gossip. Petty jealousies. You've been neglecting your students and your research. And now you're behind with the latest data analysis.'

'This is none of your business. I'm *your* supervisor, remember. I'm not accountable to you.'

He flinched and shrugged to cover it up. I'd never made a big deal of our relative positions, but guilt at missing my own deadline had ignited a blast of cold fury. I wasn't going to let Mister-Brown–Trousers-and-Coffee-Breath accuse me of letting things slide. I silently vowed to catch up over the weekend.

He tried a different tack.

'BioExpertise's stuff might be cheaper, but that doesn't necessarily mean it's the best.'

I faced him, holding my cup of steaming tea between us.

'It looks fine to me. Don't be such an old woman.'

'I don't want us to fall out over this, Tilda.' His tone had softened.

'Then let's drop the subject.'

'You've changed,' he said unexpectedly.

'What *are* you talking about?'

'You know. These last few weeks. It's been different. Are you OK? Is everything all right?'

'Of course it is. I don't know what's got into *you*. I'm not used to having you impersonate the Spanish Inquisition over lunch. Now, you'll have to excuse me. I must get on. As you so kindly reminded me, I need to write up my report.'

I strode to my office and slammed the door, locking it behind me and spilling hot tea on my hand. I swore and put the cup down quickly, dabbing my burning skin with a tissue from my lab coat pocket, then wiping my eyes which had blurred with suppressed frustration.

I thought I had been carrying on as normal, thought nobody had noticed the seismic change that had taken place. I cursed Keith, and then cursed myself for being such a poor actress. I put my head in my hands and sobbed that the deal had been done and there would be no more meetings with BioExpertise Systems, no more lunches with Michael, and no idea how to manufacture an excuse to see him again.

I wake up cold and wet. At first I think my disposable pants have leaked, then realise I'm damp all over and my nightie is clinging to my skin like a cold shudder. My body is shivering – yes, actually moving by itself – racked by a succession of small jerks and uncontrolled twitches. The downy hairs on my forearms rise like hackles. I wonder whether I'll spontaneously sit up, reanimated in a crackle of static like Frankenstein's monster. My teeth rattle to escape their prison, banging on the walls of my skull, chattering about the pain they are inflicting to the side of my head. The pounding, pounding pain.

The pattern on my curtain has come alive. One paisley swirl unfurls and slithers among the folds like a giant amoeba, waking up the others. Yellow and blue tadpoles wriggle across the material, suddenly closer and then far away, oscillating and blurring to a pinprick. And then the cold has gone and there's heat and burning and a dry desert at the back of my throat. The nurses flock and peck at me like vultures, stabbing me with their needles, scouring me with sponges.

'She's got an infection, Mr Moss... Touch and go... Urinary tract. Possibly kidney. We've taken bloods... She needs intravenous antibiotics... She's very poorly. You might want to call your son...'

And they touch me and they go, and they touch me and they go, and Oscar floats across the sky, and Claude is banging what sounds like saucepans, and then I'm all alone again with the swimming amoeba and the pounding in my temple and a burning pain deep in my loins. I want to scratch out the sting, and scream and scream and scream for the curtain to stop moving and leave me in peace. And then I'm floating on the ceiling, up in the corner. It's an unexpected development. I'm looking down at my twisted body, my eyes half-open.

I feel simultaneously heavy and solid, transparent and light. I'm both a particle and a wave, living proof of the peculiarity and mysteriousness of the quantum world. I'm Heisenberg's uncertainty principle. I'm here and not here. I'm everywhere and nowhere. I can't tell whether I'm lying on the bed or hovering by the window, and none of the medical staff seems to have noticed the increasing fuzziness of my existence. Maybe that's the problem. When no one watches over me, perhaps I've ceased to exist.

Then Claude comes and stands by the bed. He's telling me to stop my nonsense right away and come back now! He says there's unfinished business. Questions to be answered. And he's kneeling by my bedside and bending his head. And now I realise I'm in big trouble because he's started to pray.

Chapter 11

'So you've just moved in yourself?' Kiki asks, dumping her suitcase in the living room.

'I've been here two years.'

'Have you been decorating?'

'Not yet. I've bought the paint. Sorry. It's a bit of a mess. I don't get much time… I still haven't unpacked all my boxes yet. How bad is that?'

'Don't apologise. It's fine. Lovely, in fact. What beautiful pots.' She walks to the French doors and looks out at the balcony.

'My balcony garden. Yes. I love my plants.'

'I can see that. Where shall I put this?' She gestures to her suitcase. I show her to the guest room.

'I've cleared out most of my stuff. The drawers are empty. I hope it's OK.'

'It's fine, Tilda, really. I appreciate you helping me out like this.'

'I'll make a cup of tea while you unpack. Let me know if you need anything. Towels, hangers…'

'Thanks. Milky, please. With a sweetener if you've got one.'

'I'm not sure I have. Will sugar do?'

'Just this once. I'll go shopping later on. Get some groceries in. You must let me cook dinner tonight.'

I walk into the kitchen and fill the kettle. While it boils I mooch around the flat, seeing it with new eyes. The faded paint. The coffee table strewn with papers. The framed print of Guernica by Picasso leaning against the wall, still waiting for a picture hook to be hammered into the plaster above the fireplace.

'This place has bags of potential,' she says when she returns to the lounge.

'That's why I bought it.'

'I saw the paint tins in the hall. I like the colours. Would you like me to help?'

'I couldn't ask you to do that.'

'Of course you could. I'd love it! I know I work in accounts, but I try to give my creative side an airing sometimes. What colour scheme were you envisaging for this room?'

We talk about palettes and accents, the curtains and the sofa, cushion covers and ways of arranging the furniture that would make better use of the space.

'Why don't we move it around now?' she suggests.

We spend the afternoon moving the furniture. Once we've found the best position for the three-piece suite, bookshelves and desk, Kiki asks for a duster. She wipes down each book we stacked temporarily on the floor and puts it back in size order, polishing the shelves and rearranging the photographs on the top. By the time we flop back on the sofa, red-faced and dishevelled, the room's been transformed.

'Next weekend I'd be happy to start painting. All we need to do is move the furniture into the middle and put a couple of dust sheets down. The ceiling and woodwork look fine. It'll take no time at all to roller the walls with that gorgeous duck-egg blue you've bought.'

'Do you think so? I've been procrastinating, I know, but it's got beyond me now. It all seems too much by the time I come home from the lab.'

'That's because you have a very important and demanding job. Let me do this for you, as a way of saying thank you for letting me stay.'

That evening we opened a bottle of wine and sat and talked, me slumped in the armchair with my legs outstretched, and Kiki on the sofa with her feet curled under her bottom.

'Thanks again, Kiki. The flat looks better already. I can't wait to start decorating now.'

'It's much more relaxing to come home to somewhere welcoming and tidy.'

'I think I stopped noticing. Now I can see how it must have looked through your eyes. You must think me a terrible slob.'

'You work very long hours.'

'It's no excuse.'

'You know, I no longer think it's possible to have it all – career, husband, kids, a beautiful home. It's a lie perpetrated by men to keep our noses to the grindstone. And them off the hook!'

'Do I sense a Warwick rant coming on?'

'He's not worth it. But now he's finally out of my life, it's a relief to let go of trying to be the perfect girlfriend.'

'Why would you try to be perfect? He should love you for who you are. You shouldn't change yourself to suit his needs.'

'Have you ever been in love? *Really* in love, Tilda?'

'I think perhaps I have.' I pick at a thread on my skirt, thinking of the gleam in Michael's dark eyes.

'Tell me more, Dr Moss!'

'It was just one of those things. It happened. I don't know why. We don't… didn't have much in common.'

'You can't legislate for who you fall in love with.'

'That's true.'

'The heart has a mind of its own. It's shocking when it happens. Beautiful. Chaotic. The best feeling in the world. But after a while the dark thoughts come, those things you keep shut up in a box. You want to defend yourself against the pain of losing him. You try to work out what they want. What their perfect woman would be. You fill the fridge with the food they like. You put up with their stupid friends and their football. You don't place any demands on them. You watch the competition, women more beautiful and clever and successful and funny than you are. And all the time you're filing down your edges so you slot smoothly into shape, erasing your own life to fit round the contours of his. Before you know it, you find yourself living in this very small and lonely space. However hard I worked, however hard I tried to be a good girl, when it came down to it, I was no longer the woman he fell in love with.'

'Is that what happened?'

'Yes. I'd become a doormat. Plus, five foot seven strawberry blonde Charlotte Newberry happened.' Betsy jumped onto her lap. Kiki stood up and shooed her away, brushing cat hairs off her black jeans.

'I'm sorry. That's awful.'

She picked up the half-finished bottle of white wine from the coffee table and poured us both another glass before curling back down on the sofa.

'I was sorry too. But I'm no longer going to be brainwashed into thinking men are the be-all and end-all. I'm going to take a leaf out of your book and live a full professional, economic and social life on my own. I'm going to change the world to suit myself, instead of the other way round.'

'Good for you!'

'What do I want and how do I get it? That's my mantra. I'm not going to outsource my happiness to another person again.'

'Sounds a bit lonely, though, Kiki. You haven't been single for as long as I have. Paddling your own canoe gets a bit wearing after a while.'

'That's no reason to compromise. I'd rather be on my own than be with someone who's not good enough. Next time he's going to be rich, handsome and easy to manipulate.'

'Mmmm… But if you have a checklist of what you want, is that really love? Real love is about vulnerability and acceptance and truth.'

'Wow. I never had you down as an idealist. I believe you're blushing. What happened to lover boy, by the way?'

'Oh, him… we lost touch.'

'There you go, then.'

'Yes. But it was a beautiful dream while it lasted.'

She raised her glass.

'To beautiful dreams!'

'To beautiful dreams.' We clinked.

'And selfish realities,' she continued. We clinked again.

'I'm very disappointed.' Professor MacMahon is sitting close to my bed, muttering furiously in my ear. 'The bursar is fuming. Is this what it's all been about? Did you do this… this desperate thing because you've been dipping your fingers into the honeypot? It was bound to come out in the end. You had a glittering career before you. What were you thinking? If you had any personal problems or worries, you could have come to me. I'm not such an old duffer. I would have wanted to help.

'This reflects on all of us, you know. It's not just about you. I've been given a proper drubbing. Keith's back on the antidepressants. The whole department's been implicated. The auditors and the police have been checking everything. We're all under suspicion. I've come to let you know that you're now officially suspended. The bursar's put you on gardening leave.

'If you can hear me, I hope you are thoroughly ashamed of yourself. I trusted you… I trusted you.'

I remember Kiki busying herself with the painting project. The flat became perceptibly tidier over the following weeks. I began to get used to having a hot meal waiting when I returned home instead of making do with snacks and leftovers rummaged from the fridge. My papers and letters were swept into neat piles on my desk, the opened envelopes thrown away. I liked unlocking the door and discovering the rooms softly lit by table lamps, the carpets vacuumed and the cushions plumped. She'd even bought a cat scratching post to stop Betsy tearing at the carpets. I imagined the housework was her way of saying thank you.

'Warwick must have been mad to let you go.'

'He took me for granted. There comes a point where something snaps.'

'Well, I hope you don't think I'd ever take you for granted. It's wonderful how you've transformed the place. For the first time it feels like a proper home. I suppose you'll be looking for your own flat soon.'

'I wanted to do this for you. You've been such a good friend, letting me stay while I get back on my feet. Warwick's being a nightmare. He owes me a lot of money. I don't know how I'm going to get it back without going to court, and I can't afford a lawyer.'

It was then that we agreed to formalise the arrangement. For a minimal rent, and help with the cooking, laundry and housework, Kiki would become my permanent lodger. I told her she was what every career woman needed: a surrogate mother.

Chapter 12

I awake to find myself facing the window. A 'V' of geese glides across the sky. A wet leaf has blown against the window – a sycamore, I think – and sticks there like the palm of a desperate man. My father is here. The second movement of Chopin's second piano concerto fills my room with dewdrops, cool and indulgent. He no longer talks to me when he visits. He sits in the corner like a sagging leather chair, worn and creased with use and age.

He stands up suddenly when the consultant enters.

'I've got the results of the MRI scan. It's not good news, I'm afraid. There's been no improvement. There was no cerebral activity in response to my questioning, or in response to a prick to the toe.'

No! You're wrong!

'Nothing?' Dad's voice breaks.

'I'm sorry. When you've had a chance to speak to your son, we will need to have a discussion about what to do next.'

You're not looking hard enough. I'm here.

'What to do?'

'Yes. There are some decisions that will need to be made… about the future.'

'Are we talking about a nursing home?'

Oh, Dad…

'That might be an option. But you need to consider the cost.'

'The cost?'

'Yes. You would need to find a suitable institution. The National Health Service isn't here to keep people alive artificially when there's no hope of recovery.'

'You're not switching off any machines! I'm not going to let you! I'll get a lawyer!'

'Calm down, Mr Moss. It's a lot for you to take in, I know. You need to talk to the rest of the family. I can see you're not ready to make any decisions yet. We don't want to rush you. But in time, I think you will know the right thing to do. For Tilda. For your son. For yourself.'

Don't give up on me, Dad. Please.

He sits down. A strange cry comes from his lips, like an animal in pain. And he's rocking back and forth, holding his body tight, and wailing, wailing, wailing, and the doctor puts a hand on his shoulder, but won't look at him, and a nurse runs into the room to find out what's happening, and my father grips my hand, and with a strange whoosh my perspective changes and Dad looks different, like someone I've never seen before. Mucus runs from his nostrils. Veins stand out in his forehead like blue scars. His hair is white and wild. And I want to flinch from the raw intensity of his pain and pretend I'm not with him, pretend I'm not embarrassed like a teenager at his terrible lack of self-control.

I couldn't tell if Michael was interested in me as a woman. From what I'd seen, he was intrigued by everything and everybody. He regaled me with tales of girlfriends past, both before and after his wife: a sculptress, a folk singer, a vegan activist, a psychic who would regularly go into a trance over dinner.

'I put it down to indigestion,' he said.

I definitely didn't conform to type – small, colourless, detached. But when I was with him I felt the stirrings of a new me, as though I were waking up after a long sleep.

'I don't usually like atheists,' he said, smiling over his double espresso.

My heart had thudded with disappointment before I realised with a spurt of joy the implication of the word 'usually'. I was an exception.

We were sitting at the back of a small Italian café after bumping into each other in an off-licence on his side of the city. He didn't know I'd followed him on his way home from work. I told him I was looking for a bottle of wine for a fictional dinner party later in the week, and asked his advice. We finally settled on a full-bodied red for me. He bought a selection of speciality ales for himself. Our purchases were in two plastic bags under the table.

'What's wrong with atheists?'

'In my experience they're pretty dismissive of other people's beliefs, and irritatingly dogmatic about their own rightness and everybody else's stupidity.'

'I hope you don't think I'm like that.'

'Not dismissive... disapproving, perhaps. And why not? You're a scientist. I assume atheism goes with the territory. You probably find me tiresomely sentimental.'

Never tiresome, I thought. Tangling with Michael was like a bracing walk along a cliff top: invigorating, dizzying, occasionally terrifying.

'There's nothing wrong with sentiment,' I said, not quite believing the words had left my mouth. 'I try not to be a soulless iconoclast. I mean, I don't believe in the soul, so I suppose I am soulless... but I hope I'm not insensitive to other people's search for meaning. I've been on that road myself.' I spooned froth

104

from the bottom of the tall latte glass and savoured the last dregs of my coffee.

'I don't believe what you say about your soul. I see the passion in your eyes when you talk about your work. When I saw you for the first time on that podium – you remember, the conference – I was truly inspired by what you were saying. You had a clarity about you. If you, a world expert –'

'Hardly a world expert!' I gazed down at the red and white checked table cloth, discomfited by his enthusiasm.

'Yes! Yes, I believe you are. There's no need to be modest. And if you, the expert, are so sure about how life can be improved and prolonged using stem cells, then I want be part of that project in whatever small way I can. Even if it's only to stretch your budget a little further. I hope you'll find the collaboration between our two organisations helpful. I'm not just in it for the sale. I like knowing the Institute of Genetic Medicine at the university is getting a good deal, that I'm contributing in a very small way to your vital research.'

I shivered under his scrutiny, intoxicated at the intensity of his eyes, knowing he was seeing me as something more than I could possibly be.

'I think you're driven by something other than work ethic alone. Your focus. Your belief in a better world. Your integrity. I want to know what powers your engine, Tilda. What stops you becoming cynical and self-centred when you believe in nothing more than the here and now? What was it that made you ditch the idea of a Supreme Being?'

I decided to be honest. 'The death of my mother didn't help. I can't see how God could be any part of that.'

'Ah. So really, it's a matter of revenge.'

'Revenge?'

'Yes. God didn't protect you from suffering, so you punish Him by refusing to believe in Him.'

'Except that there is no God to wreak my revenge on. Just a psychological construct. Suffering is part of the random unfairness of life. I've been dedicating myself to the alleviation of that suffering ever since coming to that conclusion.'

'The mantra of the scientist: become the god you've killed off.' He had no qualms about throwing back his head and roaring with laughter.

'That's a bit much!' I objected, but it was impossible to be offended.

'Sorry. I shouldn't tease you. Sadly, you're probably right about the God question, but I still find atheism massively unappealing. There's a shocking lack of humour and poetry about the whole thing. It's difficult to be interested in the concept of nothing. How do you hold a non-belief?'

'By not thinking about it. For me, the question of God no longer arises.'

'I wish it were that easy. As I've got older, it's become a nagging question. Let me get you another drink.' He signalled to the waitress and ordered a latte for me and another espresso for himself.

'I've got some books that might help, if you're interested.'

'Books?'

'Giving scientific explanations for the existence of the universe.'

'I doubt I'd understand them. Between you and me, I'm clinging on by my fingertips understanding the equipment I'm marketing. Actually, I don't really understand most of it… but I've always had the knack of selling sand in the Sahara. That's why your input has been so invaluable.'

'You're being very hard on yourself. You've got a good grasp of scientific principles. The books I've got are well within your ability. They're aimed at students.'

'OK. I'll take a look. But the irony's not lost on me that I'm forever seeking something that's beyond my understanding.'

'Would you like me to drop them off?'

'I don't want to put you to any inconvenience –'

'It's no trouble,' I interrupted.

'I know!' He clapped his huge hands together. 'We could meet for a drink somewhere halfway between our two offices. You bring your books, and I'll bring some of mine. We'll set each other some homework. When we've read them, we'll meet up again and see whether they've changed our outlook on life.'

'What sort of books?' I asked suspiciously.

'Nothing that should intimidate your rational mind, my dear. Is it a deal?'

'Let me get this straight. I'll try to convince you of the argument for atheism and you'll try to convince me of… what?'

'Of the possibility that there are more things in heaven and earth, Tilda Moss, than are dreamt of in your philosophy.' He raised his cup in an exaggerated toast. 'Cheers, my dear! I do love a challenge. Don't you?'

'I had that Kiki girl on the phone yesterday,' Dad says.

Oscar grunts and fiddles with his cuffs. His right leg is jigging up and down.

'When were you going to tell me?'

'Tell you what?'

'That you'd been round to Tilda's flat.'

'It's no biggie,' Oscar shrugs. He glances evasively out of the window.

'I think it is. Why did you go?'

'I thought one of us should check everything's OK. We don't know this girl. She could be dicey –'

'Takes one to know one!' Dad interrupts.

107

'How do we know she's not going through Tilda's stuff? Her cheque book, her jewellery…?'

'I went last week. Everything seemed in order. I understand from Kiki you took a bag of things from Tilda's room. The police told us we should leave everything undisturbed.'

'It's for safekeeping.' Oscar puts his hand in his jacket pocket. 'Here's her iPod. I brought it with me to play some of her favourite music. Isn't that what we're supposed to be doing? Stimulating her brain… By the way, when did she become interested in jazz?'

'I didn't know she was. And don't change the subject.' I recognise Dad's tone from when we were children.

Oscar taps the screen and selects a tune. Ella Fitzgerald fills the room with a miasma of smoke and warm sugar. Her words flow through my mind, becoming my thoughts, and I feel myself becoming her music – sadder, lonelier, somnolent.

'And what about her jewellery?' Dad continues.

'It's somewhere safe.'

'Where?'

'You don't need to worry about it.'

'I knew it. The pawnbroker's! I'm not stupid, Oscar. Most of that jewellery belonged to your mother. You had no right to take it.'

'Tilda doesn't need it now… and I did!'

I've never listened to the lyrics of 'Someone to Watch Over Me' properly before. Now they're my words, words I'm unable to speak but which vibrate within. Words about Michael and my longing to have him watching over me now.

Oscar's forehead reddens. 'She was my mother too! Why shouldn't I borrow it to tide me over? I'll get it back. It's just a matter of cash flow. If you're that bothered, you can give me a grand and I'll get it back for you.'

'You put your mother's inheritance in hock for a grand?' Dad cries. 'You know it's worth at least three times that.'

'I knew you wouldn't help me. And Tilda can't at the moment. What was I supposed to do?'

'I'm sick of throwing good money after bad. Give me the ticket. I'll get it back. Not for you, for Tilda.'

Someone to watch over me.

The music slips through my fingers like a silver chain, cool and intimate.

Oscar huffs and puffs as he rummages through his wallet. Dad snatches the ticket and storms out of the room. Oscar and I are left alone with Ella Fitzgerald.

'Why couldn't you have signed those papers, Tilda? I wouldn't have let you down.'

He's staring at the monitor and the drip by my bed, chewing his lower lip.

Someone to watch over me.

He glances at my face and catches my eye in a long, assessing gaze. For a moment, I think we've made a connection. My heart leaps with hope. Then he reddens, scoops up my iPod and crashes out through the door.

The blonde woman is back.

'I'm Allegra. You must be Kiki? I've heard all about you.'

'Have you? I haven't heard anything about you.'

They circle each other like dogs, unsure whether to sniff and wag, or lunge, teeth bared.

'I'm one of Tilda's oldest friends. From Durham. We grew up together. I'm surprised she hasn't mentioned me.'

'And I'm surprised we haven't met before – if you're such good friends.'

'I've been out of the country. But we keep in touch... kept in touch. And you've lived with her for... what is it now? Four months?'

'Five.'

'I was talking to Peter the other day... her dad.'

'I know who he is.'

'Anyway, he still doesn't seem to know what happened.'

'No one does.'

'In fact, he didn't seem to know very much about Tilda's personal life at all.'

'She was very wrapped up in her work.'

'He didn't even know about her boyfriend.'

'Boyfriend?'

'Yes.'

'Tilda didn't have a boyfriend.'

'That's not what she told me.'

'What did she say?'

'If you're so close, I'm surprised you don't know about him. They were seeing each other for some months.'

'I don't believe it!'

'It's true. His name's Michael. '

I'm as shocked as Kiki looks. Who is this woman? How does she know so much about me?

'If she had a boyfriend, I would have known. He would have visited her here in hospital.'

'Unless...'

'Unless what? If you know something the police don't, then I think you should tell them.'

'I assumed they already knew about him. After all, isn't the love interest the first person they talk to in cases like this?'

'Cases like what?'

'Attempted suicide. Attempted murder.'

'You don't know that! What was your name again? Allegra? Allegra what? I'm sure Inspector Lake would like a word.'

'I'll go and see him. I want to know more about this man who supposedly loves her but never comes to visit. I'd like to give him a piece of my mind. I'll leave you two together.' She bends over my bed and looks me in the eye. I can taste her anger, peppery hot. 'Goodbye, Tilda,' she whispers, too low for Kiki to hear. 'I'll track him down. I'll make him pay. I'll make you both pay.'

Claude is arguing with a nurse. 'I'm telling you. Somebody been fiddlin' with her tubes.'

'I've sorted it.'

'It was like that yesterday. Nuffin' comin' down the tube. How she gonna get better with no liquids or medicines?'

'What do you know about her treatment? Are you a doctor or a nurse? Are you a healthcare assistant? No! You're just a cleaner-upper.'

'And I'm tryin' to clean up this mess. I've been in enough hospital rooms ta know when summat's not right. I know what a slide clip is.'

'Are you suggesting someone is deliberately sabotaging her care?'

'Maybe. How else did that clip get slid across the tube?'

'If I have any more trouble from you, I shall report you to your superior.'

'What have I done? I'm trying to help. Her line was clamped! That's attempted murder, innit?'

'You're making wild accusations. How do I know this isn't some kind of attention-seeking stunt?'

'Attention! Why would I want your attention? I just know what I knows. When I came an hour ago there was liquid goin' down the tube. Now there's none in the tube. It's been turned off. Most of it's still in the bag.'

'Perhaps the last shift changed the bag and forgot to release the slide.'

'It ain't on the notes.'

Her voice softens. 'It's sorted now. Let's leave it at that. Probably an unfortunate oversight. No harm done. But I'll keep an eye on it. All right?'

I remember the presence in my room on the night of the storm. I remember the inspector's warning. I remember the way Oscar looked at my drip, and I can't shake the sensation that someone's still out to get me.

Chapter 13

In the end, Michael suggested we go to the jazz club on Pink Lane. He didn't need to know that jazz wasn't my thing. Being with him was my thing. He picked me up in his classic 1970s racing green convertible MGB Roadster sports car, his paunch tucked under the steering wheel. If I concentrate hard, I can still smell the black leather interior. Thankfully the roof was in place because I'd made a special effort to blow-dry my hair, which had made it fickle with static. It might be early July, but Newcastle still hadn't woken up to the fact that the students had left for the summer and the weather should be improving. Michael was wearing a pair of dark trousers, a grey jacket, an open-necked black shirt and a fedora hat.

'Very jazz,' I told him.

He laughed. 'I like to look the part.'

During the drive, he steered the conversation back to my research. We talked for a few minutes but I didn't want to get sucked into work mode.

'Obviously, I can't go into the details –'

'You're right. I'm already out of my depth.'

'The university has a very strict confidentiality policy. Particularly after the Institute of Genetic Medicine was hacked last year.'

'Really?'

'Yes. Keith and I were working on something. We were just about to publish, when suddenly a researcher in Europe – Germany, Switzerland, Austria, I can't remember where – published data identical to ours. It was uncanny. The statistics matched completely. For two independent research projects to be set up in exactly the same way with the same parameters and the same statistical results is unheard of. The only conclusion we could come to was that there had been a leak.'

'Did you find out who it was?'

'No. It might have been a rogue IT student annoyed at getting low grades and tempted to earn a little cash on the side. Anyway, I changed all my passwords. Can you believe I used to use the same password for everything? 'Betsycat'. Anyone who knew I had a cat called Betsy would have been able to work that one out in five minutes. Now I have a different password for each account and document based on a little gadget I have which randomly throws up an eight-digit series of letters and numbers.'

'I'd never be able to keep track of that,' he laughs. 'The old grey matter has been deteriorating since I passed the big four-o a few years back. I can't even remember my own mobile number.'

'I have to keep a list. That's one drawback. But no one knows where it is.'

'Is the list password protected "Betsycat", by any chance?' He turned his head and winked mischievously. I gripped the seat as if we'd taken a bend too fast.

'No!' I exclaimed in mock annoyance. 'I prefer to work offline, in any case. I save everything important to a memory stick. I just don't trust all these clouds and networks any more.'

'Risky.'

'I back up regularly.'

'I'm sure you do. The trouble with any of this computer stuff – as with life in general – is that you can never entirely eliminate risk.'

I experience the scene as an outsider. It's imprinted on my memory with photographic accuracy, the lines and contours, the subtleties, the awkward flirtations.

We order a bottle of white wine and eat crab and asparagus listening to a quartet of piano, bass, saxophone and drums playing 'Cantaloupe Island' and 'April in Paris'.

A little later a woman in a figure-hugging gown takes the microphone and delivers a medley of Nat King Cole numbers. Her voice is rich and throaty, like whisky by the fire, simultaneously teasing and soothing, needling and hypnotising, until her words become my words, her voice the voice of my heart.

During the set, Michael watches the musicians, one foot slung across his knee. He nods in time with the music. An unexpected spurt of jealousy heats my cheeks. I want him to be looking at me, not gazing at blue silk falling like water through an undulating landscape.

He grips the stem of his glass in a large, bear-like hand, his face ruddy with pleasure. My stomach clenches in a spasm of desire. I have a condom in my bag, chastely wrapped and possibly close to its due date. It's impossible to imagine a scenario where I could suggest that he might like to use it. Nevertheless, I'm prepared for the possibility of passion, however remote it seems. Just the thought of it makes me breathless with excitement.

During the break he turns his attention back to me. 'Makes you believe in heaven, doesn't it?'

'I'm an atheist, remember?' I pull a book out of my handbag and slip it across the table. It's the latest bestseller from a celebrity evolutionist.

'*Cremating God,*' he reads from the cover. 'That sounds like a scorching read.'

I laugh at his terrible pun. 'It's an honest read.'

'That's one of the things I like about you. Your confidence. It's very attractive to an agnostic like me. Though sometimes I wonder if those who hold most tightly to their point of view are secret doubters, but don't want to admit it.'

'You think I protest too much?'

He ignores my question and pulls open the small rucksack he's been carrying, and puts a selection of thin books and pamphlets on the table. There's one about Transcendental Meditation, another on Buddhism and one entitled *Who Moved the Stone?*

'Here's a little collection of books I've gathered along the way. I'd be interested in your views. As you can see, I'm an eclectic agnostic. I like to keep the door ajar. I suppose it means I'm a coward.' He smiles unselfconsciously.

'Gullible perhaps, but not a coward. It takes a lot of courage to think there might be a reckoning day, a Supreme Being with his tally chart of sins and a list of names of those who are going to be let in – and those who aren't!'

'Does that idea scare you?'

'Not as much as some of your ridiculous conspiracy theories.' It was unlike me to be so bold, so flirtatious.

He chuckles. 'There speaks the sceptic. But believing there's nothing, no purpose… doesn't the meaninglessness overwhelm you?' His eyes stay fixed on mine.

'No. I believe in truth.'

'So do I.' He takes another sip of wine. His hands are huge. They look more suited to tightening wheel nuts than stroking the stem of his wine glass.

'Only the scientific method leads to truth.'

'That's an interesting argument. Did you deduce that from science? You can't prove it in a test tube. Saying only science leads to truth is a step of faith as much as me hoping I'll come back next time as a springer spaniel.' He picks up his napkin and mops his forehead. 'I prefer to imagine there's a paradise somewhere, filled with people I love and jazz bands and rock and roll and crab and asparagus and gallons of red wine and real ale and mangoes and raspberries, coffee walnut cake, roast lamb, rugby, classic cars… and where I've got a glorious six-pack and a full head of hair.'

'Don't you have a six-pack?' I ask, raising an eyebrow.

'As a matter of fact I do. A six-pack of beer!' He pats his chest and winks.

My heart thumps, every nerve ending alive.

'Surely it's better to keep wishing for something after death,' he continues, 'than to believe in a future with no love or justice or hope. I know what I'd prefer to be true.'

'Wishing for it is no reason to believe it. You're wallowing in sentimentality, Michael.' The words were out before I could stop them. 'I'm not complaining,' I smile, back-pedalling furiously. 'It's refreshing to meet someone who sees more to life than quantum theory and quadratic equations. But it doesn't make it true.'

'Maybe. But I prefer a beautiful idea over cynicism.'

'I'm not cynical. I'm just saying the kind of comfort you're looking for can only be believed if you shut your eyes, hold your nose and swallow deeply.' I sip my wine to make the point.

He didn't reply immediately. I wonder if I've gone too far. Had our friendly debate somehow turned into an argument?

'I'll get us another drink.'

I watch him walk away. He moves with territorial ease and greets the barman like an old friend. I hope he isn't offended. Why, oh why, can't I play the little woman just for once, and not make every conversation an intellectual debate in which I have to come out on top?

I can't hear what they're saying, but Michael's tone is expansive. He leans matily against the bar. I'm impatient to have him back so I can repair any damage.

I scrutinise him, unobserved from my dark corner. Beneath the heavy frame, I glimpse the young man he would have been, a broad-shouldered boy – boisterous, funny, sentimental – standing at the student bar with the collar of his rugger shirt turned up, white against a weathered neck and strong jawline. He would have been surrounded by slender girls in floral dresses who studied literature or history and went skiing with their parents every February. He wouldn't have looked twice at a girl like me, someone serious, academic, driven, sitting on a stool with the nerdy science boys, sipping half a pint of cider.

But time has been on my side. Those floral girls would now be mothers of other young men. Their waists would have widened with frothy coffees and ladies' lunches, their skins thickened through competitive parenting and the knocks of divorce. Left on the shelf, unused and unindulged, I know I don't look my age. There have been few family dramas to grey my hair. My skin's pale from years of hiding in a laboratory. I'm past the point where the latest fad matters. I dress to suit my shape (small and boyish) and can at last compete with the Mirandas and the Phoebes with their Botox, control pants and stretch marks. I'm not going to let this chance of happiness slip through my fingers.

'Atheism is like a song with words, but no music,' he says, breathless with the effort of weaving between the tables. He places a glass of white wine in front of me and sits down with his whisky. 'A meal with nutrition, but no taste. It can't say anything about good or evil, beauty or ugliness. There has to be a purpose to the whole shebang, otherwise what's the point? There's too much complexity to believe we evolved from nothing. How did fish become rabbits? What happened before the Big Bang? If the universe ticks along through rational principles, there has to be some kind of intelligent mind – Jesus or Buddha or Allah or karma.'

'That's a lot of questions. Have you got all night? Believing in everything effectively means you believe in nothing. Somewhere along the line you have to engage your critical faculties.' Again, I wonder if that sounds a little harsh, but he leans forward.

'Underneath this frivolous exterior, there's a serious man trying to make sense of it all. And my critical faculties tell me I like talking with you very much. It's exciting to converse with a woman who doesn't bang on all the time about how she's feeling and what you're feeling and what you're going to do about it. Perhaps you can convert me to a more dispassionate approach.'

'It's not a matter of conversion. It's a question of facing up to reality –'

'I've always thought reality overrated. I came to the conclusion a long time ago that human beings are completely batty so I might as well embrace the madness. Now I'm beginning to wonder if you're the first truly sane person I've met.'

The way he looks at me makes my heart stutter. I gabble to cover the expectant pause.

'I *do* believe in an eternal life of sorts. Everything on this planet was born from an exploding star. At the atomic level, all that has ever lived is still with us. Organisms decay and eventually return to their elemental structure. It takes about 50

119

years for an atom to be free from its original host. It can't remember the history of its past, and neither will we. We merely return to the unchanging pot of energy that makes up our universe.'

'All hail to the high priestess of materialism! The evangelical scientist! So it's less "dust to dust" and more "atom to atom"?'

'Exactly. Our atoms are immortal, even if we aren't.'

'It's almost romantic.'

'Hardly. Though I do think science is beautiful.'

'And what about those parts of ourselves that aren't made up of atoms? Consciousness, soul, spirit, mind, whatever you like to call it? The software that exists within the hardware of our bodies?' He raises his glass in a toast. His hand is shaking. 'And how do you explain love?'

I feel myself blushing and look away. For the first time that evening, I have no reply.

Chapter 14

There are voices all around me, whispers rising up as from a great depth. I've been somewhere else. I'm not sure where but I feel as though I've been asleep for a long time, sleeping so deeply that I wake exhausted. The scent of lavender fills the room. I'm reminded of bees drowsily nudging the flowers on my balcony. My mind buzzes with summer. I would like to slip back into the dark unknown, but the conversation grows louder.

'I would have come sooner, if you'd told me. You do know that, Peter?' It was a woman's voice, firm and reassuring.

'Yes. I should have been in contact earlier. I didn't realise... Sorry.' Dad sounds flustered.

'Not for my sake. For yours. I *want* to be here. You shouldn't have to go through this on your own. Particularly not at this time of year. You need your friends around you.'

My eyes remain stubbornly closed. However much I concentrate, I can't open the shutters. Today I'm going to have to make do with a radio drama.

'You don't know how much that means to me, Pauline. It's been... awful. Simply awful. And now the doctors are pushing me for a decision.'

'You mustn't let them! You are the next of kin. They can't do anything without your permission... not without getting a court injunction thingy. Adam's working in a solicitor's office now. Would you like me to ask him for some legal advice?'

At the mention of Adam, I finally place the voice. It's Pauline Hedges, the neighbour who was living across the road when Mum died. She was widowed herself when I was nine and Oscar was two. She had married and buried another husband since those days. Their child, a baby in my memory, would be about 22 years old now.

'That's very kind, Pauline. If you don't think he'll be too busy…'

'Nonsense. He's never too busy to do his old mum a favour.'

'If you wouldn't mind asking.'

'Of course I don't. Adam won't mind, either. Maybe you should get a second medical opinion. Doctors don't know everything. Your consultant might be wrong.'

'I'll do that. I don't know why I didn't ask before.'

'Because you're under enormous stress. The shock alone! Come here.' A heavy pause settles on the room. I imagine her pressing her bosom against Dad's chest in a suffocating embrace.

'She's so peaceful, as though she's sleeping and could wake up any time.'

'Yes,' Dad replies unsteadily.

'She looks like her mother. That fragile quality.'

'That's what makes it so hard. To lose both of them…'

'Of course it's hard. It's something no father should have to endure. You've faced loss before, but it doesn't make it any easier. I know that first-hand. Burying two husbands and now facing my old age alone. Life is a series of sorrows – and then you die! It doesn't amount to much, does it?'

'I was sad to hear about George.'

'He was a good man. We had some happy years together.'

'I'm glad. I always felt a bit uncomfortable about how things were left between us.'

'That's all in the past now. She never wanted me around, did she? She made that much clear.'

'Yes. She was a little tyrant.'

'Adolescents always are.'

'I probably should have put my foot down.'

'You put your children first. That's what good parents do. If you hadn't, Adam would never have been born. I have no regrets. The important thing at the moment is to keep you going so you're able to make the right decision for Tilda *now*. She's counting on you.'

'Yes.'

'And you must put her interests first.'

'I would, if I knew what her best interests are.'

'Time has a way of making things clear. We'll take it step by step. From now on, you don't have to be in this alone. I'll be right here by your side.'

My former life seems so distant now, as though it belonged to someone else, someone in a tattered photograph. It's a faraway place seen through a telescope. My inner world, the only one I can directly experience, is a place of uncertainty. I can't access the knowledge of what happened to me, or even prove that the past existed and this isn't a horrible nightmare. I'm adrift on fragments. Am I going mad?

Every now and then I think I've forgotten what Michael looks like. I scrabble around my memories, picking up one and then another, trying to piece together the bits of him I love – his energy, his childlike curiosity. I long for his hand in mine, for that jolt of electricity to remind me I'm still alive. Then suddenly, bam, he's with me and I remember every detail. But still he doesn't come.

Things are blurring together in strange ways. The stink of Claude's industrial cleaner scratches at my skin, disdainful of the decomposing debris on the bed. When Dad brings his CD player (my iPod seems to have disappeared forever in Oscar's pocket) I experience the taste of music on my tongue, exquisitely sharp and refreshing. I smell nervousness in the yellow swirls of the paisley curtain, and hear alarm and suppression in anything red. Green is ambiguous. The aroma of Dad's coffee is like an old friend listening to my sorrows.

Sometimes my room is as wide as a plain, the walls receding into the distance. Sometimes it's scrunched together like a used tissue. And then, suddenly, it's as bright and unforgiving as an overexposed photograph.

Days flow backward as well as forward. Memories and dreams intermingle. Sometimes I wonder what's real. Perhaps I'm only dreaming I'm in hospital. The real me is listening to jazz with Michael, not existing in a recurrent nightmare of panic and anguish. Several times I've found myself looking down from the ceiling, seeing my body as a forlorn echo of the woman I once was.

I'm changing, going beyond suffering, becoming something else. When Claude holds my hand now and lifts it to his lips, I see that I'm a creature of bones. My flesh has melted away. The skin is almost transparent, tracked by veins as blue as grief. He kisses the dry skin as though it belongs to something sacred, a royal parchment, perhaps a relic from a questionable saint. I'm an undifferentiated cell, washed of everything superficial, waiting to discover what I'll become.

Old faces glimmer at the door. Old voices talk in guilty whispers. Old footsteps hurry back to busy lives. Fireworks splash the night with colour. Blue and green and silver explosions crack the sky, wounding the stars until they bleed and my window becomes a rectangle of red. My room falls silent again. I'm weary of the routine. And still he doesn't come.

'I can't let her go.'

'She's gone, Dad. She's already gone. You need to accept it. She wouldn't want this. We both know that. Her quality of life is non-existent. There's virtually no possibility of improvement. She can't speak or move. For all we know, she might be in constant pain.'

My eyes are closed, but I smell the cigarettes on Oscar's clothes. He's changed his tune.

'Don't, Oscar. I can't bear it.'

'If it wasn't for modern medicine, she would have passed away naturally weeks ago. We could have celebrated her life, grieved for her, and begun to move on.'

'How can I move on? I still think of your mother every day – and I lost her 28 years ago.'

'I know you do.'

'If I told them to stop feeding her… well… I could never forgive myself. You can't ask a father to take away his child's life.'

'She's only here because of the hospital's intervention. They're keeping her alive artificially with all this paraphernalia. The drips, the antibiotics. If it was you, would you want to live like this? Wouldn't you rather nature took its course? We need to draw a line. Tilda has no choice, no voice. We must make that decision for her. She wouldn't want you to be sitting here day after day. She wouldn't want us to be suffering like this.'

'You don't know that!'

'Yes, I do. This is Tilda! The queen of rationality. She doesn't believe in life after death. She doesn't believe in God. You've heard her talk about death. She wasn't scared.'

'Of course she wasn't scared. She was young and healthy. If you don't believe in God or heaven or hell or judgement, there's nothing to be scared of.'

'Exactly.'

125

'But I'm scared for her. We don't know how she's feeling. What if she's frightened now?'

'She's not feeling anything, Dad. That's the point. And if she is, she would want us to let her go.'

'Don't say that –'

'She can't stay here forever. The hospital has made that clear. You're not up to trying to find a nursing home at the moment. I can't keep driving up from Manchester every week. And how would we pay for her care?'

Oscar's impatience is pulsing beneath the surface. I wonder why the hurry. Only a short time ago – was it days or weeks? – he was begging me to recover.

'There's her flat,' Dad says. 'We could sell it.'

'And squander everything she's worked for?'

'It's her money, Oscar. It should be used to look after her.'

'It's my inheritance.'

A dark red cloud settles in my head. He's come to the conclusion I'm more valuable to him dead than alive. Dust and ashes. Dust and ashes.

'Now we're getting to the truth!'

'It's not about the money, Dad. It's about Tilda and what she would want. She's not religious. She doesn't believe in the afterlife. For her it would be exchanging a life of suffering for quiet extinction. She's no longer the person she was. That Tilda's gone. We owe it to her memory. The room's empty now. It will be like… switching off the light.'

Chapter 15

It's a shock to realise I have nothing in my metaphorical bank account, no way to buy myself out of my predicament. I've always relied on my intelligence and determination to get me what I want in life. My qualifications, my reputation, my work ethic: they count for nothing now. None of them will pay the bills. I'm bankrupt, dependent on the love of my father to save me from insolvency, fearing the pragmatism of my brother who wants to cut his losses before he's dragged under too.

People say your life passes before you on the brink of death. Perhaps it's the fear that does it, the fight-or-flight instinct in a tailspin. There's no fight or feeling left. I think of the stories Dad told me about myself when I was growing up, the scaffolding of my identity.

'I've never seen a child like it!' my grandmother had complained after I refused to sleep for the first eight weeks of my existence. Underweight and overloved, I was too busy looking at the world around me to do anything more than catnap and scream to be lifted from the cot. Dad would chuckle at the memory. 'My little big voice,' he called me.

'So stubborn,' his mother-in-law complained. She can't bear to miss anything. You must give her a dummy, Laura. That'll shut her up.' But my mother would never stopper my mouth. She allowed me to have my say.

Before Mum passed away I had an imaginary friend. He was a boy about my own age with dark, untameable eyes. A teller of unexpected tales, but a good listener too. A magician. An intrepid traveller, bearding monsters in their lairs. When Mum slipped from my grasp, he disappeared too. He was part of my childhood, and I had left my childhood behind.

I was the smallest and youngest in the class at my secondary school in Durham. A little mouse with a mighty squeak. 'Incorrigible,' my English teacher once wrote on my report. I didn't care for her opinion. I wanted to impress Mr Merrick, head of science. He taught me how the world became. He explained what I saw and heard and smelled. He answered all my questions. He constructed a universe of certainties and probabilities, built from DNA and mathematical equations. I stopped having to agonise over the 'Why?' of the world. Why are we here? Why is there something rather than nothing? Why did my mother have to die? It was a relief to concentrate on the 'How' of things instead.

A degree in biochemistry. A doctorate. A job at the Institute of Genetic Medicine at Newcastle University. Lectures and seminars. Conferences. A flat. A cat. The occasional classical concert with friends. Visits to my father at Christmas and Easter, despite the fact he was only a 15-mile drive away. Visits to my mother's grave. Meeting Michael and having a new reason for living. Facing extinction and not understanding why.

I want to stamp my feet and scream, 'It's not fair!' I've always made a point of eating nutritious meals. I drank two litres of water a day. I tried to get eight hours' sleep a night. I went to the gym twice a week, not because I enjoyed it but because I've always hated team sports and had to do something to keep my body operating at an acceptable level of fitness. But I might as well have lived it up, boozing and partying every night, sleeping around, travelling the world. Michael was right: you have to live for the day, and not for the day that might never come.

Whether someone works hard or not, whether they do good or evil, are clever or stupid, black or white, male or female, it all ends the same way. What can I take with me? Nothing! Everything I own will be handed over to my father, a broken man, and my brother, who never lifted a finger in his life.

I don't know what's worse: hearing Oscar argue for my death, or hearing Dad talk about selling my flat to finance this state of purgatory in some ghastly nursing home. Although I hate every inch of this room, the thought of moving somewhere else terrifies me. And if my flat is sold to pay for my care, there will be no way back to my old life, nowhere to go home to, nowhere I belong.

On the other hand, if Dad and Oscar choose to disconnect me from the tubes keeping me alive, slow deterioration will be swapped for a sudden collapse, a big crunch, where the cosmos of my life folds in upon itself into the blackest of black holes.

What will happen to Betsy? Kiki will find a new place to rent easily enough, but it's more difficult for one cat among hundreds already dumped in animal shelters. Who will look after her? Certainly not Dad, who has a fur allergy, or Oscar, who can't look after himself, let alone another creature.

Whoever wins the debate, I'm up against a deadline. I tell myself I can cope with the thought of death if I can only find the reason for it. Or am I kidding myself? What if there isn't a 'Why?' What if the 'Why?' isn't good enough? The clock is ticking. My heart is counting down the beats of my life. I refuse to leave not knowing why this has happened, not knowing what it's all been for. I must impose some kind of order on this jumble of fragments. Find a reason. Wheedle out a motive. Dare I say it? Discover the purpose of my life. And the reason for my demise.

Chapter 16

It's morning. I have a session with a physio. I remember now that she's been before. She moves my lifeless limbs. I concentrate on each part of my body in turn in the hope that I can offer some resistance to her touch and signal my presence. But my brain and my body are no longer on speaking terms.

Two nurses come and turn me. They do this several times a day to prevent pressure sores. I'm left facing the wall. I hate it. I've examined every small imperfection in the surface many times before. The hairline cracks in the paintwork, the smudges left by careless fingers, the lump of blue putty used to stick up a picture or notice, long gone.

I will force myself to examine other cracks and smudges, the surface blemishes I've been ignoring in case investigation causes a sudden, terrifying subsidence. Who would want me dead? And why?

Money, sex and power are the usual motives – in television dramas, anyway. Laughable as it is to imagine myself provoking the kind of emotion that could lead to violence of any kind, I decide to lay out the facts dispassionately.

Firstly, money. Who could have stolen the money from the university? Who had access to the accounts?

Keith? Possibly, but it would be difficult. I was the budget holder. I kept the spreadsheets up to date and stored them on my USB. Since our argument about the contract with

BioExpertise Systems, we had studiously avoided discussing the details of the arrangement.

Professor MacMahon? He was too busy trying to avoid being put out to pasture.

The head of Finance? He was an unimaginative family man. It was impossible to imagine him planning anything so audacious, or being able to pull it off so that the finger pointed at me.

Kiki works in the Finance Office, but complex contracts with external suppliers would be way above her pay grade as an accounts clerk. Plus, I'm her best friend. She had the occasional moody moment, particularly if I came home later than expected after she had taken the trouble of cooking dinner, but we rubbed along pretty well as a rule.

I know Michael couldn't have been involved with the fraud because he had no direct access to the university bank account – unless, of course, he had an accomplice on the inside. I flinch at the thought he might have been responsible for my injuries, but I must do this properly. As the police would say, he needs to be eliminated for the purposes of my investigation.

What would he gain by my death? He had no rival. He knew that. There was no reason for him to be jealous. If anything, the shoe was on the other foot. But his disappearance is incriminating. I can't deny it any more. I'm not sure what's worse, thinking he might be in some way responsible, or thinking he might have stumbled across the perpetrator and become a victim like me.

After my bed bath, I'm propped up against the pillows. They're not concerned whether I have a good view of the room or not; they're trying to keep my lungs clear to prevent pneumonia. Even so, I'm grateful. I stare at the glass strip running down the length of the door, hoping to catch a glimpse of people passing in the corridor outside. A small boy presses his nose to the window and gives me a little wave. When I don't return his smile he sticks out his tongue. His mother pulls him away and mouths 'sorry' through the pane.

Could Michael have been trying to steal my research? Was that the reason for his interest in my work? Had he enticed me into bed for the purpose of commercial espionage? Not that much enticing had been needed. I rack my brain to think of anything I might have revealed that could be sold to a third party. Our conversations had been too simplistic. He just didn't have the scientific knowledge to understand anything but the most basic summary. More importantly, when I was with him, work was the last thing on my mind.

Oscar always needed money. But he loved and needed me more than anything money could buy. It's only now that recovery seems impossible that his thoughts have begun to turn to his inheritance. Surely he wouldn't have tried to kill me for that!

I've been moved on to my side, facing the window. This is now my favourite position. The sky is my screensaver. It reminds me that the mechanism of my mind is still switched on, the operating system merely paused to save energy. Some days the sun is white and hazy through the clouds; sometimes it's imprisoned behind a wall of grey concrete. This afternoon the wind blows. Clouds cruise past. An aeroplane draws a line across the blue. A bird swoops like a tatter of darkness. The sun is heading slowly west like a lazy Pac-Man gobbling at the sky, until it will overshoot the screen and set somewhere behind my head, leaving a farewell message in heliotrope and pink and lemon, faint echoes from a dying star.

What about power? How could that be a motive? This leads me to ask, 'Why hasn't Keith visited?' This is an obvious question. I wonder why I haven't asked it before. I've been too caught up with wondering about Michael to query the absence of the other man in my life. Maybe he *has* visited and I've been asleep or unconscious. No doubt he's under pressure, now he's in the laboratory on his own.

We've worked together for nearly a decade. The arrangement suits us both. He's methodical, reliable, capable. A gifted scientist, if a little unimaginative. I brought the flair and drive to the team – the sudden flight of insight that pushed our research beyond that of our rivals. We were close to a breakthrough, creating embryonic cells that would function as a miniature human brain. Testing on mice and rats would become redundant. We could test on living human tissue. The cure for several devastating degenerative illnesses was in sight.

Could he have been harbouring dark thoughts about his junior position? Although he's my assistant, there had never been a serious disagreement between us or any hint of professional jealousy until I became involved with Michael's scheme. But he wouldn't be human if he didn't sometimes dream of fame and fortune, of having his name on the top of the papers instead of mine. Perhaps my links with a commercial organisation – my 'compromise', as he chose to call it – had made him think beyond the university walls. The multinational biomedical giants had deep pockets and ruthless hearts. Had he tried to steal my findings and claim them as his own? Or had he devised an elaborate fraud, hoping to place the blame on my shoulders and pocket the cash himself? But what am I thinking? This is Keith! Bridge-playing, bird-watching, corduroy-wearing Keith!

Our temperaments suited each other, up until the last few months. I know he sensed the change in me. I couldn't hide the light that glowed under my skin when I caught myself thinking of Michael. One morning, Keith complimented me on my new hairstyle. Nothing unusual in that, except a primitive female sensitivity registered an interest that had not been there before.

I caught his glance of surprise when I arrived at work wearing lipstick in anticipation of a business lunch with Michael and the head of finance at the university. Our relationship had always been strictly business; now there had been a few tentative suggestions of dinner, which I managed to deflect without hurting his feelings. There was certainly nothing to suggest the kind of sexual jealousy that could lead to him pushing me off my balcony.

And who is Allegra? Why does she visit? She told Dad she knows Kiki. She told Kiki she knows Dad. But does she know any of us? And how does she know about Michael?

The sun is setting. Is it even the same day as the one I awoke to this morning, when dawn broke with a burst of cool bird song and I began my investigation of likely suspects? Days might have passed since then. They blur into an endless loop. I can't remember what happened yesterday or the day before that. My mind is too busy trying to solve the riddle. Time is short. Soon it will be midnight and I shall turn into a pumpkin, glass slipper smashing on the pavement. I know what's waiting. I've pricked my finger. I've eaten the poisoned apple. I'm facing the jaws of that aged dragon and hoping against hope someone will rescue me in the nick of time. Whether a rescuer arrives or not, one of my tomorrows will never come. The sun will rise and fall. I won't be here to see it, but it will happen just the same.

Chapter 17

'OK. We're both here now,' Dad says. 'If you're expecting a decision today, I'm telling you I'm not ready, whatever my son says.'

'Mr Moss –'

'And what's this DNAR on her notes? I know what that means. Do Not Attempt Resuscitation. Is that your idea? Well, you can take it off. I want to talk to the hospital chaplain. And I'm going to speak to a lawyer.'

'That's not why I called you in.' The doctor shifts from foot to foot. The dark shadows that always flutter around his form are nervous.

'I hope you've got a good reason for dragging me all the way here from Manchester,' Oscar fumes. 'I have a life, you know. This better be important.'

'It is. There's been a development. As you know, Tilda had an infection last week. We tested her urine and took some bloods and swabs to decide which antibiotics to use. We weren't sure if she picked it up from the feed.'

'If there's been any negligence…' Dad begins.

'No. Not at all. When the lab came back to us there were some anomalies, so we did another test to confirm the findings.'

'Is she getting better?' Oscar asks.

'You might want to sit down, Mr Moss.'

'It's bad news, isn't it? I can't bear any more.' Dad perches on the visitor's chair. Oscar steps forward and places a hand on his shoulder.

'I don't know if it's good news or bad. She's pregnant.'

'Pregnant!' Dad and Oscar exclaim in unison.

'There must be a mistake,' Dad says.

'There's no mistake. I palpated her this morning. I'm guessing she's about four months gone.'

I don't remember him touching me. It must have occurred in a gap in my consciousness. I'm glad. His presence alone fills me with apprehension; the thought of him touching me conjures an image of a scavenger pecking over a corpse.

'She'd better be at least four months pregnant, or I'll be calling the police,' Dad says.

'I don't like what you're insinuating.' The doctor clenches his fists, takes a breath. 'I've booked her for an ultrasound scan tomorrow to get a more accurate date and to check what's what. It's a miracle she didn't miscarry after the fall.'

Dad puts his head in his hands. 'I'm sorry... I was out of order. I can't take this in. Not Tilda.'

'You don't think your precious girl can get herself pregnant?' Oscar says bitterly. 'Perhaps you think she'd have to be unconscious before she let anyone lay their hands on her. She's not so perfect now, is she? She makes mistakes too.'

'Be quiet!' Dad shifts in the chair to look up at Oscar. 'Did she have a boyfriend? Is there something you know that you're not telling me?'

'Don't try to push this on to me! I know as much as you do.'

'We'll know more tomorrow,' the doctor states. 'I'm not allowed to divulge confidential patient information, but I'd like to suggest Inspector Lake be informed. The presence of a lover might shed some light on what has happened to your daughter and why.'

I'm dreaming that I'm lying on a four-poster bed draped with silks and velvets. I'm wearing a long white gown. My hair spreads like a stain over the pillow. Outside the window a forest of thorns grows thick and dark. I'm alone and asleep, dreaming that Michael will come. I know he's out there searching, riding through the forest, hacking at the thorns. If only he would come. If only he would find me and kiss me and rescue me from this castle of death.

I wake suddenly. It's a clear night. I sense there will be frost. A small part of the Milky Way can be seen through my hospital window, speckling the sky with pricks of light. Hundreds of billions of stars are blazing, most of them unseen by the human eye. I know that in ten billion years the majority will have faded from sight, victims of the second law of thermodynamics. But still the Milky Way will continue to sparkle. New stars will be born to take the place of those that have died. And that is the nature of things.

I'm no longer alone in this prison. A new star is being formed, a fuzzy blob of primordial material, hot and energetic, is recycling matter from the dying supernova of my body. From an evolutionary perspective I'm fulfilling my destiny, passing my genes along the chain of blind process. I think about the generations that have gone before, passing through time, passing through women's bodies. Now I'm the one to have been reduced to a vessel, like so many before.

I wonder if Michael will come now there's a child to be considered. I remember him talking about the failed attempts at IVF undertaken with his wife. The calendars, the injections, the blood tests, the clumsy invasions. I'm childishly pleased I have something of Michael's in my body that she never had in hers. Surely he will come now that I've proved his fertility.

'It's a miracle anyone gets pregnant!' he had exclaimed. 'And yet it happens all the time, inadvertently... a drunken one-night stand, two kids mucking around. When everything's working as it should, there's an elegance to the process that science will never be able to replicate.'

I smiled indulgently. 'Maybe. But we'll be able to eradicate the cruelties of nature. Muscular dystrophy, Mitochondrial disease, Huntington's, Parkinson's, Down's…'

'I wonder what sort of world that will be.'

'A happier one.'

'Maybe. A less caring one, I imagine.'

'I disagree. It's because we care that we want to prevent the suffering in the first place.'

Prevent the suffering. How is it possible to prevent suffering? His child will be born into a world of immediate loss. If I die, I'll be like a character in a fable, someone talked about in hushed whispers. Even if I'm still around to see my baby grow, I won't be able to care for it. I'll be a tedious burden to be visited in my nursing home, dutifully kissed on a Sunday afternoon. And what if the embryo has been damaged by the trauma of my accident or can't develop properly inside an immobile body? What if it's been affected by the X-rays, the medication and the MRI scans? Better to terminate now to prevent the pain. It would be the logical decision.

I shrink from the thought as soon as it invades the space in my head where I now exist. I've had enough of death. This is life! Something fresh and unsullied. Another beating heart. Michael's child, the fusion of our DNA, conceived in love and growing against the odds. Tomorrow I'll have a scan. We'll find out whether or not the foetus is developing normally. The doctors will make recommendations. My family will agonise over the possibilities. Once again I'll be helpless to influence the decisions that are being made about my body. Dad and Oscar and the doctors will choose: life for the baby and a few more months of existence for me… or an abortion.

Chapter 18

It's after midnight. He stares into his empty whisky glass. The band has finished their set and packed away their instruments. Lyrics and harmonies still drift between the tables, but they're now being piped through the music system, loud enough for the words of the song 'Don't Blame Me' to insinuate into my consciousness but soft enough for us to be able to talk in low murmurs.

'Looking back, I wonder whether I've ever experienced unconditional love. Or given it for that matter.'

'Maybe you haven't met the right person yet.'

Or recognised them when they're under your nose.

What started out as a light-hearted conversation about love songs through the ages has turned into a discussion about his love life.

'That old cliché. I'm not talking about "the One", whoever that is. I'm talking about having the unconditional love of my family and my friends too.' His words are beginning to slur.

'Of course your parents loved you.'

'When I was passing exams and scoring rugby tries and earning good money. I'm not so sure when I was bumming around the world and dating unsuitable women.'

'They were just being protective.'

'Perhaps. But I wasn't able to provide the longed-for grandchildren. All in all, I think I was a bit of a failure as a son.

Particularly at the end.' He stirred the melting ice at the bottom of the glass with his finger. 'Sometimes I wonder whether I know what love is.'

'You mustn't be so hard on yourself. I know you do.'

'I'm talking about real love. Not the "I'll do this for you if you do that for me" kind of relationship. I've come to the conclusion that women only wanted to be with me in the past because I was tall and athletic and knew how to have a good time.'

'You don't have a very high opinion of women!'

'I'm not talking about you. But when I think about it, most of my relationships have been pretty shallow. But that's probably a reflection of me.'

'What about your wife?'

'She wanted kids. I think she stopped loving me when she realised I couldn't give them to her.'

'That must have been tough.'

'Yes. I want to be an end in myself and not a means to an end.'

'Don't we all?'

'But now I wonder if I wasn't doing the same thing. Maybe I only loved her because I liked trying to fix her problems. I wanted to rescue her from the anxiety that stalked her all her life. I needed her to need me. She made me feel good about myself.'

'But you did love her.'

'I thought so at the time. But perhaps my need to be the centre of attention, to make sure everyone around me is happy, is because deep down I hate myself.'

I reach forward and take his hand. 'Oh, Michael...'

'You know who your friends are when you're divorced. I was a miserable grouch after the split and everyone disappeared into the woodwork. They wanted the old Michael – the great adventurer, the comedian, the "eat, drink and be merry for tomorrow we die" raconteur. Now I try to enjoy people for who they *really* are, and hope they'll return the favour.'

'Of course they will… I will.'

He squeezes my hand. A pulse beats like a moth at the base of my throat. 'Thanks, Tilda. That means a lot.'

He leans forward, strokes my cheek. His fingertips are dry and papery. I can't meet his eyes. The intensity is unbearable. I sense rather than see his head moving closer to mine. At the last second I look up, an undetectable movement that closes the gap between our lips.

A fluttering in the pit of my stomach pulls me back to the present. For a moment I'm in the overlap. The shadows of the jazz club haunt the white corners of the hospital. Michael, transparent, sits next to my bed, holding my hand, gazing into my eyes. I try to grasp him but he's fading into nothing, until all that's left is a faint smell of whisky and the echo of a song. Don't blame me.

Someone has stuck a rope of threadbare tinsel around my window frame. It looks as though it's been in and out of a box in the attic for at least a decade. There are Christmas cards on the sill: a penguin, a robin, a fat Father Christmas. A picture of Mary bending over a manger, another unmarried mother giving birth in a place she would rather not.

Pauline picks up my limp hand and gives it a squeeze, releasing a strong sensation of vanilla. I'm reminded of mixing bowls and oven gloves and licking the spoon with Mum.

'She's as cold as ice! She can't go out in the corridor in just this nightie. She'll catch her death! Sorry, Peter. That was tactless. You know what I mean. Has she got a dressing gown?'

A burst of irritation jolts my eyes open.

'I don't think so. She hasn't been out of bed since it happened. It didn't occur to me she might need one. It's so hot in here. I bought her some new nightdresses…'

'Of course you did. I'm not criticising *you*! I'm not sure the nurses are looking after her properly. She can't speak up for herself. I know they're busy, but they really should make sure she's warm.'

Pauline disappears from view. I hear what I imagine to be the door to my bedside cabinet click open.

'There's a cardigan in here. Is this Tilda's?'

'I think so. Yes… I don't know how it got there. Maybe Kiki brought it in. Perhaps it was what she was wearing when it happened. Look!'

'Don't upset yourself. It's just a small stain. It might not even be blood. I'll take it home to wash afterwards.'

'Shouldn't we give it to the police? It might have forensics or something.'

'I hadn't thought of that.'

'I don't know how the police came to miss it.'

'I suppose they were concentrating on searching her flat. But she needs to wear something now. Let's pop it on and worry about what to do with it afterwards. For all we know, they've already checked it out. It's not our fault if they've been incompetent. Help me put it round her shoulders. That's right.'

Dad and Pauline stand either side of the bed and take me by the elbows. I slump forward, doubled up over my chest like a rag doll. The cardigan, an old friend, hugs my shoulders. Pauline smooths it down to my waist and picks up my left arm, heavy as sleep, and pushes it down the sleeve. Dad follows her lead and thrusts my right hand into the other sleeve, awkwardly yanking the material up and over the tubes and my elbow. Pauline wallops the pillows behind me and I'm dragged back up to recline on the bed.

'There you go. Nice and cosy. She looks much better, don't you think?'

'Yes. She looks more normal now.'

'Exactly! I think it's important to make an effort, not just to keep her warm but so the nurses know we care. They need to understand she's loved. She's still a person. Less chance of any funny business that way.' She pulls the blue wool across my chest and does up the buttons. The urge to push her away is so strong that for a moment I believe I've done it. Then I realise she's straightened up of her own accord. 'Perhaps we could buy her a nice bedjacket at the weekend? I'll help you choose. We can wrap it up and you can give it to her when you visit on Christmas Day.'

'That would be nice. Thank you, Pauline. If her mother were here –'

'I know. But we're here. It's going to be all right.'

The door opens with a swish of cool air. A couple of porters arrive with a trolley. I'm rolled aboard like an old rug. Pauline fusses with the blanket, tucking it round my legs for modesty. When one dead arm falls off the edge to dangle like the limb of a corpse in the mortuary, she picks it up gently and places my hand in the cardigan pocket to keep it in place.

My fingers brush against something small and cold and hard. And something smooth and thin. An image of my memory stick and Michael's business card bursts before my eyes. They've been here with me in the hospital all the time. My latest research, my budget spreadsheet, some personal correspondence: all saved on something the size of a cigarette lighter.

The police and Professor MacMahon have been searching for my USB. It's now within my grasp. Do I want them to find it? My body heats with embarrassment as I ponder the dossier of information I've collected about Michael – a couple of headshots copied from the internet, a brief biography gleaned from the company website, his LinkedIn profile, a letter I wrote to him but didn't have the courage to send, selfies of us together. All saved on my memory stick.

I know how it will look to other eyes – mad, obsessive – but I've been trained to collect and arrange data and make decisions based on empirical research. Why not bring the same method to bear on my personal life? Selecting a life partner is one of the most important decisions a human being can make. And it was the only way I could channel the rush of unrequited attraction I suffered in those early days.

But I want them to find Michael and bring him to me more than I want to protect my privacy. The porters bang the trolley through the door and rattle me down the corridor. The stick is jolted next to my palm. I command my fingers to curl shut. *Right hand little finger. Right hand ring finger. Right hand middle finger. Right hand index finger. Right hand thumb.*

Dad and Pauline's footsteps trot behind. The world is racing very fast, a blur of sights and sounds and smells jumbled into a current of chaos. A corner is taken with a lurch of fear as I rock on the trolley, my muscles unable to compensate for the loss of balance. The USB slips to one side, next to my thumb.

We reach what I assume to be the ultrasound department. Oscar is sitting in the small waiting area.

'What's she doing here?'

That's what I'd like to know.

'You remember Pauline Hedges.'

'You didn't answer my question.'

'She's here to offer me some support.'

'What am I doing here, then? I'm not a complete waste of space, you know. This is a family matter.'

For once, Oscar and I are on the same page.

'Pauline's practically family. She's known you and Tilda all your lives.'

'I'm happy to wait outside, Peter –'

'No. You stay here. We need a woman's perspective. You know what sort of questions we should be asking.'

A young sonographer, pretty and hygienic, floats before my swimming eyes. She ushers us into a tiny room. There's a scattering of small talk, but their words flutter away and are lost when she loosens the blankets around my legs and wheels a pair of stirrups to the bed. She gently takes my left foot in her hand.

Please, no. Not in front of my father and brother!

'Son of a biscuit! She's not giving birth now, is she?' Oscar exclaims.

The girl turns to face him. 'Because of her recent injuries, I want to check for any internal abnormalities. Also we ask our ladies to drink at least two pints of water before they come in. A full bladder pushes the uterus forward, making the image clearer.' Oscar winces when she says the word 'uterus'. 'Dr Moss is on a drip and has lost all bladder control so that's not been possible. For these reasons, I'm going to have to use a transvaginal probe.'

'Not with me in the room!' The air stirs as Oscar strides towards the door.

'If the men want to stand behind the curtain while I set things up, we can preserve everyone's dignity. Would Mum like to stay with me to act as a chaperone?'

'I'm not her mother,' Pauline says. 'But I'm happy to stay. I've seen it all before.'

You've not seen mine before! I rage.

The nurse yanks the curtain across the door with a metallic *ssshhhh*. Dad and Oscar disappear. I put myself in a different place mentally and ignore what's going on down below. My body hardly seems mine any more. I'm going beyond embarrassment.

'We didn't have these in my day,' Pauline says.

'It's quite straightforward. We're just checking that all's well with baby. I'll also measure the head and the length of the thigh bone to date the pregnancy. You can come back now, gentlemen,' she calls.

Dad and Oscar reappear in my peripheral vision and stand next to Pauline near my head. All three look across my body at the computer screen. I'm lying on my back and can't turn my head to see.

'There's the heartbeat. It's looking strong. It's not twins. Just the one. Here's the head. You can just see a little hand moving here.'

'I can't make head nor tail of it,' Dad says. 'I hope it doesn't have a tail…'

'Was that meant to be a joke?' Oscar grumbles.

'No.'

'It takes a bit of getting used to,' the sonographer replies. 'This is the spine. I'm checking the vertebrae. Down here you can see the kidneys. They're a little dilated. It looks as though baby needs a wee.'

A pair of hands gently turns my head to the screen.

'There you go, Tilda. Is that better?' Pauline says.

'She doesn't know what's going on, you know,' Oscar snipes.

'Maybe not. But a mother should see her own baby, all the same.'

Suddenly, I'm overwhelmed with thankfulness that Pauline is here. I know the theory behind ultrasound technology. Sound bounces off tissue like an echo in a cave. And now my heart is calling out into the darkness.

Is anybody there? Anyone at all?

I see a grainy black and white image on the screen. A smattering of white on black like a constellation of stars, or frost on a car windscreen, or the fuzzy darkness that descends over my eyes just before I lose consciousness. And then the flurry of snow coalesces into a line. A limb. A head. Not a collection of cells. It's my baby.

'Everything looks fine. By my calculations she's about 19 weeks pregnant.'

'That far along!' Pauline exclaims.

'Obviously!' Oscar mocks. 'She's been in the hospital nearly 15 weeks!'

'No need to be unpleasant, son. Pauline's only saying.'

'Yes. Well, *I'm* only saying.'

'I meant that there's nothing of her,' says Pauline. 'Shouldn't she be showing?'

'She's lying down,' the sonographer says. 'If she were able to stand I think you would notice a small bump. Do you want to know the sex?'

'Do we?' Dad asks.

'Don't you think you should be asking me, Dad?' Oscar bites. 'It's none of her business.'

'Of course… I'm sorry.'

'I don't want to know. It will only make it harder,' Oscar says.

'Make what harder?'

'The abortion.'

'Who says she's having an abortion?' Dad says.

'You can't seriously think she can have a baby. Look at her!'

'It's not your decision.'

'I'm thinking about Tilda. You can't put her body through this.'

'We don't know what Tilda would be thinking. For all you know, she might have wanted this baby.'

'Do you think she knew she was pregnant?' Pauline interjects.

'When was she brought into hospital?' the sonographer asks.

'21st August.'

'She would have been about three or four weeks pregnant. She wouldn't have known, unless she was trying for a baby and took a pregnancy test very early.'

'That's unlikely.' Oscar says. 'She was wrapped up with her work. Her career came first.'

'You don't know that. When did you last speak to her?'

'When I pitched to her the nightclub investment –'

'I mean *really* speak to her,' Dad emphasises, 'to find out about her life and how she was feeling about things, not tell her about yours.' There's an uneasy silence. 'I think I've made my point!'

'Why don't we all calm down,' Pauline says. 'This is a very emotional moment. We're looking at a new member of your family. A precious gift.'

Oscar exhales.

'You're right, Pauline,' says Dad. 'I'd like to know. Please tell us. Is it a boy or a girl?'

'It's a girl.'

'A girl,' Dad breathes. 'A little piece of Tilda.'

Chapter 19

I'm lying in his arms. His nose is red from the sun and he still has grass in his hair from our picnic. My face rests on his chest, and rises and falls with each breath he takes. His heart is beating in my ear, strong and steady. When he speaks, his voice reverberates through the bones in my temple.

'I can't understand why you weren't snapped up years ago. You're brilliant, beautiful –'

I snort and smack him playfully in the ribs. 'Apparently I intimidate men. Are you intimidated?'

'I like to live dangerously. But you *are* beautiful, Tilda. You have to learn to accept a compliment when you're given one. I'm sure you've left a trail of broken hearts in your wake.'

I laugh. 'Hardly. I'm a matter-of-fact sort of person. Not romantic at all. I don't think I inspire the kind of feelings that are likely to break hearts.'

'I don't believe that! So, how many relationships have you had?'

'Not many. I don't suffer fools gladly. Men my own age have always seemed weak and needy.'

'I'm glad you're appreciating the benefits of an older man,' he whispers.

'I think it's a consequence of having had to grow up very fast.'

'Because of your mother?'

'Yes. It's difficult to have close friends when you've lost a parent. The problems your contemporaries are dealing with – spots, crushes, puppy fat – appear pitifully trivial in comparison with what you've been through.'

'You're making me sad.' He hugs me tight to his side. 'I don't like to think of you like that.'

'Like what?'

'Vulnerable, alone, grieving.'

'I was very capable.'

'I don't doubt it.'

'I didn't realise it at the time, but my mother was preparing me for my future bereavement. She used her pregnancy as the reason why I had to do more around the house. She would send me off with a shopping list to the corner shop. I learned to cook –'

'But you were only seven!'

'Yes. Beans on toast. Omelettes. That sort of thing. Suddenly she no longer took me to school. I walked there and back. I started looking after Dad long before she died.'

Michael shifted on to his side to look at me. 'I don't understand. I thought she passed away in childbirth. How did she know in advance she was going to die?'

'She was diagnosed with breast cancer in the first weeks of her pregnancy. The doctors recommended a mastectomy and chemotherapy, but she wouldn't hear of it because of Oscar. She could have had an abortion, had the treatment and survived. But her religious beliefs meant she wouldn't consider a termination.'

'How dreadful! Did you know about this at the time?'

'Yes. I was the kind of child who needed to understand what was happening. She didn't want me to be afraid. She told me everything about her condition except that it was breaking her heart. She told me everything about dying, except that it would shatter my own.' We lie in silence for a few moments while he takes this in. 'Afterwards I thought perhaps she didn't care that she was leaving us behind. It was as if death was no great thing. Just a blip to be managed.'

'I'm sure that's not what she intended. She was trying to prepare you as best she could. It must have been agony for her.'

'I see that now. But at some level I internalised that she loved Oscar enough to give her life for him, but she didn't love me enough to want to stay.'

'Oh Tilda! What a burden to carry. That must have had profound implications on your relationship with your brother.'

'Yes and no. He doesn't know. Dad and I sort of made the decision not to tell him about the cancer.'

'Sort of?'

'Neither of us liked talking about it. It was easier to leave out the details. The cancer was very aggressive. By the time Oscar was born, it had spread to her liver and bones. She died a few weeks later. It was bad enough that he grew up thinking Mum died giving birth to him. He was a highly strung child. However much we tried to reassure him it wasn't his fault, it's been a blight on his life. I don't know how he would react if he knew the truth. That she didn't have to die at all.'

'Shouldn't you give him that opportunity? After all, your mother was upfront with you. Shouldn't you be upfront with him? Don't you think he has a right to know how much she loved him?'

'It's not as straightforward as that. You don't know Oscar.' I stood up and pulled on his dressing gown. 'Let's eat. Shall I cook an omelette?'

'She couldn't help it, you know.'

'I know that.'

'She had an impossible choice. What would any of us do in the circumstance?'

'Have you got any cheese?'

'She had to follow her conscience, Tilda. That's all any of us can do.'

'She believed God would work it out for good. Let's just say I had a hard time seeing how any of it was for our good. Let's not talk about it any more. I'm hungry.'

'I'm just trying to understand. You mustn't cut yourself off from the empathy of others –'

'I'm not looking for empathy, Michael. Or sympathy.' Uncharacteristically I let his dressing gown slip over my naked shoulder and gave an exaggerated pout. 'Just get out of that bed and find me some eggs!'

I'm back in my hospital bed. My cardigan is in my bedside cabinet. The excitement of the scan seems to have put all thought of handing the jacket over to the police for forensic analysis out of Dad's mind. Michael's business card and my memory stick are still in the pocket.

'You can't take the baby away from her,' Pauline says. 'What if she recovers and discovers you've given permission for the child to be aborted? Do you want to be answerable for that? What about the father? He needs to be informed. He will have a view.'

'This is nothing to do with you,' Oscar snarls. 'None of us knows what Tilda would want.'

'Doctor, what are the risks of continuing with this pregnancy? Is it detrimental to my daughter's health?'

'It's an additional strain on her system, which is already fragile. There's a strong chance of a premature delivery or a stillbirth. If she were to reach anywhere near full term, we would have to perform a Caesarean, and that carries its own risks – even for healthy mothers.'

'There! It would put Tilda at risk,' Oscar declares.

'Yesterday you were arguing to have her life-support machine switched off. *That* would put Tilda at risk!' Dad retorts.

'I'll leave you to discuss this among yourselves. You can ask the nurse to page me when you've made your decision.' The door opens and thuds shut.

'I grew up without a mother. I wouldn't wish it on anyone else.'

'Are you saying you'd rather not have been born?'

'No, I'm not saying that. I'm saying that it's been like a jinx, following me everywhere.'

'This is not the same thing at all,' Pauline interjects. 'It's not the child's fault Tilly is injured and in hospital. We could keep your sister alive *in order* for the baby to be born. The child would always know how much she was wanted.'

'Why are you still here?'

'Do you want me to leave, Peter?'

'No. I want you to stay. You were good friends with Laura before she passed. What do you think she would have thought?'

'She would have fought for her granddaughter. She would fight for them both. You know she would.'

Oscar swears.

'This is your sister and your niece we're talking about,' Pauline declares.

'This is grotesque. Tilda's brain-dead. Haven't you been listening to the doctor? All I want to do is show her some respect. Let her slip away with dignity.'

'Pauline's right. Your mother would never have agreed to an abortion. She was against it in principle for religious reasons. I've never told you this, Oscar... but the doctors told us that carrying you was a risk to your own mother's health. She loved you too much to listen to their advice. She went ahead. When she held you in her arms, it shone from her face that she had no regrets. Even when... even when...'

153

'Oh, Pete…' Pauline moaned.

'Come on, son. Perhaps I should have told you before. No one blames you for what happened. You were wanted… *are* wanted…'

Muffled sobs reverberate through the air.

'There, now. We must be strong for each other. Strong for Tilda… And strong for her baby. She might be the only piece of Tilda we have left. She's her legacy.'

Chapter 20

My hospital room has become my theatre. It's a minimalist set –
white walls, harsh lighting, a cheap yellow and blue paisley
curtain. Actors troop across my eyeline, enacting tedious dramas.
Doctors poke and prod. Nurses tut and fiddle with tubes. My
father oscillates between hope and despair. I recognise the
desperate intensity of his vigil, the unbearable desire that I will
answer his love with a sign. Time inches somewhere, nowhere,
with little to show for his devotion. I must face the truth: I'm
living in a Tom Stoppard play. The reviews are terrible – and
with an audience of one, it must be a flop.

Sometimes the inspector comes to sit with me at the end of
the day. He's scrolling through the messages on his phone now,
catching ten minutes of quiet before returning to his wife and
children – at least, that's what I like to think he does. He comes
to find peace. To empty his mind of the sordid horrors he's
confronted with every day, to purify himself before he goes
home.

His mobile rings. 'Hello, love. Yes… I'm at the hospital… I'll
be home about 8.30… The scientist who's in a coma… No. No
change. But the nurses stopped talking when I walked past. I get
the feeling there's something they're not telling me. I'll find out
soon enough… What's for dinner? OK. Give the kids a kiss
from me…'

He scratches his stubble and begins to call another number. Before he's connected, his sergeant bangs through the door.

'I thought you might be here, sir.'

'What can I do for you, Stevenson?' He puts his phone in his jacket pocket and leans back in the chair.

'We've had a report of a missing person. A girl, aged 13. She didn't come home from a friend's house in the Wallsend area last night,' he pants.

'Family argument?'

'Not according to the parents. Uniforms visited this morning. Mum and Dad say it's completely out of character. Younger brother says he knows nothing. The girl's mobile is going straight to voicemail. They've contacted all her friends. She's never stayed out all night before, except for prearranged sleepovers. They're frantic.'

'It's probably nothing, but you can't be too careful. Has anyone been to the school?'

'Not yet.' He looks down and reddens.

'Why not?' The inspector sighs in annoyance. 'It'll have to wait until it's open tomorrow. Get on to it first thing in the morning. In the meantime, arrange for uniforms to go door to door tonight. Ask the neighbours to search their garages, sheds and gardens.'

'Yes, sir.'

'These things are usually a storm in a teacup, but she might be hurt or hiding somewhere nearby. We don't want her spending another night away from home if we can help it. We need to get the community mobilised... Go on! Get to it. You know the drill... Oh, and Stevenson! If she doesn't turn up tonight, when you go to the school tomorrow, find out about... what's her name?'

'Jennifer Allen.'

'Find out about Jennifer's behaviour in lessons. Ask whether she seemed worried about anything. Talk to her classmates. See if anything's been happening on social media that could have upset her. That should put the wind up her mates if any of them are lying and someone's letting her sleep on their bedroom floor.'

Stevenson hurries through the door. It swings shut. The inspector takes his phone from his pocket.

'Donald! Lake here… I've got a missing girl. 13. I need a list of everyone in the Wallsend area who's on the Sexual Offenders Register, particularly those who are interested in young girls. Thanks. Email it to me can you? I'll be back at the station in 25 minutes.'

He looks down at the phone in his hand for several seconds before making another call. 'Hi, love. Sorry, I'm not going to make it home in time for dinner. Put mine in the microwave and I'll heat it up when I get in. Don't wait up… It can't be helped, I'm afraid. Love you.'

He doesn't know I listen to the expression in his eyes. I see his pain, his anxiety. I don't answer back or make demands. I remind him that there are worse lives to live than his own. I'm his perspective.

Allegra and Oscar have walked into my room together, wrapped up in coats and scarves, carrying disposable coffee cups from the League of Friends café. It's a relief to have something to watch, a conversation to overhear, although in their different ways they both bring a shadow of foreboding to my room.

'I live round the corner from Tilda and Kiki,' she says.

'Dad told me he met you. I remember you because he said you were into homeopathy. Classic joke! Tilda hated that sort of stuff. And Allegra – well, that's not the sort of name you easily forget.'

'I suppose not.'

'I bet you had some ding-dong rows.'

'Not really. We talked about other things.' She takes off her coat and slings it on the bottom of the bed, on top of my feet. She stands and gazes out of the window.

'Like what?'

'Oh, you know, the usual. Diets, fashion, men.'

Oscar laughs, unwinding his scarf. 'I'd like to have been a fly on *that* wall!' He casually throws the scarf over my drip stand.

'I'm more a friend of Kiki's,' Allegra back-pedals, 'but when I heard what happened to Tilda, I couldn't stay away. If there's anything I can do to help –'

'I think it's gone beyond that now.'

'What are the doctors suggesting?'

'Nothing, really. I don't think there's anything more they can do other than keep her stable like this.'

'That's typical! They shouldn't give up on her just because surgery and medication haven't worked. Human beings are a delicate holistic balance of mind, body and spirit. As I was saying to Peter… your father… I could try a little Thought Field Therapy, or some essential oils to stimulate the inner reaches of her mind.'

'If hearing you say that doesn't thrust her out of bed like a jack-in-the-box, nothing will!'

'OK!' she huffs. 'So what do you think should happen?'

'I think they should let nature take its course. I don't say that lightly – she's my sister, after all – but she wouldn't want this. It's not respectful. She's gone and she's never coming back. We need to be allowed to grieve… and move on.'

'You need closure. I think you're being very brave… and loving.'

A sad smile twitches at the corner of Oscar's mouth. 'Thank you. I just wish Dad could see it that way. He wouldn't listen to

158

the doctors when they tried to suggest withdrawing treatment, and of course it's not going to happen now.'

'Why not?'

Oscar sips from the small hole in the plastic lid. 'Because of the baby.'

'Baby?'

'Yes. Tilda's pregnant. Didn't Kiki tell you?'

'She's having a baby? Are you sure? How's that possible?'

'It's Tilda, so who knows? She's been a dark horse. I can't imagine her letting anyone get that close, but presumably it happened in the usual way.'

'I can't believe it! She's having a baby… When?' She sits down heavily on the chair next to my bed.

'Middle of April. If they let it go that long. And if she doesn't miscarry.'

'Four months' time.' Allegra puts her coffee on the floor and leans forward to touch my stomach. 'And have you any idea who the father might be?' Her hand is heavy. I instinctively shrink inside myself.

'No. You?'

'No.'

'Perhaps it's the immaculate conception!' Oscar says, trying to be funny, but his words leave a lingering aftertaste of dandelion on childish fingers, or fennel, or bitter herbs.

Stevenson is muttering to Inspector Lake. They are discussing the missing girl. The inspector shrugs off his coat and hangs it on the back of the chair. Before he can sit down, the door swings open and a nurse enters.

'Oh! Sorry. I didn't know you were here, gentlemen. Did you want to speak to Dr Arnold?'

'He wants to talk to me. He left a couple of messages for me to contact him. We were passing the hospital so thought we'd swing by. The nurse on reception is letting him know we're here. Has there been any progress?'

'Not really. Dr Moss opens and closes her eyes. Sometimes she moans but she doesn't seem to recognise anyone or respond to people's questions.'

'She hasn't regained consciousness?'

'No.'

'I thought there might have been a change. I'm in the middle of another investigation. I haven't got time to hang around here.'

'I think you'd better speak to Dr Arnold. He should be along in a minute.'

The inspector sighs.

'Bad day?' the nurse asks as she checks my IV line.

'You could say that.'

'I read about the missing girl in the newspaper. If I were her mum I'd be beside myself.'

'She *is* beside herself.'

'Any leads?'

'I can't really discuss the case, but no, not yet. You tell the parents not to give up, but we've been here too many times before. We're all imagining what might have happened to that poor child.' He steps towards the bed and stands over me. 'At least her father knows where this one is. The worst is behind her.'

'I'm not sure that gives him any comfort.'

'No... But sometimes I envy her lying here. No pressure. No deadlines. Just peace. No worrying about whether or not you can get to where you need to be before the monster does what monsters always do, scared witless you won't catch him before he does it again.'

'I know what you mean,' his sergeant interjects. 'It's waiting for the call that they've found the body that gets to me. The not knowing, and the hope that everything might be OK… Even though you know it won't be, you cling to it anyway.'

'Telling the parents that their child has been devoured by evil. That's the worst,' the inspector continues.

'It's always terrible giving bad news to relatives,' the nurse says.

'And is Dr Arnold going to give us bad news today about Dr Moss?'

'He should be here in a minute. Can I get you a cup of tea?' she asks.

'Black coffee, please.'

'Tea for me,' the sergeant says. 'Just as it comes. No sugar.'

The nurse leaves.

'However bad a day we've had, we still get to go home to the wife and kids,' the inspector says, looking down at me. 'When you're dead, you're dead for a long time.'

The two men walk to the window and gaze out at the darkening sky, their backs to me.

'So what's the latest news from the Fraud Squad?' the inspector asks.

'The university received a letter saying BioExpertise Systems was changing its bank account details. All that was needed was an official-looking letterhead. It must have been good because it was taken at face value by the drones in the college Finance Department. The bogus bank account was called BioXpertise, without the first letter E and with the letter X being capitalised instead. When the counterfeit invoice was sent to the university asking for payment in advance as per the contract, it was processed for payment. With Dr Moss incapacitated here, no one chased up the delivery until it became obvious she wasn't going to return to work in the next few weeks. That's when it emerged that BioExpertise Systems had never been paid. They were still waiting for official confirmation of the order.'

'What happened to the money?'

'It was deposited in the bogus account and immediately transferred to Switzerland… and you know how cagey the Swiss banks are. I doubt we'll ever find it.'

'The question for us is how does this link in with what happened to Dr Moss? Was she involved with the theft? Did she discover someone else was involved? Or is it a complete coincidence that she's lying here practically dead? How helpful are the guys in the Fraud Squad being?'

'Not too bad at the moment. They seem up for sharing information. I guess it goes both ways. They'll want to know about anything we dig up.'

'She doesn't seem the type, does she?' the inspector muses. 'Usually fraudsters have expensive tastes – foreign holidays, luxury cars, designer clothes. I'm not sure what she would spend the money on. Her life seemed pretty dull, to be honest.'

'I've been doing some digging on the family. Apparently her younger brother is up to his armpits in debt to the wrong people – the type you don't even owe an apology to, let alone nearly £100,000.'

'That begs another question, Stevenson. How much does Tilda Moss love her brother?'

My mind is overloaded with new input: seeing the baby growing inside me, listening to Dr Arnold breaking the news of my pregnancy to the policemen, trying to contain my anger and disbelief at the university fraud, hearing Dad and Pauline's endless speculation as to who the father might be. Then there's Dad's relief at my stay of execution, Oscar's churlishness, Pauline's simple belief that everything happens for a reason, and perhaps my condition is a blessing in a disguise, and now we have something to look forward to, and can you believe it's Christmas next week?

Then the routine settles back to normal, and the renewed silence of my room is unbearable. I want to scream with boredom! It's like standing in the middle of a desert while everyone else is back at the oasis, talking about you around the water cooler.

I push myself to the periphery of my vision, attempting to move my eyes, which are stubbornly fixed on the least interesting part of the room – the ceiling. I count again the bolts that hold the tiles in place. Two bolts on each side. Eight per tile. Each pair of bolts is also shared with the tile next door. Eight tiles wide, ten tiles deep, 80 tiles in total; 284 bolts. Two of the tiles above my bed are translucent glass rather than plastic, with light bulbs behind. They stare down at me like two square eyes. At night they can be dimmed to become two square moons.

The hush of the heating system is getting on my nerves. A deep tone is overlaid by a higher-pitched and irritating shush, like water running in a cistern long after the toilet's been flushed. Every five minutes the shush stops and the low throb becomes part of my breathing until I lose all consciousness of the sound.

And the waiting and the longing and the wishing remind me of childhood Decembers, of writing letters to Father Christmas, of counting down the days on the Advent calendar, of fingering the parcels under the tree. Festive nostalgia and fantasy sneak in the back door with a flavour of cinnamon. Like Pauline, I imagine myself buying wrapping paper, sherry, bin liners and cranberry sauce. I set out a table for two. Candles on the table, mistletoe hanging by the door. It's our first Christmas together. Michael buys me a ring...

Then the heating system starts up again. Shush. Shush. Like tinnitus. Like a worm burrowing into my brain. I remember that I gave up believing in Father Christmas a long time ago. I remember that I can't have been a good girl, because if I had been, all my wishes would have come true.

A clamour of carols echoes down the corridor, along with the smell of warmed-up sprouts and plastic meat. I can't be sure, but I don't think the man with the white beard and blood-red coat bothered to visit my room. I caught a glimpse of him striding along the corridor, sack over his shoulder, a nurse in an elf's hat trotting by his side. No doubt they have good children to visit.

Dad's working his way through a box of chocolate liqueurs. I smell the brandy and cherries, taste the darkness and the soft pink syrup that pops in your mouth like a boil. He told me Pauline is spending the day with Adam. Oscar has foisted himself upon a long-suffering mate for the festive season.

Dad unwrapped a new radio/CD player for me earlier, together with an Ella Fitzgerald compilation disc, presumably because Oscar still hasn't handed back my iPod. He's also given me a bike lock. He threaded the cord through the radio handle and locked it to my bed so nobody can steal it.

'It was Pauline's idea. It's so your room's not so quiet when we're not here. She thought it would be good for the baby, good for you, to have the stimulation.'

We listen to the Queen's speech at three o'clock. Absurd how the rituals continue, despite the circumstances.

Then in a blink there are fireworks in the sky, and I hear voices from the nurses' station singing 'Auld Lang Syne'.

The old year goes. The new year comes. There's a dying and a new start, and I'm stuck between the two, hoping for a cup of kindness. Hoping I'll never be forgot.

I remember drunken voices singing another song. It's Saturday, 11th August. My 35th birthday. Kiki has arranged a surprise supper party for me at the flat. She's invited Dad and Oscar, Mrs Squires from next door, Keith, Professor MacMahon and his wife Marjorie, a couple of colleagues from the Institute of

Genetics, and a lab technician from the university I occasionally lunch with.

Michael had planned to take me out to dinner that evening, but when I saw Kiki flushed and furtive in the kitchen earlier in the day, I knew something was up.

'You must have guessed I would be planning something,' she laughs after I wheedle it out of her. 'I saw the new dress hanging in your room. Don't tell me you didn't buy it specially! What gave me away?'

It was a green silk 1950s-style cocktail dress, cinched tight at the waist, with a full skirt down to just below my knees. The stiff material rustled voluptuously as I tried it on in the shop, and lent me curves I didn't possess.

'Oh, I don't know... the extra food,' I hedge, not having noticed anything until I caught her trying to hide a tray of canapes in the fridge.

I don't want her to see my tears of frustration, so I make an excuse about soaking in the bath and doing something special with my hair. I turn on the taps to cover my voice, sit on the closed toilet seat and ring Michael.

'Don't worry. We can have dinner another time. I'm glad your friend wanted to do this for you.'

'But I want to be with you,' I protest.

'I know. And I'm going to miss you dreadfully.'

'Are you sure you can't come?'

'What do you think your colleagues would say if I was there? It would look a little irregular. I'm just a supplier, remember. Do we really want to face everybody's questions?'

'I suppose not. But I'm very cross. I bought a new dress, specially.'

'Then I'll look forward to seeing you in it. I can take you out for Sunday lunch instead.'

'It's not really a Sunday lunch kind of dress.'

'I'm intrigued, Dr Moss,' he says suggestively. 'Just try to enjoy yourself.'

'Well, I won't,' I sulk. 'And Kiki's used up all my bubble bath again.'

The doorbell rings at eight o'clock on the dot. It's Keith, carrying a bunch of flowers and a bottle of wine. I'm secretly pleased at the expression on his face when I open the door.

'Wow! You look different.'

'Thanks. I'll take that as a compliment.'

I introduce him to Kiki, who sent him an email invitation via the university intranet but hasn't met him before. Mrs Squires arrives almost immediately, probably having heard the bell and the voices through the adjoining wall.

The French doors are open. A bird is calling in the dusk. Earlier in the afternoon there was a summer shower, and now the stillness smells of wet leaves. Betsy has been banished to the bedroom. Mrs Squires dislikes cats and still hasn't forgiven her for jumping across to her balcony and doing her business in a tray of tomato seedlings back in April.

A year ago, I wouldn't have believed I would be standing in my living room, a glass of rosé in my hand, surrounded by family and work colleagues admiring my appearance and that of my flat – polished and plumped to perfection, courtesy of Kiki. I would have been secretly delighted that someone had thrown me a birthday party, and be relishing the office gossip, the thrust and parry of scientific debate, hearing Marjorie MacMahon give Kiki a recipe for a lamb tagine, and Dad telling Mrs Squires the benefit of switching electricity supplier. But instead I'm edgy with frustration. It's an effort to keep smiling and nodding. I wonder how long the guests will stay, and whether I'll be able to sneak out and drive across town to Michael's apartment after Kiki goes to bed.

Oscar arrives late and grabs a tumbler and a bottle of gin, ignoring the tonic. He walks over to my iPod docking station. 'Haven't you got any proper music, Tilly?'

'I like Albinoni.'

'Alby who?'

'Tomaso Giovanni Albinoni. He's an Italian Baroque composer. Leave it alone.'

He throws himself into a chair and pours himself a full glass, placing the bottle next to him on the bookshelf.

After a buffet of smoked salmon, sweet chilli chicken wings, couscous, garlic bread, salad and a selection of cheeses, Kiki conjures a chocolate cake and everyone sings 'Happy Birthday'. I'm made to open my cards and presents. Dad gives me a cheque as always. I unwrap the usual selection of smellies and chocolates. Inside Oscar's card is a ticket for a free quad bike safari, obviously typed by him and printed on his PC.

'But it's in Manchester!' I exclaim.

'That's where I'm running the expeditions. I've hired a bit of wasteland on the outskirts of the city, next to a canal.'

'Sounds delightful!'

'Don't be like that. You'll love it. You can bring any of your friends.' He raises his voice. 'How's about a quad bike safari, everyone? You could get a lift down with Tilda. Let's make it a group jolly. It's only 65 quid each for an hour. Come on, Keith. Sounds tempting, doesn't it? Wouldn't you like the chance to cut up your superior and come out on top for once?'

I cover the embarrassing silence by opening a gift box. The professor and his wife have bought me an edition of *The Times* dated the day I was born. The paper is passed around the group, generating a tedious flurry of comment on the value of the pound and the FTSE 100.

People begin to drift away after eleven.

'Can I stay the night?' Oscar asks grumpily from the depths of the armchair.

'No. I don't have a spare bed any longer. I have a flatmate now.'

'A matflate?'

'A flatmate. Kiki. She lives here.'

'Does she?'

'Yes, and she doesn't want to wake tomorrow morning and have to look at you half-naked on the sofa, stinking of booze and garlic.'

'Oh, I don't know,' Kiki calls from the kitchen.

'You should have checked with me first. You really are the limit, Oscar. You can't just expect to crash here whenever you want.'

'I couldn't ask you because it was a *surprise* party, remember?'

'All the same…'

'But I'm too drunk to drive.'

'That's why I've taken your keys from your jacket and given them to Dad. He's agreed to take you home to Durham with him tonight.'

He swears. 'Do I have to?'

'I heard that, son. I'm not as deaf as you think.'

By 12.30, Kiki finishes clearing the lounge, stacking the dishwasher and wiping down the surfaces. I told her to leave it until the morning, but she refused.

'I don't want you getting up early tomorrow and doing it. This was your birthday treat. I don't want you lifting a finger.'

'Thanks, Kiki. I'm really grateful. It was lovely.'

'Yes, it was, wasn't it? I enjoyed meeting everyone. It's good to be able to put faces to the names.'

I'm not aware that I've spoken to her about my family and colleagues very much, but I let it go. I'm not even sure how she managed to draw up the invitation list. But her recent heartbreak has left her a little down, and I can see that meeting a few new people has done her good, even though I now recognise them for what they are, a collection of duffers, drips and drunks.

Once alone in my bedroom, I ring Michael to see whether it's too late to come over. His mobile goes straight to voicemail. No doubt he has switched it off and is fast asleep.

Dr Arnold arrives with a pack of student doctors. They crowd near my bed like wolves around a kill while the Great One explains my condition.

'She's in a vegetative state. As well as the damage from the fall, a recent MRI scan revealed that her brain is beginning to atrophy.'

'What about an EEG?' a pretty intern asks.

'Good question. That's an electroencephalogram for those of you with your mouths open, catching flies.' There's a ripple of uncomfortable laughter. 'Dr Moss had several EEGs in the early weeks following her trauma. At different times they revealed normal continuous generalised slowing, intermittent generalised slowing, background slowing and suppression, and both alpha and triphasic waves. In other words, underlings, I concluded that the EEG findings were too variable to be of diagnostic value… In addition, I've had nurses sitting in half-hour shifts noting down her movements and trying to ascertain whether she's trying to communicate.'

This is all news to me.

'Unfortunately,' he continues, 'the family are struggling to face up to the reality of the situation. Everybody's an expert these days. In the past, doctors were the authority on patient care. It's a different world now. It's not helpful when relatives Google medical information. For example, in this case, the father is keen for his daughter to be diagnosed as being minimally conscious, probably because it leaves him with a sliver of hope.'

'How can you differentiate between the two conditions?' a bespectacled student asks.

'It's a fine line. One could argue either way. This patient does open her eyes, but she can't move them and doesn't blink. She makes noises, but not in response to external stimuli. As far as I'm concerned, an occasional groan doesn't prove cognitive awareness. I also have to bear in mind the fact that there's no legal way to end the life of someone who's minimally conscious. It's much more straightforward with PVS, where a decision can be taken about whether a life should be prolonged beyond the point it's worth living, and feeding can be withdrawn.'

The pretty intern lifts her pen to attract the consultant's attention.

'Yes?'

'How's that decision made?'

'Sometimes it's a question of economics. That's the harsh reality. There has to be a ceiling of care where rehab is impossible. Part of your job as doctors will be to consider the impact of unsuccessful life-saving interventions on the hospital budget. Basically, you've got to be prepared to play God.'

A bearded intern hangs back in the corner. Unlike the consultant and other student doctors who are all wearing open-necked, short-sleeved shirts and smart trousers, he's wearing an old-fashioned doctor's coat. It's dazzlingly white against the dark hair on his collar. He looks like a walking advertisement for washing powder, or a new boy anxious to impress. I'm reminded of someone from my past, but can't recall who. He hovers in the background while the consultant drones on.

'This is an interesting case because we've just discovered the patient's pregnant. This raises a whole host of other issues. In my opinion, it's highly unlikely for the pregnancy to be successful, and the additional strain on the patient's body will probably hasten her demise. For there to be any improvement in her condition, a termination would be the best way forward. However, as I've said, the family's wishes have to be taken into consideration, difficult as it may be for the hospital to accommodate.'

I switch off, too depressed to listen to a discussion about how little my life and the life of my baby are worth.

As the interns file out of the door behind Dr Arnold, the bearded student hangs back, turns and smiles at me. I smell sunshine and ozone and warm bread. My ears are filled with the rush of a hot breeze over water. He nods slightly, acknowledging my presence. My heart soars. This time, someone with medical expertise, someone other than Claude, believes in me.

But after he's left, doubt creeps in like a thief, stepping softly, intent on stealing my hope. If none of the other students recognise my presence, how can he see me, a small pip within a smashed and rotting fruit? Was he really smiling at me? Perhaps he was thinking of his girlfriend, or his plans for the weekend. Or perhaps he was merely laughing at my predicament.

Chapter 21

I'm no further along with my investigation. Retrieving my memories is a haphazard process. My brain stubbornly refuses to fast forward. It's still piecing together the corners and edges, gradually moving towards the black hole at the centre.

Days pass in a somnolent blur of shifting dreams, then suddenly there'll be a break in the cloud. A brilliant shaft of light will strike through the veil and illuminate a moment in perfect detail. Early one morning a petite woman passes my door dragging a small case on wheels. Her scurrying trot clicks an image into place. Like Alice in Wonderland, I follow the rabbit back down the tunnel of my past.

Michael is planning a trip to London. There's a big exhibition at Alexandra Palace. The thought of him returning to his old haunts and his bohemian friends fills me with anxiety. He might awake from the enchantment that has befallen us and see me again as a business contact, a dowdy academic, instead of a woman breathless with love.

To be away from him even for a couple of days will be agony. The passionate afternoons and intimate evenings at his flat have become an addiction. Without thinking of the implications, I decide to surprise him. I cancel a meeting with a PhD student I'm supervising and pack a small flight bag early on Thursday morning to catch the 08.59 train to London King's Cross, arriving at 11.51 where I change on to the Underground. The

Victoria line takes me to Finsbury Park where I switch platforms to the Piccadilly line for Wood Green station. I spurn the free shuttle bus and stride up the hill and through the park, pulling my overnight bag – toiletries, a change of clothes, a new negligee – to burn off the anticipation firing my blood.

An ice cream van chimes. The wheels of my case rattle self-importantly along the concrete path, releasing the stink of hot tar. Children dart like flies around overladen mums with buggies, shrieking at a game of chase beside a cushion of summer bedding plants. Heat prickles under my arms. My blouse is sticking between my shoulder blades. The temperature is at least ten degrees warmer than it would be in Newcastle, and I'm already missing the edge of freshness I've left behind. At the summit, I stop to catch my breath.

Summer shimmers over London like light on water. A great panorama spreads beneath my feet, a counterpane of dusty trees and semi-detached Edwardian villas. In the distance, skyscrapers float above suburbia like Neolithic monuments, vast and incomprehensible. They rise out of the miasma of diesel, indifferent to the incense of the city – the prayers of the people for wealth and power and success.

I turn to face the palace, its yellow brickwork glowing in the light. The ornate red and white decoration, the arches and pillars and the recessed rose window, are part Victorian railway station, part Italian opera house, part neo-classic cathedral. It's a fitting place to surprise my Michael, another English eccentricity: overwhelming, larger than life, unclassifiable.

I step through the doors and into a domed courtyard of glass and wrought iron. Immense palms stretch to the ceiling. My heels tap across to the ticket stall. I imagine a rendezvous in the foyer of a grand hotel on the French Riviera. For the first time I feel the glamour of love, the lightness, the style of it.

Once through the main exhibition hall, the atmosphere changes. I'm back in a twenty-first-century world of science and marketing. I wander along the aisles, pretending to view the exhibits. It's hot and crowded, but I'm grateful for the anonymity of the throng. I consult the exhibitors' map and follow the route to his stand.

I stop, suddenly unsure, and survey the BioExpertise exhibit from behind a promotional banner. I see him immediately. He's towering over a woman in a turquoise blouse and figure-hugging skirt. It's the girl from the Expo, the one I overheard calling Michael a pseud as he stood on the stage to introduce the equipment sponsorship programme.

Something about the way they laugh together pulls me up short. A dark shadow moves deep in my gut. A snake of fear uncoils and slithers up my throat, catching my breath. Being here is a terrible mistake. What will she think of me turning up like this with my overnight bag? How will Michael react? He'll be astounded at my indiscretion. Part of me wants to disappear into the crowd and slink home. Another needs to look him in the eye to find out whether I've anything to worry about. I decide to wait until he packs up for the day. I'll surprise him once we're alone.

I drag myself to the cafeteria and sit brooding over a pot of tea and an overpriced sandwich. When the crowds begin to thin, I creep back to my position behind the banner. Michael has rolled up his shirt sleeves and loosened his tie. The girl is tidying a rack of promotional leaflets. After a few minutes he picks up his jacket and slings it over his shoulder. They say a few words. He grabs his briefcase and strides towards the Palm Court, waving a casual goodbye.

I hurry behind, keeping my distance through the exit and down through the park. His pace slows. His shoulders stoop, his body slackens like sails without a wind. The afternoon heat is sucking the vigour from his body. He cuts across the grass,

174

ignoring the paths, taking the shortest route to the main road. He's heading for the station, probably to catch a train to his hotel. I'm unsure what to do, whether to catch up with him with some lame excuse as to why I'm in London, or give up and go home now I know he's left the bimbo behind. He descends the steps to the platform. Either way, it looks as though we are both taking the westbound train towards King's Cross station.

He sits heavily and pulls a newspaper from his briefcase. I stand at the far end of the carriage, just able to glimpse his frowning face from behind a couple of tourists hanging on to an overhead strap. I've never seen him look so despondent. I hope it means he's missing me. I long to squeeze his hand and tell him I've been missing him too, but the whole thing has become ludicrous. I've left it too long. The spontaneity has gone, along with my nerve. There's no way to explain how we've come to be travelling in the same carriage together.

The train lurches to a stop after a couple of stations. He staggers to the door, thrusting the newspaper back in his bag. I push past the tourists and follow him down the platform. When he reaches his destination, perhaps I can come up with some kind of story to explain how I managed to track down his hotel. He plods through the ticket barrier and out into the street. Maybe I can convince him he let slip where he was staying. Or I could tell him I inadvertently saw it written in his diary. We walk past a few seedy shops and turn off the main road on to a residential street. He looks exhausted. Perhaps he won't question my presence, just sink gratefully into my arms, into a bed, and rest beside me with my hand stroking his forehead.

He crosses the road. I remain on the other side, shadowing him like a faithful dog, struggling to carry my bag to avoid drawing attention to myself with the noise of the wheels. Eventually he stops at an imposing terraced house and pushes open the gate. It doesn't look like a hotel. I creep forward, hoping he doesn't turn and look behind. He rings the doorbell. Perhaps he's visiting friends. Possibly he's visiting his ex-wife. My stomach begins to churn again. After a couple of minutes, the door opens. Standing on the step is the most beautiful woman I've ever seen. Dark hair swept up, olive skin, an expensive dress clinging to her slender frame. He walks past as though he's expected. The door slams behind him. I stand on the pavement, bereft.

I arrive home just after nine. Kiki emerges from her bedroom. 'I wasn't expecting you tonight. I thought you were away at a conference.'

'I came home early. The keynote speaker was... tedious... and I think I'm coming down with something.'

'You gave me such a fright. I thought you might be a burglar.' She pulls her dressing gown tight around her waist, flustered.

'Burglars don't come through the front door with keys.'

She fidgets with her belt. 'You *are* looking a bit peaky. Perhaps you should have an early night. I was having an early one myself.'

'Yes. I'm going straight to bed. Sorry to have scared you.'

A noise sneaks from her bedroom.

'No worries,' she says, blushing.

'Oh! I didn't realise you had a visitor. Would you like to have the flat to yourself?' I want nothing more than to crawl into bed, but find myself saying, 'I can go and grab myself something to eat at the pizza place down the road.' My eyes begin to well with tears.

'Of course not. You're poorly and this is your flat. Perhaps I should have asked you, but as you said you were going to be away, I —'

'You don't need to ask my permission to have a friend over. This is your home. I'm happy for you.'

'We were going to pop out later anyway to get something to eat. You get your head on that pillow. Give us a few minutes and *we'll* go and get a pizza instead. I promise to be quiet when I come back *alone*,' she emphasises with an awkward smile, 'so as not to wake you.'

'Thanks, Kiki. I really appreciate that. I feel deathly.'

She retreats to her bedroom. As she opens the door I catch a glimpse of a pair of men's trousers folded neatly on her chair. I turn quickly, not wanting a stranger to see my watery eyes, and embarrassed I might catch sight of more than I bargained for.

I hardly slept the night after my visit to Alexandra Palace. When I did I dreamt of a woman with hair as black as a raven's wing and lips as red as blood. *'Mirror, mirror on the wall, who is the fairest of them all?'* I knew it wasn't me.

I phoned Keith the next morning to say I was coming down with a virus. I had planned on pulling a sickie anyway, hoping I would be in a hotel room with Michael. I certainly felt unwell. My eyes were swollen and sore. My nose was blocked and my head pounded to the beat of betrayal and despair.

At a quarter past eight, Kiki slammed the front door behind her. I shuffled to the kitchen to make myself a cup of tea. Betsy sat primly by the swing bin, licking her paws and wiping them behind her ears, ignoring me completely.

I carried my mug back to my room and placed it on the bedside table. My overnight bag was unzipped on the floor where I had pulled out my toiletries the previous night. Black lace spilled from the opening. I yanked at my new negligee and buried it in the bottom of my knicker drawer, unable to bear the sight of my crumpled hopes, my unworn dreams.

Huddling under the bedclothes, I sipped the hot liquid and reviewed the situation. Michael didn't know I'd followed him to London. As far as he was concerned, nothing had changed between us. Perhaps nothing *had* changed, except for my mood. And my faith in him.

It was unusual for me to make a judgement based on my emotions. My habit was to gather data and calmly survey the results. But Michael had spun my world on its orbit, and I no longer knew which way was up. What was the evidence for any betrayal? He had entered a house belonging to a beautiful woman. That was all. I might have jumped to the wrong conclusion. It could have been his sister or his niece, though her exotic appearance spoke otherwise. He hadn't told me he was visiting anyone in London, but then why should he? We weren't living together or married. We were two mature adults who had recently begun a secret affair. We didn't live in each other's pockets!

Perhaps it was an innocent business appointment that he would tell me all about on his return. Keep cool. Bide my time, that was the key. All would become clear, one way or the other. As clear as a microbe under a microscope. I would make sure of it.

Chapter 22

'Her mother wouldn't have agreed to an abortion. She believed in the sanctity of every human life.'

'It's not my place to question your decisions. I'm just here to ascertain the facts.'

'I'm sorry, inspector. It's been a long day. My son...'

'He doesn't agree?'

'Let's just say he's having difficulty with this unexpected turn of events. As we all are. We didn't know she was in a relationship. I've asked the doctor about the night she was brought in. He was quite sure there were no signs that she might have been... might have been –'

'Sexually assaulted?'

'Yes.'

'I can put your mind at rest on that account, sir. There was no evidence of a sexual attack. In fact, there is no real evidence pointing to what happened that evening. If it wasn't for the fraud committed against the university – which could be an unfortunate coincidence – my superior would have probably wound down our investigation. Put the whole matter down to misadventure.'

'He wants to close the case?'

'Not yet. After the baby's born we can order a DNA test to find out who the father is. That might shed some light on the matter. Violence is usually about sex or money. We've got substantial sums missing from the university, and now we have confirmation of a sexual relationship.'

I've become an incubator of the truth, which swells inside me waiting to be delivered. It's a waiting game now. Is it my imagination or are the medical staff handling me more gently? The nurse who had previously accused me of diverting resources from children with cancer pats my stomach gently.

'How you doing in there today?' she coos.

It's no longer about me. Something new and innocent is growing, a dewy white mushroom on the dungheap of my decaying frame.

'The police are extremely concerned about the whereabouts of 13-year-old Jennifer Allen. She was last seen walking home from a friend's house at about 6.30pm on 8th December in the Wallsend area of Newcastle. Police are appealing to the public for any information. Jennifer has shoulder-length brown hair, hazel eyes, and wears a brace.'

Dad switches off the radio. 'That poor family. When you lose your own daughter, it makes it all the more horrific when you hear of others going through the same thing.'

'You haven't lost her, Peter. You mustn't give up hope.'

'Whatever happens, she's never going to be the girl she was.'

'Perhaps not. But she'll always be your Tilda.'

An unforgiving light, cold and white, tracks across my hospital window. My eyes are watering. I wish I could blink the tears away. A stream of salt dribbles into my neck.

'Look! She's crying!' Dad exclaims. The sound of a chair scraping back lifts the hairs on my arms.

'The sun's in her eyes,' Pauline says. 'I'll close the curtain.' She stands and yanks the yellow and blue cotton along the ceiling track until it shades my face. 'There. That's better.'

Dad shuffles to my side and leans over, wiping my cheeks with his handkerchief as if I'm a child.

'But what if she *is* crying?' he says. 'What if she knows what's happening to her and can't reach out to us?'

'You mustn't upset yourself, Peter.'

'I can't help it. Not knowing if she has any kind of awareness... it's tormenting me. Feeling so helpless...'

'Then you must *do* something. Tell her how much you love her. Tell her how special she is and how you'll never give up on her. You must keep telling her every single day. You must talk to her and play her music and hold her hand and –'

'Yes. Yes, of course. You're right.' He takes my hand. 'My dear heart... My beautiful girl... You know I love you. It goes without saying. And your brother loves you. And your mum, rest her soul.' He mops his own eyes with his handkerchief. I hear the click of a switch and my new Ella Fitzgerald CD begins to play, 'Come back to us, Tilda. If you can hear me, give my hand a little squeeze.' The words from 'Someone to Watch Over Me' curl in the corners of the room, stroking the ceiling and falling down like blue rain.

'Please try. We're all waiting. We all want you back,' Pauline whispers.

'I miss you so much.' Dad tightens his grip. I fear he'll crush my fingers to a pulp. 'Tilda. Wake up, darling. Wake up! It's time to wake up! Are you listening to me?'

'Gently, now.' Pauline hovers at his side, holding his elbow, patting his shoulder.

'You'll do as you're told, young lady... or... or...' He drops my hand, sobbing. 'But it isn't enough, Pauline. My love isn't enough! It can't reach her.'

'You don't know that. You mustn't give up hope. Never that. I'm sure at some deep level she can sense you're here. And it gives her comfort.'

'It's useless.'

'Hush, now. Don't upset yourself. Tilda wouldn't want that. You're doing everything you can. Nobody could be doing more. You're running yourself ragged.'

'I wish it was me on that bed.'

They both stand over me, watching, their hands entwined.

'Of course you do. We would all spare our children's suffering if we could. But it was just the sun in her eyes. A reflex.'

'Yes. Maybe it was a reflex.'

Pauline leads him back to the chair. While their backs are to me, water oozes from the corner of my eye and runs down the side of my face and into my ear. It's a real tear, but they're too busy hugging each other to notice.

'Tilda, dear. Would you like me to line up some peer reviews for your paper?'

'It's fine, thanks, prof. I think I'll wait for feedback post-publication.'

'Don't you think that's rather a risk?'

'Maybe, but safer than the risk of my findings being leaked. You know what a load of gossips that clique can be.'

'I don't want you to publish something prematurely that you'll later regret. We can't see our own blind spots, Tilda. You have to be absolutely sure of your thesis. It's the university's reputation too.'

'I'm well aware of that. But given the current climate of leaks and computer hackers, I'm not willing to chance it.'

His lips tightened as if he didn't trust himself to reply. He picked a dead leaf off the African violet on my desk and scrunched it in his hand, rolling it into a small ball before dropping it in the bin.

'You know best, I'm sure, my dear. I just don't want you going down a path you'll later have cause to regret. You can't turn back the clock. Once it's published, you won't be able to put the genie back in the bottle.'

I can't sleep. The memories of my trip to Alexandra Palace are too raw. First, Michael leaning too close to his work colleague. Then his visit to the house in St John's Villas, Holloway. Who was the woman who opened the door? They hadn't kissed or shaken hands, but he had walked in confidently, as though he was a familiar visitor.

I wait until after one o'clock the next day. I've decided I'll ring to ask how the exhibition's going. He'll think I'm on my lunch break. In reality, I'm still in bed, dishevelled and unwashed, having rung Keith to confirm I've come down with a bug. He sounds genuinely concerned. Guilt nags at my stomach. I'm not used to telling lies.

I select Michael's name from my contacts list and tap the telephone icon. After a couple of rings, a woman answers.

'Hello.'

'Hello,' I reply automatically. 'Can I speak to Michael Cameron, please? Is this the right number?'

'Mike can't take your call at the moment. Do you want to leave a message?'

The proprietorial tone of her voice annoys me.

'Who am I talking to?'

'His wife.'

The two words plunge like pebbles in a pond, the ripples expanding in successive waves of pain... *His... Wife.* Not 'his ex-wife'. *His wife.*

'No message. I'll catch up with him later.'

'Do you want to leave your name?'

'I don't want to disturb him if he's not at work. I thought he was running an exhibition.'

'He is. We're just having a spot of lunch together. He's in the little boys' room at the moment. You could try him later this afternoon.'

'Thanks.'

Even at that moment I'm thanking her. Thanking her for speaking to me, thanking her for offering to pass on a message from her husband's lover, too diffident to break with conventional politeness and scream for his heart to be served up on a skewer.

I throw my mobile across the bedroom. It strikes the mirrored wardrobe door with a crack. The glass shatters into a spider's web of lines and angles, my shocked face reflecting in a dozen shining facets.

Chapter 23

The jealousy that flared that day returns, fresh and stinging as a slap. I'd forgotten the incident. Now I've remembered, I feel betrayed all over again. He was with his wife. He'd been lying all the time. I'd been taken for a fool – me, Dr Tilda Moss, PhD, tough-minded rationalist – duped like an airheaded romantic by a whiff of testosterone, a lopsided smile, a tantalising self-deprecating twinkle in his eye. I wonder it has taken me this long to remember. Some primitive mechanism has been protecting me, keeping me hoping, keeping me waiting, keeping me alive until the time when my shattered mind could absorb the shock of his treachery.

How can I go on living? The pain is too raw, too crushing. Why try to fight? Better to give up and slip away now, if only I knew how to do it. Nothing matters. There was never any point to it, no higher meaning than a biological urge. I should have known that more than anyone, but I'd allowed myself to be swept along by an impossible dream.

My stomach flip-flops. A sickening sinking sensation makes my monitor protest with a series of high-pitched bleeps. A nurse comes and checks my blood pressure.

'What are you doing to your mummy, little one?' she croons, patting my stomach. 'You stop that now. Go back to sleep.'

Then I realise. The strange flutters visiting in the night, the unexpected warmth curling in my belly, are not yearnings for my lover. They've been the first tentative strokes of my child, swimming in the ocean of my inmost being.

I'm glad of the distraction, and turn my thoughts away from Michael's betrayal. My ability to compartmentalise different areas of my life, and switch off my emotions at will, has always been my strength – or perhaps my weakness.

I think of my baby, floating in the dark peace of my womb. Does she marvel at the fingernails she's growing? Does she question the uselessness of her lungs and her eyes and her vocal cords, faculties that have no purpose yet but are being prepared in readiness for her next life? Life after birth. She can't conceive what's coming, that one day all her life supports will be torn away and she'll be ejected into the light. Will she feel it as a violent death, this being born? I know there's an infinitely richer life waiting for her than the one she now lives, but if she were given a choice between staying where she is and moving through the terror to something better, what would she choose? What would I choose?

The hospital sheets are clinging to my body. The swell of my stomach is noticeable now. Despite the warmth of the room, I long for the heaviness of a plump duvet, the comfort and the softness and the feeling of home. I'm sick of camping under thin blankets. I want to slink away like a wounded animal and hide in a dark place where no one can find me.

The house I inhabit is crumbling around me. Webs hang from the ceiling. Evil thoughts are roosting in the chimney. There are problems with the plumbing and the electrical supply. But there's a tiny creature hiding in the skirting boards, scurrying in the loneliness of the empty rooms, those echoing spaces that were once so full of hope and joy. The demolition order has been given. Once she's been rescued from the ruins, the wrecking ball will swing. I'm being kept alive for her sake. I have no choice but to go on, a prisoner against my will.

My visitors are fewer now. My friends and colleagues are moving on with their lives. The Victorian circus has left town. I'm old news. The world is a greyer place. My yellow and blue curtain no longer shimmers. It hangs limp and faded, transparent in the afternoon light. I dream the names of people I no longer remember. I drift through thousands of hours of stillness. Perhaps I only exist in a physical state when people come to visit. Unobserved, I float in the realm of the immaterial, neither a particle nor a wave, but a shallow breath waiting to be released. Then someone comes, and I am again a lump of misshapen clay.

The young doctor in the white coat slips through the door more frequently now. At first I wonder if he's here to observe my movements, to spot the 'cognitively mediate behaviour' my consultant couldn't find. But he never says anything, doesn't even check my notes or the readings on the monitor. I'm annoyed he seems to be using my room for his lunch break. He sits and eats a crusty roll, drinks from a bottle of water. The smell of the fresh bread is agonisingly fragrant. Sometimes he brings a book and studies the pages intently. One day he's visibly moved by the story. Occasionally he glances at me as though he wants to share a private joke.

Why don't you read it out loud, if it's so funny?

Dad still comes for an hour or two every day. He listens to the cricket on the radio. England are playing Australia on the other side of the world. I hear the heat shimmering on the willow with each thwack of the ball.

Some days Pauline appears, bringing tins of home-baked rock cakes for Dad. They sit together talking banalities. I no longer listen. I no longer care that they're holding hands. They whisper to each other but I can't hear what they're saying over the racket of the radio.

The hourly news bulletin reports that Jennifer Allen is still missing. I recognise the inspector's voice at the press conference. His words cut cleanly through the click and whirr of the cameras. 'As you are aware, we have conducted numerous searches for Jennifer during the last two months, including house-to-house, aerial searches and the use of police dogs. We are grateful to the community for their support and urge people in the Newcastle area to continue to be vigilant. However, we are now widening our search. Someone in the country must know where Jennifer is. At the moment this is still a missing person investigation, but as time passes we are becoming increasingly concerned for Jennifer's safety. I would urge people to come forward if they have any information that might help our investigation.'

The report cuts to her father. 'Jenny. Please contact us. We miss you. We love you… We can't live without you. If you hear this, please ring home. It's been too many days and we don't know where you are. Please come back to us. If anyone knows where she is, please bring our beautiful Jenny home.'

Oscar is in my room. I haven't seen him for a while. He's unshaven. He looks tired.

'It's hard for me too, Tilda.' he mumbles. 'Dad doesn't care. I can't talk to him any more. Never could, really. You were always the one who translated between us. He's with Pauline all the time now.' He curses and stares intently at the monitor bleeping in the corner. 'It's obscene, keeping you going. I know you would have hated the thought of ending up like this.' He strokes the tube running from the drip bag. 'You should have the right to die with dignity. I know you best… but they won't listen. I'm your brother, for goodness' sake, and I have no say at all! I'd get a lawyer if I could afford one.'

He stands, shuffles over to my IV bag and examines the tubes carefully. I know what he's thinking. I always could. I watch from a cold distance, as though his actions have nothing to do with me. He wipes his hands down the sides of his trousers. He steps towards the bank of plug sockets on the wall. He's out of my line of vision now, but I smell the scarlet heat of his intentions.

Claude enters with a bang. Oscar jumps back and sits down on the chair.

'All right?' Claude nods.

'Yes, thanks.'

'It's a cold one, innit?'

'Yes.'

'They say there might be snow.'

'Yes.'

Claude pushes a large microfibre brush around the floor and under the bed, taking his time. 'Visiting hours be over, mister.'

Oscar looks at his watch. 'Oh, yes. Of course.' He picks up his coat from the end of my bed and winds his scarf around his neck. He pecks me on the cheek. 'Goodbye, Tilly.'

When he's gone, Claude leans the brush against the wall and stands next to the bed.

'You're welcome, girlie… It was nothin'… Any time… Think of me as your guardian angel.'

And strangely enough, I do.

I awake to the sharp tang of cut stalks. From the corner of my eye something yellow droops down from my head. While I've been sleeping (or whatever it is I do when the darkness descends and I'm lost in a swirl of images and sounds), I've been propped up on the pillows, facing the door.

Dad and Pauline stand next to each other at the foot of the bed. He's wearing a suit. His receding hair has been neatly combed across his forehead. She's resplendent in hat and floral two-piece.

Oscar shifts from foot to foot by the window. 'I don't know why you have to do this here. Or now. Or at all! No one needs to get married these days.'

'You know why. I love Pauline. And I respect her too much to ask her to come and live with me without promising her a lifelong commitment.'

'You're rushing into it,' Oscar objects.

'No, we're not. Pauline and I go way back. I should have had the courage of my convictions and snapped her up when you and Tilda were children.'

'You don't need to explain yourself,' Pauline says.

'Yes, I do. Marriage isn't fashionable. But I believe it's the foundation for a satisfying relationship. It's not an optional add-on, like a conservatory or a loft conversion that you only get around to once you've finished all the other home improvement projects.'

'Save the sermon, Dad. We all know what this is about. You're only marrying her so you will have a better chance of being granted guardianship of Tilda's baby.'

'That's a consideration, certainly. Pauline knows that. But she knows my feelings for her too. What else would you have me do? See the child put up for adoption? She's our flesh and blood. And I don't see you stepping forward to help.'

'Me! How can I bring up a child?'

'Exactly. Pauline loves children. It will give us both a purpose in life once Tilda has... you know, once...'

'Just say it. Once Tilda's dead.'

'Yes.' Dad winces.

'And what about me? When you, Pauline and the baby are playing happy families, who's going to care about me?'

'You're going to be part of that happy family,' Pauline says. 'You'll be the adored son and uncle. There's enough love to go around.'

Oscar snorts and the door swings opens. A chaplain in vestments enters, followed by a nurse and a young man who kisses Pauline on the cheek.

'Hello, Mum.'

'Hello, darling. Thank you for coming at such short notice. Oscar, you remember my son, Adam.'

The two men shake hands and exchange reluctant pleasantries.

While Dad, Pauline and the nurse chat to the clergyman by the door, Oscar pulls Adam closer to the head of the bed.

'What do you think about all this?' he whispers.

'I couldn't be more delighted for Mum,' Adam replies stiffly.

'I hope you haven't been encouraging them in this madness. The idea they can be parents all over again at their age! It's ludicrous.'

I'm feeling dizzy with confusion after so many days on my own, or with only a nurse or Dad for company. My senses are overwhelmed with stimuli. The fragrance of aftershave and perfume. The smell of irritation. Words echoing round the room, muffled then clear, reverberating in my head, floating free, then captured and understood. I hear Dad thank the chaplain for making the arrangements so quickly. The nurse compliments Pauline on her appearance.

'I've been advising them on the legal situation, certainly,' Adam says. 'Social services will be involved as soon as the baby is delivered. It's important to have their application for a residency order ready before then.'

'I don't understand what's in this for you. Can't you see we risk being disinherited?'

'I'm interested in Mum's happiness, not her money. My dad left provision for me, as I know your father is leaving provision for you.'

'Great! So now you know *my* private business.'

Noticing the raised voices, the clergyman opens his arms in a conciliatory gesture. 'I think everyone who is going to come is here: the happy couple, the best man and the two witnesses.'

'And my daughter. Our bridesmaid.'

'With daffodils!' the chaplain enthuses.

'Yes. They're my favourite.' Pauline steps towards me and fiddles with the yellow shape flopping by my ear, which I now realise is a daffodil. 'Such happy flowers. It won't be long until spring.'

'Indeed. So if we're all ready, let's begin.' He passes a small pamphlet to everyone, opens a larger book and begins to read.

'The grace of our Lord Jesus Christ, the love of God, and the fellowship of the Holy Spirit be with you.'

'And also with you,' Dad, Pauline, Adam and the nurse reply.

'In the presence of God, Father, Son and Holy Spirit, we have come together to witness the marriage of Peter and Pauline, to pray for God's blessing on them, to share their joy and to celebrate their love.'

I'm trying to grasp the tableau before me. The wicked stepmother – Oscar's black widow – has claimed my father at last. He's sacrificing a comfortable retirement for a treadmill of feeds, nappies and tantrums. As if he hadn't done it all before, raising Oscar on his own while battling with a precocious and grief-stricken teenager.

'Marriage is a gift of God in creation through which husband and wife may know the grace of God. It is given that as man and woman grow together in love and trust, they shall be united with one another in heart, body and mind. It is given as the foundation of family life in which children are nurtured and in which each member of the family, in good times and in bad, may find strength, companionship and comfort, and grow to maturity in love.'

Pauline leans closer to Dad and squeezes his arm. There are tears in her eyes.

'First, I'm required to ask anyone present who knows a reason why these persons may not lawfully marry, to declare it now.'

Suddenly I'm scared my little brother might say something, find an objection and scupper the plan for my baby. Pauline isn't a wicked stepmother. Maybe, if I hadn't objected to her so much when I was a teenager, we might have been a happy family years ago. Perhaps my brother wouldn't have gone off the rails, smoked pot, dropped out of university and spent the last decade chasing a succession of get-rich-quick schemes.

Oscar grimaces and stares out of the window.

'Peter and Pauline, I now invite you to join hands and make your vows, in the presence of God and his people.'

They face each other and promise to have and to hold, for better, for worse, for richer, for poorer, in sickness and health, until death takes them in his arms and scatters their bodies and their love on the wind. And I can't help thinking about Michael and the hope I secretly had of standing next to him in a register office, pledging to cherish him with all of my mind and all of my heart and all of my strength until death dragged us both to oblivion. And I wonder whether anything would have been different if I had held out for a commitment before jumping into his bed.

Oscar is fiddling in his top pocket. He resentfully passes a ring to Dad, who slips it on Pauline's finger. For the first time I register my father's expression. After so much pain and grief there's a flicker of something else. The man he used to be. Younger. Happier. And I wish it was me who had given him that glimpse of joy. I've been so wrapped up in my own anguish I haven't noticed the story unfolding at my bedside. I am looking at the face of a man in love.

Afterwards, Pauline lays her bouquet on my bed and places my hands so it looks as though I'm holding it. Dad takes a photo on his mobile phone. I imagine I look like a scarecrow.

'She looks beautiful,' says Pauline.

'Yes. And so do you.'

'Thank you, darling.'

They kiss. I wish I could avert my eyes.

My fingers tingle against the soft, waxy petals. The scent of freesia spirals through the room and dances with the aroma of decay that permanently curls around my bed. I'm not a scarecrow; I'm a corpse holding my own funeral bouquet.

I've been walking through a wood, a red cape around my shoulders. A wolf is howling in the distance and I'm following the sound. I know there'll be a devouring. It's inevitable. I knock at the door. I see through the disguise easily, the euphemisms and platitudes that surround the monster. Let's cut to the chase. Forget about the eyes and the ears, and focus on the teeth. It turns out there's no need to chew. One swallow is enough to complete the circle.

I'm back inside a belly, where it all began. I'm not scared, just very, very tired. Too tired to sleep. I wait for closure, for assimilation, wrapping my cloak of blood around me. Then another howl, so close that the reverberation shudders through my body. Something rips. A shaft of light dazzles. Someone reaches in. I kick and scream, not wanting to leave the hot darkness, and find myself awake and gasping in my hospital bed.

The night is filled with impending doom. My back and legs are aching. My head is pounding. I wonder why my bladder hurts and why my ears are ringing. Is my blood pressure too high or too low? Are these the normal symptoms of a pregnant woman in a persistent vegetative state? Or perhaps I've come down with another infection. It might be sepsis.

I don't know why I'm so frightened. It was just a dream. A silly fairy tale. An annoying story that puzzled me as a child because of the logical impossibility of pulling a human alive from the stomach of a wolf. But it's in the middle of the night that the certainties I have slip away. Dark thoughts riot and trample my reason. There's no way of dissipating the fear that's coursing through my veins. I can't roll over or punch the pillow. I can't scream or cry. Alone and overwhelmed, even the most enthusiastic atheist might begin to believe they've been singled out by a merciless deity. It's the primeval urge to blame something, anyone, for the suffering being endured.

Do you have to grow old before you can understand life? Is that why the old certainties are dissolving around me – naturalism, atheism, the pre-eminence of the material world? The place where I exist is not a physical space. As Michael said, there are more things in heaven and earth than I could have dreamt of in the past. This intangible realm of emotion and memory, thought and belief, is as real to me as the DNA I handled in my lab. There are precious things here, and fearful things too, things that swim in the darkness, monsters waiting to surface if I stand too close to the edge.

Perhaps I set myself too high. I've tampered with nature, manipulated the microscopic structures of the universe for my own ends. I gave myself the task of destroying death itself and now it's coming back to bite me. If the gods are punishing me for my hubris, I've nothing to bargain with. My hands are empty. My intelligence and qualifications count for nothing here. My money, my friendships: they won't save me. The baby is a temporary reprieve. And now my father is beginning to move on with his life. He's learning to let me go.

I'm too young to die, but too old to ask the simplistic questions. Where did I come from? Where am I going? What happened to me between the two? I'm stuck in the hinterland, not quite believing I'll perish here, but knowing I'm hardly alive. I'm vacating my life, little by little. I hope I've been right about the essence of things, and that the only thing that awaits is oblivion.

White flakes illuminated by the distant glow of the street lights wheel out of the darkness and tap at my window. I tell myself I'm not scared of death. I just don't want to go alone, like this, unprepared and in the dark. Or perhaps it's not the dying I'm frightened of, but the possibility of recovery, that the woodcutter will come and resurrect me after all.

It's morning. The sky is the colour of dirty dishwater. It's still snowing, a white drizzle now instead of the fat flakes that wheeled in the night. I'm feeling a little better. The pain in my back has lessened to a dull ache, and my terror has turned to gloom. I'm ashamed that I allowed panic to overwhelm my long-held beliefs even for a moment, but cannot escape the feeling that my inner world seems increasingly at odds with the outer world of scans and drips and investigations. Nothing is verifiable. I can't demonstrate to the medical staff that I'm aware of what's going on. Their equipment and knowledge are unable to reach me. I put my faith in science but it's letting me down. It's as though I'm existing in another realm. I'm a wisp of smoke, an oscillation, a sense of déjà vu, a ghost in a broken machine.

And now the bearded doctor is standing by the door. I notice a splash of blood near the hem of his jacket. I'm reminded I'm not the only one who suffers in this place, and wonder who the blood belongs to. Are they still alive? Or are they dead? Or are they like me, neither one nor the other, a Schrödinger's cat stuck inside a box – both alive and dead at the same time, at least until someone opens the lid.

He's looking into my eyes as though trying to unlock a puzzle. Or is he urging *me* to solve the conundrum instead? Questions tumble through my mind. What happened? What was the point? What am I? How can I escape? I'm frustrated by the limitations of my perspective. Like my baby, I can't see beyond my own experience. She hears my heartbeat as the recurring background to her world, like the sun rising or the rain falling. She cannot know she's reliant on me entirely for her life and growth. If someone asked her, 'Do you believe in your mother?' she wouldn't be able to comprehend the question. She doesn't recognise that her own reality is proof of mine. Can a baby come from nothing? Can life leap spontaneously out of arbitrary disorder?

I shrink from the direction my thoughts are taking. The doctor looks away, disappointed.

Dad arrives after lunch as usual with his newspaper and switches on my radio for the latest cricket score. He's not taking even a day off for a honeymoon. He doesn't attempt to talk to me. We ran out of conversation a long time ago.

'I understand congratulations are in order.' The inspector sits opposite.

'Thank you.'

'I spoke to your wife on the phone. She said you'd be here. There's been a development in the investigation. I thought you should be the first to know.'

Dad switches off the cricket. 'Go on.'

'Have you heard of a Michael Cameron?'

'No. Who's he?'

'An employee of BioExpertise Systems. He was their senior sales executive. He worked closely with your daughter on a contract to supply the university with scientific equipment. It was an irregularity with a payment relating to this contract that led to the university losing half a million pounds.'

'It was him! I knew it couldn't be my Tilda.'

'We're still trying to establish all the facts.'

'Have you arrested him?'

'He flew out to Switzerland the day after your daughter was injured.'

'Why's it taken you so long to work this out? If someone does a runner, it should be obvious they're guilty.'

'He's been on our radar for some weeks. I felt it best not to release the information to the public in case it spooked him.'

'I'm hardly the public!'

'No. Perhaps I should have been more candid. He resigned from BioExpertise a couple of weeks before Dr Moss ended up in here. He didn't work out his full notice. Then he just vacated his flat and handed his keys back to the landlord without any explanation. He might have been completely innocent, of course, but it looks suspicious.'

Dad curses. I'm shocked to hear the ugly words on his lips.

'It was all a set-up; he used my poor girl to gain access to the money. Perhaps she found out what he was up to. She might have confronted him. That's just the kind of thing she would do. She liked to have things out in the open.'

Now I know the truth. Michael betrayed me. At best I was just his bit on the side. At worst, he purposely set out to seduce me so he could defraud the university. At the very worst, he bears responsibility for my injuries. But it's difficult to square this conclusion with the man locked in my memory.

'We need to find out how well they knew each other. Nobody at the university thinks they were anything more than professional colleagues.'

'Have you asked Kiki?'

'She says she knows nothing. She's quite upset at the moment. She was the one who paid the phoney invoice. She didn't pick up the small spelling difference in the company name.'

'Another innocent victim!' Dad growls. 'Just tell me you've found him.'

'He booked a one-way ticket to Zurich on 22nd August and stayed one night at a hotel near the airport. After that we lost track of him. We put in a formal request for assistance from the Swiss police and applied for an international arrest warrant. They got back to me yesterday.'

'Have they got him?'

'No.'

'Why not?

'Because he's dead.'

Chapter 24

A sudden pain radiates from my back and across my stomach. He's gone. I'll never see him again. In spite of his betrayal, I realise how much I've been longing for him to walk through the door. If anyone could have reached into my mind and brought me from the brink, it would have been him. His rueful smile, that boyish guilt, his recalcitrant charm would have catapulted me from the bed. I would have ranted and screamed and punched his enormous chest before sobbing into his arms and forgiving him. That's how badly I've fallen. I've become one of those women, the ones who take their abusers back. Better the devil you know, better a devil you love, than no one.

My mind tells me I should be satisfied, even pleased, at his demise. He deserved it, didn't he, for what he did? But I can't gloat. There's no pleasure in his fate. The pain of his death is so much worse than his desertion, because there's no possibility of him ever coming back.

The discomfort in my ribs returns, squeezing my heart in a tightening vice. A memory unexpectedly jolts into place. A memory of an earlier agony. The memory of a fall. A dark thing lies ahead, but I must follow the path to the truth, wherever it may lead.

It's Monday afternoon, 21st August. I've sent an email to Professor MacMahon and Keith, cancelling a meeting to discuss our current project. I told them I have an urgent dental appointment. I've arranged to meet Michael at my flat. He travelled back from London yesterday and this is my first opportunity to have it out with him. Is he still married or not? Does he care for me at all, or is he that sad cliché – a middle-aged man having a jolly with a younger woman?

I want to be sure we won't be disturbed. He's not been to my flat before but I can't bear to meet him at his apartment, the place where we shared those intimate moments of bliss. Kiki is going on a date with her mystery man straight from work tonight and won't be home until late. When she returns, we can down a bottle of wine and curse all men to Hades.

Another pain brings me back to the present. The recurrent beep of the monitor races with my heart. Suddenly a high-pitched shriek fills the room. At first I think it's me, then I realise it's a medical alarm. A nurse runs into the room

A doctor arrives, one I haven't seen before. He places a stethoscope on my stomach, conducts a brisk examination. 'She's gone into labour,' he tells the nurse.

'It's too early.'

'She needs to be transferred to the maternity unit to see if we can halt the contractions. We'll need to start steroids immediately. Ideally she should have these for 24 hours before the birth to help the baby's lungs mature. Can you arrange a trolley, please? I'll make sure there's a bed for her downstairs.'

I sink back into my newly retrieved memory, imprinted now with photographic accuracy. It's a long-running script. I'm searching for the moment when I could have done things differently, that turning point where I could have altered destiny and set myself on a different path, a parallel universe where Michael and I could have been happy and together, where I wouldn't have been smashed to the ground like a wind-blown apple.

I needn't have worried that the flat might not be tidy. Kiki has been busy as usual. I'm glad. It helps that everything looks under control. He mustn't see the pain and chaos in my heart, the shattered crockery, the dirty corners, the shameful secrets in the back of the cupboards. I must appear invulnerable if I'm to survive the encounter.

The bell rings. I walk to the door with the tread of a death-row prisoner.

'Professor!'

'Hello, Tilda.'

'What are you doing here?'

'I received your email cancelling our meeting, but it's imperative we talk before I go off on annual leave tomorrow. I took the chance you might be home. Might I come in?'

I look at my watch. 'I don't have much time. I have an emergency appointment with the dentist. He's fitting me in after the surgery closes.'

'Yes, I know, but I won't keep you a minute. It's important.'

He pushes past, walks into the living room and sits on the sofa. I silently curse and follow, but pointedly don't sit down. Michael could arrive at any moment. I can't imagine what the professor will think if he discovers I've been having an affair with an employee of BioExpertise Systems. My integrity will be compromised. He might insist on an investigation into whether there's been a conflict of interest in the drawing up of the contract between Michael's employers and the university. There would be the embarrassment of everyone knowing details of my private life, then finding out I'd been taken for a ride by a duplicitous rogue.

'I know you've been very conscious of the security issues at the Institute of Genetic Medicine – and quite rightly too. I'm not sure what those bods in IT actually do all day. It hardly inspires confidence, does it?'

'No.'

'So I completely understand the measures you've taken to restrict access to your research. However, as your superior, I think the time has come when I need to step in and insist you share your findings with me. I represent the Institute to the grant-making bodies. They need to have some reassurance that their money's been well spent, that you've been able to make real progress.'

'I have. I promise you. Quite frankly, the results are staggering.'

'I'm glad to hear it. Very glad. And what does Keith think?'

'I haven't shown him the final analysis yet.'

'Perhaps that's wise. Not that I'm casting any aspersions in his direction, but we've been here before, haven't we? We're all vulnerable to cyberattack. However careful we are, it just takes a moment of complacency, not logging out properly or leaving a laptop unattended. And Keith can sometimes be a little naïve about these things.'

My eyes automatically flick to my desk in the corner where my personal laptop sits in full view. Next to it, Kiki has placed the morning's letters in a neat pile. She must have thrown the opened envelopes in the recycling bin before departing for work, because I remember leaving them strewn on the top in my haste to be on time for work. And next to the pile of letters, lying in full view, is the red USB stick I use to back up my files. I look away before the professor sees the direction of my gaze.

'I'm sorry, but I really have to go in a minute –'

'Yes, of course. I just wanted to say that although I've agreed with your approach up to now, I think it's time I saw the data. I know you don't keep anything on the server at the university, and I'm sure you wouldn't want to send it to me as an attachment. However, I've bought my own little memory stick.' He takes a black USB from his top pocket. 'Perhaps you could download the files on to it. I'll review your findings tonight, let you have any feedback, and then delete the files immediately to be absolutely on the safe side. I realise you can't be too careful.'

'Sorry, but I just don't feel comfortable –'

'This isn't a request, Tilda. It's an order. The university's reputation is at stake. If you publish something that hasn't been thoroughly reviewed, we could end up a laughing stock. I'm thinking of you. You have a glittering career ahead. I don't want to see it ruined by an avoidable blunder.'

I walk slowly towards my desk as though I'm considering his words. My back is to him and I'm blocking his view. I take a tissue from my cardigan pocket and wipe my nose.

'There's no need to be upset, my dear. I'm not cross with you.'

I quickly turn to face him, holding his gaze steadily, hoping he doesn't notice that my hand has grazed the desk and scooped up the USB. I drop it swiftly into my cardigan pocket.

'It's not that, professor. I'm afraid it's too late. I submitted my research for publication last week. I took the view that I'd rather look an idiot than have my work stolen again.'

He stares at me for a few moments, visibly stunned, the colour draining from his cheeks.

'I'm very disappointed, Tilda. Very disappointed indeed. I deserve better than this.'

'If it turns out there are errors in my findings, I'll take full responsibility. I'll make it quite clear that neither you, nor Keith, nor anyone else in the Institute is to blame.'

'This is personal ambition gone mad! We're a team, Tilda. I thought you understood that. I feel you've stabbed me in the back.'

'I'm sorry you're taking it that way. I've thoroughly acknowledged my debt to the university. I see it as a win-win situation. I've made sure the department will take credit for any success without bearing any of the risks of failure.'

I stride to the front door and open it. 'I really have to be somewhere else now. Goodbye, professor. I hope when you've had time to calm down you'll be able to forgive me. I took the course of action I thought best.'

Another contraction engulfs my body, stealing my breath until an ancient reflex pushes the air from my throat with a deep groan. I'm on a trolley being wheeled into the lift. I gaze at my reflection in the mirrored wall, surprised to see my outer self after so long examining the inner workings of my mind. My hair is longer and sticking to my forehead. My arms are as thin as a skeleton's, my stomach absurdly distended like that of a malnourished child. My eyes are grey stones. There's nothing to indicate the fear and pain, the terror for my child and the overwhelming grief that Michael is dead. All these months of waiting and yearning have been in vain. He was never going to come. He had gone on ahead. I know now that whatever his treachery, I will never stop loving him.

I close the door on the professor and go to the fridge. There's a half-finished bottle of white wine in the door. I pour myself a large glass and slump down in the armchair, exhausted.

I lied. I've been so distracted by recent events with Michael that I haven't got round to submitting my paper to the eminent scientific periodical waiting to print it. I've spoken to the editor, a good friend from my undergraduate days, and know that once he receives my findings they'll be safe from plagiarists and thieves. He wants the scientific scoop of the decade too badly to leak it to anyone else. I vow to visit him in Edinburgh at the first opportunity to hand over my data.

I'm jerked from my thoughts by an unearthly whining coming from the balcony. It's Betsy. She's sitting the other side of the French doors, staring at me with cold blue eyes. I'm not surprised she's angry. Kiki must have locked her out for the day. I've remonstrated with her a couple of times recently about her attitude to the cat. 'She's a house cat. She's never liked going outside, even as a kitten.'

'The fresh air's good for her. It's dry out there. She has her basket, litter tray and water. And it stops her clawing at the curtains.'

'She's 11. She just wants to sleep on my bed.'

'The soft furnishings tell a different story! Have you seen what she's done to the sofa?'

I imagine Kiki must have had quite a struggle to catch Betsy and deposit her on the balcony. Whenever I've tried – attempting to keep her away from my newly painted walls, for instance – I've always ended up with a line of scratches for my trouble.

I unlock the doors and push them open. Instead of walking in and curling round my legs, the cat jumps onto the balustrade, tiptoeing disdainfully along the edge.

'Sorry, old girl. Don't blame me. Blame the lodger.'

I stand and look down at the communal garden below. Michael should be here any minute.

My mobile rings. I walk back into the sitting room and take it from my handbag.

'Hello, Oscar,' I sigh.

'Hello, Tilly.'

'It's not a great time at the moment. Can I ring you later?'

'It's never a great time.'

'Don't be like that. I'm just about to start a meeting. I'll ring you tonight, I promise.'

'It might be too late by then.'

'Too late! What do you mean? What's the matter?' There's a long pause. 'It's not that nightclub nonsense again, is it? I told you what I think about that.'

'I know you did. But you're not being fair to me.'

'Fair to you! You're the one asking me to invest a large part of my savings in some hare-brained scheme.' I hate always being the voice that bursts his bubble, but I can't contain my exasperation.

'It isn't hare-brained. And it's not fair that you won't give it proper consideration. I'm your brother, after all. This is my opportunity to make some real money.'

'Or lose all of mine.'

'Give me some credit! I thought you would want to support me in this. I promised the others I'd be able to raise the funds.'

'You shouldn't have made promises on my behalf.'

'What am I going to tell them?'

'You're going to tell them, "No can do."'

'They're not the sort of people you tell that to.'

'Oscar! You really are the limit. I haven't got time to try to sort out your stupid dramas.'

'But what am I going to do? They're expecting me to have the money this evening.'

'Go to the police.'

'I can't do that!'

'If you feel threatened, you must report them. It's just like the bullies at school, remember? You have to stand up to them. As soon as they know you're broke, they'll drop you like a hot brick. Now I've really got to go. I'll speak to you later.'

'Can I come and stay with you tonight?'

'No, you can't. Go and stay with Dad if you're that worried.'

'I hate you! I really do.'

'Don't be like that –'

'You couldn't care less about me. It would serve you right if you never saw me again –'

'Oscar!'

'Then you'd realise what having a brother means. But it would be too late! You've had your chance to help. You're choosing to pass by on the other side of the street. Be it on your own head, then. I hope you're satisfied.'

The line goes dead.

I toss my mobile onto the sofa and look at my watch. Michael's late. I smooth down my hair. Betsy's crying from the balcony again. The door's open. I don't know why she doesn't come in. When I investigate, I discover she's jumped the gap to next door's balcony and is standing on Mrs Squires' balustrade, staring balefully at the chasm between us.

'What are you doing over there, you naughty girl?' I hold out my arms and make encouraging kissing noises to coax her back.

Her tail sways back and forth, a calculating expression in her eyes.

'Come on. You can do it.'

But she turns and sashays away from me, balancing like a gymnast. Mrs Squires' glass doors are closed, but her kitchen window is ajar. Betsy sits on the wall, staring inside, then glances at me defiantly.

'Betsy! Don't you dare!'

I run into the kitchen and grab a tin of tuna, frantically twisting the tin opener until I've made a jagged tear in the top. I race back to the balcony and begin spooning the fish into her bowl.

'Teatime! Teatime, Betsycat!' I call in an encouraging sing-song voice.

She stands slowly and picks her way back along the edge.

I sit on the high balcony wall, my feet on the rickety wrought-iron patio table, and lean over the gap, holding the bowl of fish towards her. She sniffs dismissively, tantalisingly out of reach.

'Yummy, yummy. Come and get it.'

Submitting to my entreaty as though she's doing me an enormous personal favour, she leaps the gap and lands safely on the wall next to me. I scoop her up with one hand and put the bowl on the table. The table legs wobble beneath my weight as I stand and prepare to jump to the floor.

A loud knock at the door. Startled, Betsy flies to my chest. Her weight is dragging the cardigan from my shoulder. She scrabbles higher, her claws digging into the base of my neck. Instinctively I wrench her away from my clothes with both hands. The patio table shifts. Another knock at the door.

'Tilda. It's Michael. Are you there?'

I pull Betsy from my body and throw her to safety. The squirming ball of fur flies towards the clutter of plant pots by my French doors. She twists mid-air at an impossible angle. My heart lurches, then calms as she rights herself and lands on all fours. I step back to try to steady the table, my arms circling.

And then I'm looking at the guttering and the sky beyond. From a distance I hear my table tumble over with a clatter of metal on tiles. I'm falling through the gap between the balconies.

I register a glancing blow to the side of my head from the edge of Mrs Squire's balcony. The clouds, purest white, rush away from me into the blue. There's wind in my ears. My body is weightless. I'm falling backwards with my arms and legs outstretched like a giant X. I try to imagine how Betsy turned in the air and landed the right way up but my body won't respond. Then a lurch of horror when I realise there's nothing to do but fall, nothing to do but wait for the crash. It seems as though I'm dropping for an eternity, but it's only a few seconds before I smash onto the hardstanding area used for drying laundry and storing the bins.

It doesn't hurt. Nothing hurts. I'm looking up but I can't move. I wonder how long I've been here. I hear a phone ringing. I recognise the ringtone, the first notes of 'Fly Me to the Moon'. It belongs to Michael. I'm surprised to hear his voice nearby, yet echoing from a great distance. Perhaps from the moon. Or from the stars that are dancing like drops of blood before my eyes.

'Hello, doc… You didn't need to ring. Everything's fine. Really. I was going to talk to her about it tonight, but she's not in.'

His voice is coming from the other side of the garden gate. He must be standing by the communal entrance door at the side of the flats

'It might have started like that… Of course I wanted to pick her brains. Who wouldn't…? That's unfair! What would you do if you met someone conducting groundbreaking research into stem cell technology? It was too good an opportunity to miss. I'm only human… I never asked her directly… I don't think she suspects anything… I'm fully aware of your reservations… I'm taking care of it… OK, OK. I'll be in touch. Bye.'

And suddenly everything hurts. My leg, my ribs, my head, my heart. And the clouds are turning black. And the sky is turning the colour of blood.

Chapter 25

Dad and Pauline are dressed in green scrubs with masks over their faces. For a moment I'm confused as to whether I'm still in the past and in hospital following my fall, or have returned to the present.

'Aren't you going to give her an anaesthetic?' Dad asks.

'That won't be necessary,' the doctor replies from the other side of a screen. 'I paged her consultant, and he assures me she's completely unconscious and unresponsive to pain. We need to operate now. The baby's in distress. The heartbeat has dropped. That's our priority at the moment.'

A sharp slice across my abdomen cuts the breath from my lungs. I feel the squelch of blood. Black spots dance before my eyes.

Please no!

The agony is shattering. My heart leaps in my chest like a trapped animal.

Why are you doing this to me? I've been a good person. I don't deserve this. Nobody deserves this!

Bewildered, I thrash and writhe in the corners of my mind, trying to find a place without pain, a place of unconsciousness. And for the first time I long to die, anything but endure another moment of this torture.

Anything but this.

'Her heartbeat's dropping.'

'Stay with us, Tilda,' Dad cries.

I'm too tired to struggle against the pain any more. Darkness washes over me in a burning wave. And then I feel the pull, a separation. Something rips apart.

A cry, faint at first. A cry that claws at my heart like Betsy's paws on a cushion.

The medical staff murmur to each other on the other side of the screen. Dad hugs Pauline close to his chest. They're both weeping. The woodcutter has torn Red Riding Hood from the belly of the wolf.

'Here she is,' a nurse says.

Dad takes the bundle and gazes down. Pauline peeps over the top of the blanket, gently pulling the material away from my daughter's face.

'She's beautiful, Peter.'

'Yes. She's perfect. Just perfect.'

The baby is bustled away by the midwives. I'm being stitched up like an old toy whose stuffing is spilling. I feel every thrust of the needle. I can't see any more. The darkness is absolute. I know there's something more important than the pain but I can't remember what it is. My breathing has dipped to a shallow rasp. I'm sinking under the weight of the agony. There's nothing to hold on to any more.

'She's going into cardiac arrest… I'm sorry, you'll have to leave, Mr Moss.'

'Tilda. Tilda!' Dad calls over the shriek of the medical alarm. 'You have to save her. The DNAR's been taken off her notes. I'm begging you. Don't let her go.'

Rough hands pound my chest. An electronic buzz accelerates to a high-pitched wail.

'Clear!'

For a split second I look down and see a small crowd of medical staff standing over a corpse. The space that surrounds me thins. Everything's fading like the evening light. The dark presence I felt on the night of the storm is circling in the shadows.

'Clear!'

Whoosh! A hot charge surges through my chest. I jerk upwards. My eyes open. With a sharp tug I'm plunged back into a vortex of pain and unforgiving light.

'It's all right, everyone. She's back.'

After so many months alone in my cocoon, the heavy days and hopeless nights, the revelations of the last 24 hours have overwhelmed my ability to think. Emotions ricochet around the pinball machine of my mind, striking bells, lighting bulbs, in my frantic attempt to play out the game and improve the score.

I'm a mother! My baby is alive and has been taken into special care as a precautionary measure. Dad and Pauline are with her. I'm the husk that has been left behind, broken peel that's given up the sweetest fruit and been tossed aside to rot.

Nobody tried to kill me. It was a stupid accident. It was my stupid cat. All these months of searching have led to this. I'm the victim of a banal and random mishap. I'm strangely deflated. I'd imagined myself the centre of a dramatic intrigue, a vital piece of data under examination. The attention of the police lent significance to my predicament. Now I learn I'm not even important enough to be murdered.

What was the point of any of it? Of my birth, my work, my ill-fated love affair? Michael is dead. My attempts to conjure him from memory and dreams have failed. He has eluded me, leaving behind a ghostly trail of longing and regret. My own stupidity has lost me my life when I was on the brink of a major scientific breakthrough, when I was on the brink of love. I missed our final meeting. What would I have said to him? What would he have said to me? Would he have denied he was still married?

Would he have protested his innocence? Or would he have confessed to seducing me for money, for my research, owned up to being a conman and a thief? There would be no closure now. I would never know if he loved me, even a little bit, even enough to give a higher meaning to the last months of my existence.

The police will never be able to discover what happened. There was no intruder; there was no witness. I was alone with Betsy. Dad and Oscar will be left with a scab to be scratched that will never heal, their questions forever unanswered. The police have been on the wrong track from the start. The parameters of their investigation have been incorrectly set. My accident had nothing to do with the fraud at the university, or my research, or my secret affair. The data was corrupted by a random anomaly: Betsycat!

Chapter 26

The baby begins to cry. Dad looks at Pauline anxiously.

'Here. Let me.' She cradles the bundle before turning towards
me. 'Now she's out of special care, she should be formally
introduced to her mother.'

I'm propped up on pillows with my old cardigan round my
shoulders. My stomach is sore, but I imagine several days have
passed since the Caesarean.

Pauline unwraps the front of the blanket and places the
squirming infant on my chest. Her naked cheek rests on the skin
above the neckline of my nightie. She smells of freedom, of fresh
sunshine on grass. Small cries of protest sputter from her throat.
Pauline places my arm so it looks as though I'm holding her, and
tilts the baby towards me so she's looking into my eyes. I see my
reflection in her dark pupils. A hush falls across the room.

'Look! She knows it's her mummy,' Dad whispers.

'She should have this, at the very least. Smell her skin. Feel
her heartbeat.'

A small hand flails against my bosom, but I'm lost in her eyes.
I'm dazed by the marvel and the mystery I see in their depths,
unprepared for the torrent of love that wells within me, enlarging
my heart so I think it will explode with joy and pride. And
something else. Shock. She has Michael's eyes, but the
expression is her own. For the first time in my life I see what

215

I've never seen before. I'm in the presence, not just of another person, but of a living soul.

It's strange to imagine the cells I manipulated so calmly in a test tube had the potential to turn into something so wonderful. I want to say 'thank you', but to whom? I want her life to be blessed with health, happiness, protection and love. It's absurd! A mechanistic universe can't watch over her; it doesn't care whether I love her or not. I'm experiencing a biological urge. Nothing more. But for the first time in years I have the unsettling feeling I've glimpsed something of the divine.

'Take a photo, Peter. A picture in her mother's arms, a memento for her to keep. Let me tidy Tilda's hair.' She pulls a scarf from around her neck. 'She can wear this.' She drapes the silk around my head. 'There. That's better. It all looks less clinical now.' She smooths the bedclothes. 'Take the picture while Tilda's eyes are open. You wouldn't know she's unconscious. We must capture this moment... for the baby.'

Dad's hand is shaking. He points his mobile towards us. I hear the snap and whizz as the picture is taken.

'Don't let her think Tilda died in childbirth,' Oscar says from the door.

'We won't. We'll say she kept her mummy alive. Come and meet your niece, son. Come and meet Millie.'

Pauline scoops the baby up and gently passes her to Oscar. My arm flops to my side, empty, resting on the outside of my cardigan pocket. A small raised ridge tingles against my fingers. I know what it is. The repository of all my secrets.

Once again I automatically move around the circuit, testing the connection. *Right hand little finger. Right hand ring finger. Right hand middle finger. Right hand index finger. Right hand thumb.* Oscar sits on the end of my bed with a soft thud, Millie pinned awkwardly to his shoulder. My fingers jerk forward into a partial claw, dragging the USB up and half out of the top of the pocket.

'Careful, son.'

'He's fine,' Pauline soothes. 'You're doing a great job. You're going to be a wonderful uncle.'

Cool plastic touches the tip of my index finger. My heart leaps to my throat. Did I move my hand with the power of my mind, or was it just the aftershock of Oscar's weight? *Right hand little finger. Right hand ring finger. Right hand middle finger. Right hand index finger. Right hand thumb.* A barely perceptible twitch and the USB moves a millimetre closer to my palm. For the first time since I've been in hospital, I'm faced with the possibility of doing something for myself, making a modification, changing an outcome, altering my destiny.

A see-saw of anxiety and exhilaration rocks the room. My eyes blur. The risk of failure. The risk of the USB falling into the wrong hands. The risk of doing nothing at all. I focus on my hand, blocking out the murmured conversation of my family. I must collect the scattered fragments of my strength and assemble them for one final push.

'You wanted to see me, Mr Okeke.'

'Yessar.'

'You could have come down to the station. Spoken to my sergeant.'

'Don't do police stations. Had a baaaad experience once, innit. I wanted to speak to you here. Man to man. I wanted Doctar Tilda to know I'm taking care of her business.'

'You said it was important.'

Claude takes his hand out of his trouser pocket. Sitting in the middle of his palm is a red memory stick.

'What's this?'

'Found it yesterday.'

'Where?'

'In Doctar Tilda's hand. She were holdin' it. Holdin' it tight.'

The inspector takes the USB and turns it over.

'I always shakes her by the hand when I've finished cleaning up,' Claude continues. 'I likes to be polite. Her fingers was never all curled up so tight before. I pulled them open for her… in case it hurt summat.'

'Is it your job to touch the patients?'

'Not touchin'. Showing respect for the dyin'. Just a little handshake between friends. Before she crosses over to the other side.'

I remember all the times he raised my hand to his lips, the fear I felt when he first approached my bed, and how that fear has gradually slipped away until I've grown to think of him as my guardian angel.

'So she didn't have it before yesterday?'

'No. I think I would have seen.'

'Have you looked at what's on it?'

'Maybe.'

The inspector runs his hand through his hair in annoyance. 'It's a serious matter to tamper with evidence!'

'Not tamperin'. Just checkin'. Didn't want to waste your time if it was nothin'. It be just hows I found it. Lots of documents, but you can't open any of them.'

'So they're password protected?'

'But they belongs to her all right.' He jerks his head in my direction.

'Have you any idea how it could have come to be here? In her room? In her hand?'

'Nope!'

'And who visited yesterday?'

'Ask them nurses. I'm just cleanin' up, innit.'

The door opens. Kiki appears, carrying a pink helium balloon. I smell her surprise when she sees the two men. She hasn't visited for a while. Her hair is longer, blonder. The inspector takes an evidence bag out of his pocket, slips the stick inside, and seals it.

'Thank you, Mr Okeke. We'll have to take a formal statement. I'm going to have to ask you to visit the station tomorrow. My sergeant will see you then. I'll make sure there's no trouble.'

Claude shuffles away, passing Kiki at the door.

'Miss Halliday!' the inspector calls in greeting. 'You can come in. We've finished.'

'Inspector… I just popped by to meet the baby. But I see she's not here.'

'She's down in the maternity unit. Mr Moss and his wife are probably with her. I think they're being allowed to take her home at the end of the week. I'm glad I've bumped into you.'

Kiki's eyes narrow.

'I wanted a quick word.'

'I've already spoken to the police. Someone in the fraud department.'

'And now you're speaking to me.' The inspector's tone bears an undercurrent of steel.

'Perhaps I should have questioned it,' she gabbles, 'but the letter looked authentic. I knew how important the deal was to Tilda. So I made the changes to the bank account details and paid the invoice straight away. She wanted that equipment. It was a routine transaction. I might lose my job because of this! I've been given a written warning. When I find out who's responsible, I'm going to make sure they swing!'

'You can leave that to us –'

'Well, you're taking your time about it! How many months is it now?'

'So you don't believe Dr Moss was involved in the fraud?'

'Of course not!

You tell him, Kiki!

'She's the victim here, remember. When you find the person who hurt her, you'll find the thief. It's obvious.'

I'm pathetically grateful for her loyalty.

'You can stop looking at me like that. I have a cast-iron alibi,' she continues. 'Don't you think it haunts me that I was out enjoying myself on a date while Tilda was lying in a pool of her own blood?'

The inspector's phone rings. Kiki sits by my bed and fusses with my blanket, straightening the creases.

'Lake here! Is it Jennifer? Oh, right,' he says gloomily. 'What have the Swiss police got? OK. Ask them to email the details. I want a full report.' There's a long pause. He taps his foot impatiently. 'I see... yes... OK. By the way, Stevenson, I've located the USB. The one Dr Moss used to save her research... I'll explain when I get there.' He hangs up and turns to Kiki. 'You'll have to excuse me. I've got to get to the station.'

She shrugs. 'Whatever!'

As soon as he's gone, Kiki rummages in her handbag for her own mobile. She punches a button.

'It's me. The police have found her memory stick... How should I know? I searched the flat from top to bottom! Calm down... We don't know that... I'm in the hospital. I've just overheard that policeman talking about the Swiss police.' She swears viciously. 'For goodness' sake, Keith. Don't be such an old woman... OK, OK. I'll pack a bag. I'll meet you at the airport. I don't know... Anywhere! Does it matter? Somewhere without an extradition treaty with the UK. Google it!'

I'm feeling very tired. Everything's unravelling. Nothing's as I thought it was. I spent so many years training myself to be objective, and yet I've failed the most important test. I've trusted the wrong people. Michael betrayed me. Now Kiki and Keith.

How could it have happened? I haven't been a bad person. I've kept my nose clean and worked hard. I've paid my taxes. I've been a responsible adult, recycling my yoghurt pots and cardboard. I've even donated my body to medical science, though I wonder whether they'll want these broken fragments now.

Who was I to lecture Oscar on the suitability of his friends? My choices have been just as bad. There must be something defective in my make-up, something missing. Emotional intelligence, perhaps. How could I have been so blind to the truth? Michael never loved me. Kiki never liked me as a friend. Keith's true colours have leaked through his white coat and folded trousers at last. I was a target. Nothing more. Prey for the predator, part of that ruthless evolutionary jig where only the fittest survive to dance another day.

I make a quick mental calculation, amazed at the ease with which I can still juggle the numbers. I've been alive for 35 years and seven months. Taking into account leap years, that's about 12,784 days. How to quantify my worth? Should I use the number of exams I've passed? Perhaps the money I've earned or the amount of tax I've paid? Can I measure the meaning of my existence by the loose change I've dropped in a charity bucket? By the number of friends I have on Facebook, the number of followers on Twitter? The papers I've published? By achievements, by possessions, by success? By nights and mornings, by cups of coffee, by the love I've given and the love I've received?

I thought I was good – not perfect, but better than most – but that's not true either. I've misjudged myself as much as I've miscalculated others. I never really went out of my way to be helpful unless it suited my own purposes and it wasn't too inconvenient. I didn't phone Dad as often as I should. I've been impatient with my brother, resentful of his dependency. And now it's too late to do anything about it.

There's no point thinking like this. If the universe is morally neutral, it's not a question of value or length or depth; in the great scheme of things my existence amounts to nothing. Zero. Zilch. And now I'm going to die.

My little universe is doomed. I can only watch and wait for the end. I would like to maintain some objectivity, analysing the data of my decay. I long to be able to transmit my findings for future posterity. Old habits die hard. I will continue to observe the cataclysm as carefully as possible, hoping against hope I will rise miraculously from this bed of suffering to share my experience with the world.

In the meantime, I suppose I must prepare myself for a move. I need to sort and pack up the baggage of my life. What's to be thrown and what's to be kept. I must collect what's valuable – my mother's love, my father's devotion, the miracle of my daughter, the sharp rush of affection for my little brother, the exasperation, bitterness and fierce devotion, and the endless longing for Michael – and hold it close like a talisman as I cross the final border. I never thought I would be so superstitious, as if such intangibles could keep me safe. But I need something warm to shroud my soul: the knowledge of how much I've been loved and the love I've given to others.

My abdomen hurts, the stitches itch. I'm very tired. I mentally climb the rungs of my ribs, past my grazed heart, to a quiet space in my head. That unsteady feeling comes, the one that rocks me to the edge of sleep. I imagine I'm a sailing ship, a thing of rope and bleached bone, sails flapping loose, then tautening with the wind. The air feels thinner now. Perhaps I'm smelling land ahead. Soon I'll reach my destination and the long voyage will be done.

Chapter 27

'Rather than bring you all down to the station, I thought it would be better if we met up here. I know the family is under a great deal of strain at the moment. I understand Dr Moss's condition has deteriorated overnight.'

'She's very weak,' Dad replies. 'Dr Arnold says it's the shock of the Caesarean. Her organs are beginning to shut down. He's had to put her on a ventilator.'

'I'm very sorry to hear that.'

I realise I've been intubated. I'm no longer breathing on my own. My body has given up. An endotracheal tube is going up my nose and down my throat. I know enough about hospital procedures to understand this is a short-term option. If it had been decided to ventilate me long-term, I would have been given a tracheotomy.

'Thank you... I think we all knew this time would come. We're just grateful she held on so long. For Millie's sake.'

Pauline is feeding the baby with a bottle. The soft sucking noises tug at my breast. Oscar is leaning against the wall, shoulders hunched forward, his hands shoved in his trouser pockets.

'Our investigation has progressed very quickly during the last week. I thought you should be fully briefed before the media becomes aware of developments. As I mentioned on the telephone, your daughter's memory stick has unexpectedly turned up.' He pauses, but nobody comments. 'We still can't understand the whys and wherefores of how it came to be here in the hospital, but needless to say our computer forensic experts have reviewed the contents. There have been some very unexpected and enlightening discoveries.'

'Please tell us, inspector,' Pauline says.

'Firstly, we were able to use the small notebook of passwords from Tilda's flat to open her directories. Substantially there were three different types of document. Her scientific research, some spreadsheets relating to the departmental budget, and some personal documents including details of a private email account she used to communicate with Michael Cameron.'

Oscar swears under his breath.

'That monster!' Pauline mutters.

'I'll leave you to make up your minds on that question when I've shown you an email he sent to Dr Moss on Thursday 24th August.' He opens his briefcase, takes out a sheet of paper and passes it to Dad.

Dad takes it with a shaking hand and looks at it silently.

'Out loud, Dad,' Oscar demands.

Our father clears his throat. 'My dearest Tilda. By the time you read this letter, I will be turned back to stardust, and scattered on some nice flower bed in Switzerland. Let me explain.

'A little while ago I was diagnosed with motor neurone disease. At first I thought the old knees were going – too much sport in my twenties – but then my hands started shaking and I began slurring my words. I've always enjoyed a pint, but I was beginning to look like a lush! I've been visiting a private doctor in London. She did some tests and was good enough to lay it out straight. I only had another year at best.

'I like to think of myself as a classic car. Things are wearing out and it's impossible to find replacement parts. It's no longer worth investing in temporary repairs, and I don't want to be tinkered with any more, in any case. The great scrap heap is waiting, and I want to go while I'm still enjoying myself. With a bang and a roar, not a whimper.

'When we first met, I wanted to pick your brains about your research, to find out whether gene therapy would be an answer for me. I quickly saw that the solution would be too long in coming, though I believe one day it will come. I should have left you alone after that, but I confess I enjoyed talking with you about matters of faith and science. And then those precious moments we shared together. What can I say? You're simply marvellous in every way, my darling Tilda.

'These last few weeks a great calm has settled upon me, so different from the restlessness and searching of my past. Like you, I've become convinced we are alone on this planet, and always have been. There's nothing to fear in death. Thank you for releasing me from months of suffering and setting me free.

'I hope you don't think I'm a coward because I couldn't face living out my life to the bitter end. I didn't want to be treated as a child, which is what would have happened. I care about you too much to let you watch me fade away, like you watched your mother all those years ago. I know you would have stuck by me and sacrificed your own work to care for me. Perhaps we might have ended up hating each other. In any case, what you are doing is *too* important. I believe one day you'll make a discovery that will banish diseases like motor neurone for ever. You mustn't be distracted from the task by a mouldering old baggage like me!

'I know you would have supported me in the decision I've made. Your pragmatism has been such a comfort. I kept my plan a secret because I didn't want anyone to be prosecuted for helping me. I hope you'll forgive me for that. I did knock at your flat on Monday night as agreed, but there was no reply. I was hoping to see you one last time, but perhaps it was better you were out. Saying goodbye is the one unbearable thing about this process. I might have been tempted to change my mind. I'm selfish enough to have melted into your arms, pretend none of this is happening, but I care for you too much to drag you down with me. I believe my feelings for you have been the one pure thing in my life. You helped me find the treasure I've spent all these years searching for – the capacity for unconditional love.

'I hope I live on in your memory as a happy time in your life. Please don't grieve. I've lived everything to the full. Like most people, I've had my share of sadness, but I've also climbed the heights. Think of me with affection and go on to do great things.

'Remember how much I love you. I wish you only good things for the future. Be happy.

'I leave my heart in your hands. With all my love. Michael.'

An earthquake of emotion rocks through my body. He loved me! He loved me! He didn't abandon me in my time of need. He exited my life without knowing about my accident, and more permanently than I'd imagined.

Oscar snatches the paper from Dad. 'What does this mean? Is this some kind of joke?'

'It's no joke,' the inspector declares. 'We've discovered that after staying one night in Geneva, he hired a car and drove to Forch, a village ten kilometres south-east of Zurich. He checked himself into a clinic. They've confirmed a long-running correspondence between the two of them about his deteriorating condition. They have copies of his medical notes from a Dr Olivia Garcia, a private consultant working in the Holloway area of London. On this evidence, they agreed to euthanise him. He took a lethal cocktail of drugs the following day. He died at 9.10am. He was cremated on 28th August.'

A great sadness descends. He didn't tell me, hadn't trusted me. He bore his death sentence alone. I rerun a conversation in my head.

'Cell death is a natural process,' I told him. 'Older cells are more likely to suffer genetic damage, so they need to be eliminated before they harm surrounding tissues.'

'Now you're saying death is good.'

'For the rest of the body, yes. Not perhaps for the individual cell. Call it a sacrifice for the general good. Does that sound heartless?'

Why didn't I realise these were pressing issues, not philosophical musings or chat-up lines? He was searching for the possibility of a cure, searching for certainty about the beyondness of things.

'But why would he steal the money if he was about to croak?' Oscar asks.

'He didn't steal the money. We arrested Catherine Halliday and Dr Keith Gadson at Newcastle International airport yesterday morning. They were on their way to Havana.'

'Kiki!' Dad exclaims.

'Yes. And Dr Gadson, your daughter's assistant. It appears they've been in a relationship. We suspect Miss Halliday was the lead party in the fraud. Dr Gadson caved immediately and has confessed to everything. It was a moment of madness in an otherwise solid career.'

'Keith Gadson?' Oscar repeats. 'Not that nerdy bore who was at Tilda's birthday bash? He wouldn't have the nous to pull off something like that.'

'We think Miss Halliday was the mastermind of the fraud, although Dr Gadson unwittingly gave her the inside information necessary for her to pull it off. Apparently he was pretty fed up about the university's deal with BioExpertise Systems. His moaning about it probably gave her the idea in the first place.'

I don't care about any of this now. Didn't you hear Michael's letter? Didn't it break your heart? I would have looked after him. I would have reviewed his hospital notes and fought for the best treatments. I would have held him close in the night and told him I would never let him go.

It was better when I thought he had betrayed me. I'd rather see him as my enemy than think of him as a corpse. At least my anger kept me warm. Now I'm frozen with loneliness. Why is everyone talking about Kiki and Keith? Can't they spare a thought for the man who loved me? Don't they realise what's happened? A light has gone out. Everything's grey.

'I can't believe it of Kiki,' Dad whispers. He pulls a handkerchief out of his pocket and dabs his forehead. 'She always seemed such a nice girl.'

'We've been doing a bit of digging.' The inspector pulls out a notebook and flips through the pages. 'My sergeant spoke to Miss Halliday's previous boyfriend, Warwick Foster. Apparently she'd been taking money out of his online bank account without asking him. When he discovered this, he chucked her out. That's how she managed to end up homeless. She moved in with your daughter pretty much straight away. It seems she's the type to always land on her feet... but not this time.'

A spurt of anger penetrates my grief. I'm not angry with Kiki and Keith. I don't care about them at the moment. I'm furious with Michael. He didn't let me comfort him, didn't give me the opportunity to demonstrate the extent of my devotion. His flight to Switzerland was a wasted gesture. He thought he was releasing me to a better life, but instead I'm facing what he would have faced – a slow, painful death with total loss of control. If only he had told me the truth earlier, we could have faced death together, clinging to each other in the storm. Because he took matters into his own hands, he isn't here to watch over me now.

'How did she do it?' Oscar asks.

'She probably stumbled across correspondence from BioExpertise lying around the flat. I understand your daughter often took her work and laptop home with her. Miss Halliday was able to create a convincing counterfeit letterhead. Using this she sent herself a letter at the accounts department requesting that the university change the bank account details. She issued a fake invoice, forged Dr Moss's signature as authorisation, paid £500,000 into the bogus bank account, then transferred the funds immediately to a Swiss bank account she had previously set up. To deflect suspicion from herself, she took Dr Moss's identity when setting up the BioXpertise bank account. Living under the same roof, she had access to your daughter's birth certificate, utility bills and other documentation. As far as the bank was concerned, a respected scientist was setting up some kind of private consultancy firm. It all looked routine. However, examining the spreadsheets your sister kept on her memory stick, it's pretty clear that any transaction shouldn't have gone through until several weeks later.'

'She's a clever girl,' Oscar mutters.

'Wicked girl, don't you mean,' Pauline declares.

Oscar ignores the interruption. 'I wonder why she hung around to get caught?'

'We think she was planning to leave Newcastle pretty quickly after swiping the money, but changed her mind when Dr Moss ended up in hospital. Her bank records reveal she had booked a one-way flight to Spain, leaving on 26th August. She cancelled it on the 22nd. She must have thought it would look suspicious if she did a runner just after her flatmate was critically injured. And Dr Gadson was her alibi. She wanted to keep him onside. It's one thing to commit a relatively small fraud; quite another to be accused of attempted murder.'

'Small fraud!' Oscar exclaims.

'In the grand scheme of things, yes. She could have disappeared overseas quite easily, safe in the knowledge that the resources needed to apprehend and extradite her would probably exceed the amount she stole.'

'And geeky Keith Gadson was going with her,' Oscar scowls.

'No, I don't think so. They weren't what you would call a match made in heaven. Dr Gadson says he knew nothing about the theft until Miss Halliday broke down and confessed the day after she visited Dr Moss in hospital for the first time. Apparently she was quite shaken, though still clever enough to manipulate him into believing it was partly his fault for explaining the deal with BioExpertise to her in such detail. She told him the theft would teach the university a lesson and stop them getting involved in similar schemes in the future. Because he didn't report her immediately, it became more and more difficult to extricate himself. She said he had become part of a conspiracy to defraud the college, arguing they would both go down if it was discovered. I think they hoped Dr Moss would get the blame for the stolen money and they could go on with their lives as if nothing had happened. When we arrested him, he was in a complete panic. He was almost relieved to be caught.'

'But was it Kiki who hurt Tilda?' Pauline is holding Dad's hand. Millie is asleep in the crook of her arm.

'She has an alibi,' the inspector replies.

'Was she with Keith?' Dad barks.

'Yes.'

Oscar punches a fist into his open palm. 'Surely that doesn't count now!'

'Miss Halliday left work at 5.35pm on 21st August. Her boss was able to verify the accuracy of her time sheet as they stopped and chatted for a few minutes in the stairwell about the month-end accounts. She met up with Keith and had dinner with him in a noodle bar in the centre of Newcastle. CCTV shows they arrived at 6.16pm. The waitress confirms they were there until about nine, as does the credit card transaction. By then, Tilda was in an ambulance on the way to hospital.'

'Are you saying there's no link between what happened to my daughter and the fraud at the university?'

'They appear to be two completely separate incidents. The only overlap, if you can call it that, is that Dr Moss's inability to defend herself offered them a better chance of passing the buck and escaping justice.'

I tune out their voices, weary of the discussion. I have more important matters to consider. Would I have wanted Michael with me in the hospital, seeing me like this? Suddenly I understand the thought processes he was juggling – what was best for him, and what was best for me. Perhaps it *is* better he never knew of my fall. I've been spared the guilt and frustration of watching him suffer as he sat by my bedside watching *me* suffer, seeing him exhaust himself like Dad, endlessly waiting and sickening at the roller coaster of hope and despair. On the other hand, he never knew he was going to be a father. He missed having his heart pierced with joy at the sight of Millie. Ultimately, our love for each other was left untested by the tragedies and delight of life. It will remain this perfect thing, still in the box, unwrapped.

The inspector's voice breaks into my thoughts. 'This is a lot to take in, but there's something else you should know.'

'Go on,' Dad says. 'Let's get it all over with in one go.'

'Her USB also contained the conclusions of her recent research, and all the statistical data on which it was based. I've already had her superior, Professor MacMahon, on the line asking to see a copy. However, Dr Moss also wrote up a detailed report of security concerns within the Institute of Genetics. It seems the results of a previous project were stolen by a private corporation. She's produced a comparison of the data.

Unquestionably there's been a leak. The similarities are striking. We've decided not to release the findings of her current research to the department until the university has conducted a thorough internal investigation.'

'Hear, hear!' Pauline says.

'Yes. We owe it to her to protect her intellectual legacy,' Dad says. 'Her name can live on... live on...'

'Precisely!' Pauline interjects. 'Her name will live on as someone who pushed the boundaries of human knowledge. She's helped in the fight against disease and misery. What greater testimony to her life than that she left the world a better place for being in it?'

'But wait a minute,' Oscar says. 'We still don't know who hurt Tilda.'

'That's right,' Dad pressed. 'Who did it, inspector?'

The inspector rubs his unshaven jaw and sighs. I smell his exhaustion, a mixture of chalk and sweat.

'That, unfortunately, we still don't know.'

Chapter 28

I'm sleeping more and dreaming less. I have the sensation of floating in the shallows, my legs barely touching the seabed. The waves are pulling me from the land. If I relax completely I could be borne away by the tide and sink into deep waters. But something holds me back. I'm snagged on a doubt.

I wonder what thoughts passed through Michael's mind as the poison flowed into his system. Did he stick to his resolve and abandon all hope of eternity? Or did he regret his decision when it was too late to go back? I want to beg his forgiveness for not making life good enough for him to want to stay with me, for not giving him a good enough reason to live, just a reason to die.

I didn't tell him that every minute of life was precious. Instead, I was the one to convince him there was nothing beyond this world. My rigid atheism was his downfall. In my arrogance to win every argument, I swept away the psychological constructs that would have given his life and his death meaning. Believing in a universe without intentionality or moral categories, I decided that the death of a man was no different from the death of an ant.

I gave him my certainty; he bequeathed me his doubt. Now I've experienced the mutability of things, the shifting and sliding of time and space, agnosticism seems a more honest position to take. I've been existing in an immaterial world. I've looked down from the ceiling at my broken body. I've died in the delivery room and been brought back to life. I've seen the reflection of God in my daughter's eyes. I've sensed Michael with me, a ghost in my dreams, an echo from the next room. I hope he's alive somewhere other than my memory, but I guess there's no hope for him. If there is a God, surely suicide puts him beyond the pale.

But the ripple of his laughter shivers over my skin. His voice resonates in my mind. *And what about those parts of ourselves that aren't made up of atoms? Consciousness, soul, spirit, mind, whatever you like to call it? The software that exists within the hardware of our bodies? And how do you explain love?*

I stand at a door, one I'm reluctant to open. Changing my mind is not something I'm used to. It's a terrifying proposition. I might turn the handle and find it's been closed for so long that the hinges have rusted shut. Or it might be locked, with no hope of finding the key. Or I might open the door and discover something... something... something too overwhelming to contemplate.

Is it a weakness to hesitate before drawing a final conclusion? Isn't that part of the scientific method, to question everything, to test a hypothesis to destruction? If I'm right, and there's nothing after death, I'll never have the pleasure of saying, 'I told you so,' and believers will never know they've been mistaken. But if I'm wrong and this life has been something utterly other than I observed it to be – a realm of blessings and punishments, miracles and signs, a battle between good and evil – then I've flunked the exam. In any case, why would I want to spend an eternity with a God I didn't want to get to know in this life?

I give my wayward mind a stinging slap. I don't want to look at the accounts, the debits and the credits. I can't think about the pile of just desserts I might have piled up. Face the facts. Michael is never coming back. My old life is never coming back. Maybe death is better than life after all. If only there's a way of being sure there isn't something worse on the other side. I want a guarantee of oblivion with no possibility of an avenging spirit who might damn me to a cold eternity without love.

I used to think my feet were on solid ground. I couldn't understand those who chose to leap into the abyss of faith. Now I know there's no solid ground. From the moment I was born I've been falling off a balcony. I've had no choice in this, except in the style of the fall. My life has been a series of twists and turns to try to prolong the descent, not just for myself but for others too, hoping I might be able to discover a way to escape the final crash or to make the landing painless. I've told myself the impact will be immediate, leading to extinction, but this too is a matter of faith just as much as belief in a great Catcher who might pluck me from the air in the nick of time.

Allegra pulls a chair very close to my bed and leans her head next to mine. For one horrifying moment I think she's going to kiss me.

'The police came to visit me yesterday,' she murmurs in my ear. 'I knew it was bad news when I saw them at the door. They told me to sit down, asked if I was on my own, you know, like they do on the telly. They told me everything. They told me he killed himself…' Her voice rises to a harsh whisper. 'Because of *you*! He didn't want *you* to be worrying about him. He didn't want *you* to be inconvenienced by his illness, so he took himself off to die among strangers in a cold room, with no comforting words, and no one to wish his soul well on its journey back to the Great Mother.'

My heart turns to ice. I'm alone with a mad woman. If anyone walks past my room and glances through the glass panel in the door, they'll think she's a friend or family member telling me how much they care, how much they miss me, how much they want me back. There's nothing I can do to raise the alarm. I've never felt more helpless.

'What kind of hard-hearted control freak are you that he couldn't tell you he was ill? He spent his last moments all alone… We saw each other over the summer, you know. Even after the divorce, I thought it would always be Mike and Allegra. He told me he had fallen in love with someone else. I didn't believe it. And when he told me the kind of person you were… well! What was he thinking? I knew no good would come of it. You can't trap a deep spirit like Mike's in a box and expect him to thrive.'

She takes my hand and begins to pick at the plaster holding my cannula in place.

'He sent me a letter, telling me to stop phoning him, telling me to accept the divorce. He didn't say he was unwell… But I could have saved him. I'm a healer. It's what I do. You have no understanding of the power of the human spirit to restore itself. If he'd told me, I would have done everything to make him better. He could have come back home.'

Perhaps that's why he didn't tell you!

She peels off the plaster.

What are you doing?

'He said it was goodbye, but I didn't believe it. He always came running when I needed help. He was that kind of person. He would never stand by and watch another person suffer. His heart was too big. So I knew something was wrong when he stopped returning my calls. I've got a sixth sense about these things. I knew you had to be responsible. So I made some enquiries and found out Mike had disappeared off the face of the earth… and you were here in the hospital. I thought you'd done for him somehow, and in a way you did.'

She yanks out the cannula in one excruciating tug.

No! No! No!

'You deserve everything you've got. It's karma. You can't escape it. *You* deserve to die, not him.' Each word is accompanied by a spray of spittle on my cheek.

She stands and takes a step to the bank of plugs by my bed and turns each switch off one by one.

Help me! Somebody help me!

'We still loved each other. We just couldn't live together any more. There'd been too much pain…' She pauses for a moment. Her voice softens. 'And now you've had his baby, the baby I've been yearning for. Mike's baby.' She sits back by my bed, a speculative look in her eye. 'They say being a mother is the hardest thing. It's not. *Not* being a mother is the hardest. By rights, the baby should be mine. I loved Mike more than you – 17 years together! Four cycles of IVF. All the heartache… I've earned the right to have a baby. You don't deserve to be a mother.'

Don't you even think about Millie! Why aren't the nurses coming? Surely an alarm must be registering at the nurses' station.

'Hello.'

'Oh! Hello, Oscar.' Allegra coolly turns her head to the door.

'Have you been here long?'

'Five minutes.'

'You heard the good news, then?'

'What news?'

'About the baby.'

'That's one of the reasons I've come. To see the baby. What did she have?'

'A little girl. We're calling her Millie.'

Oscar, look at my hand. Look at the monitor. Can't you see what she's done?

'Congratulations. That's a sweet name.'

'Thanks. Dad and Pauline are on their way up from the maternity unit with her. The midwife said she'd wheel the cot up so they can sit with both of them at the same time. They've been trying to split themselves in two, visiting both the patients.'

Help me, Oscar!

'How is she… the baby, I mean?'

'Four weeks early but feeding, pooing, crying. The usual stuff. She's small but unusually resilient. Like her mum.'

'I'd like to see her.'

'If you hang around for ten minutes, they'll be here soon.' He pulls the other chair up to the bed and sits down. 'It's been crazy… What's this?' He picks up my hand. 'Why's the needle out?'

'Don't worry about that. It's fine. I was thinking about what you were saying last time we were here together. You know, about how the doctors have given up. I wanted to help. I spoke to your dad about letting me do some Thought Field Therapy with Tilda. I know what I'm doing. I've been tapping the meridian points on her hands and upper body. The needle was interfering with her chi, the life force flowing through her body. I slipped it out.'

'I don't think you should have done that –'

'The nurse can put it back when she needs it.'

'And why's her ventilator been switched off?'

'Oscar, I'm trying to help. This paraphernalia was getting in the way. Remember when you said it wasn't respectful to Tilda, that she wouldn't want to be kept alive artificially? You were right. I feel it in my spirit. I know her soul wants to be healed or set free, not stuck in the no man's land between life and death.'

'Now, hang on –'

'Don't be scared for her. I've been tapping into the perturbations that are the root cause of her emotional and spiritual blockage. It's not just about the physical, you know. She's had a terrible trauma. I'm trying to remove the deformities in her thought field.'

238

'But you can't just disconnect her. She'll die!'

'I'm giving her the choice. She may come back to us, or she may choose to be released from her suffering...' She leans across the bed and touches his hand. 'Oscar, you wanted this, remember? You love her like I do. Let nature take its course. It's the kindest way.'

'This is my sister you're tampering with! What gives you the right?' He jumps up and presses the emergency button to call a nurse.

Allegra leaps from her chair and dashes to the door. Oscar grabs her arm and spins her round.

'Let go!'

'No, you don't. I'm getting hospital security.'

The door swings open. A woman in a tunic appears, wheeling a clear plastic cot ahead of her. Dad and Pauline follow through the doorway.

'What's going on?' the midwife exclaims.

'Call security. She's trying to kill Tilda!' Oscar shouts, his arms around Allegra's struggling body.

The midwife tries to retreat with the cot, but Dad and Pauline are blocking her exit. She pushes the cot into a corner and Pauline stands in front of it to protect the baby.

'It was him! I was trying to stop *him*!'

'Oscar!' Dad booms. 'What are you doing?'

'She's switched off the ventilator and disconnected the drip.'

'Do something!' Pauline cries.

Oscar pins Allegra's arms to her sides. She kicks him in the shin. He winces but manages to push her back against the wall, pressing her face into the paintwork, and wrenching one arm behind her back.

'It wasn't me, Dad, honest... I wouldn't...'

239

The midwife is fumbling with the ventilator plug. A nurse arrives in response to the alarm. Dad speaks to her in hurried bursts, but I can't hear what he's saying.

'It has a back-up battery. She's still getting oxygen,' the nurse shouts above the obscenities Oscar and Allegra are screaming at each other. The midwife stands aside. The nurse punches the soft touch buttons to recalibrate the settings on the machine. Once the reassuring beep of my heart returns, Dad yells at the midwife to go and get help.

'We'll make sure no one leaves... Call the police.'

She rushes through the door. A thin wail rises from the cot. Pauline bends over and picks up the baby, pulling a pink blanket round her tightly.

Allegra stills, her eyes on Millie's face. 'That's my baby. She should have been mine. Mine and Mike's.'

'Are you insane or something?' Oscar huffs as Allegra attempts to reach the child. 'She's Tilda's baby, and my niece. And I'm not going to let anybody do anything to hurt my family ever again.'

Claude comes with his electric polisher. It hums around the room; he hums above the vibration. Once he's satisfied with the result, he unplugs the machine.

'We is born to trouble as sure as sparks fly upwards,' he declares. 'Ain't that the truth! I hear all about the hubbub you been causin', missy. The police have arrested that woman. Gonna be charged with assault or attempted murder, they say. Your brother sure thinks he saved the day. Keeps braggin' to them nurses 'bout what a hero he is, innit.

'I'm saying a prayer for your soul, girlie. You be the little seed that's been dumped in the muck and covered in darkness. Remember what old Claude say. Life springs, missy. Life springs from the darkness. You can't achieve it. You can only receive it. That's what the Bible say.'

Someone has been in my room, switched my radio on and left. I'm listening to a stream of dreadful pop songs interspersed with adverts and inane banter. There's a local and national news report, and a weather and traffic update from the Newcastle area on the hour and half-hour.

At ten o'clock, I'm startled from a daydream by the clipped tones of Inspector Lake. 'I can confirm that a bag containing body parts in an advanced state of decomposition was discovered by a dog walker by a culvert near the Ouseburn railway viaduct yesterday evening. Although a post-mortem has yet to take place, items of clothing have led us to believe it's the body of 13-year-old Jennifer Allen, missing since 8th December.'

Sorrow fills my room. I hear it in the inspector's voice, a grey cloud in a malicious sky. He has a more important case than mine to pursue now, and I know he'll embark upon it with steely determination and a jaded heart. What a waste of a young life, a bud on the cusp of blossoming, all her tomorrows snatched away. How can I complain when I've had more than twice the years she had, seen my body grow to maturity and my mind become strong, given my heart in love and my body in desire. The pity of her loss is unbearable.

The background drone of the newsreader is suddenly pulled into focus. 'Following investigations into a half-a-million-pound fraud at the Institute of Genetic Medicine at Newcastle University, two employees have now been arrested. Keith Gadson and Catherine Halliday were due to board a flight to Havana when police intercepted them on Wednesday. The Institute of Genetic Medicine has been the centre of several overlapping investigations, first into the circumstances surrounding life-threatening injuries sustained by top scientist

Dr Tilda Moss, who fell from her apartment balcony and remains in a coma in Newcastle hospital, and also an investigation into plagiarism of her groundbreaking genetic research. Departmental head, Professor Ian MacMahon, has been suspended pending an internal enquiry by the university.'

Another tinny pop song stirs the air. I'm very tired. Tired of living, scared of dying. I've worn myself out with the waiting. But I sense it's coming to an end.

Chapter 29

The most important people in the world are gathering in my room – Dad and Oscar, Pauline, and baby Millie, who's snuffling into her chest.

The only one missing is Michael. I wish they could have met him. They would have loved him too. I conjure again the memory of our picnic and our first night together. It runs like warm butter through my body.

The hospital chaplain arrives with Dr Arnold and a nurse. I idly wonder whether we're going to have a christening. Oscar pulls Dad to one side.

'What were you thinking, Dad!' he hisses, jerking his head in the direction of the clergyman.

'We used to go to church when your mother was alive. She was always very keen.'

'But I never went, did I? You gave up on the whole thing, remember?'

'This is not about you. And I still believe, in my own way. I want to do this properly now, for your mum's sake and for my sake, as well as for Tilda's. The only reason I stopped going to church was because Tilda couldn't bear to set foot in the place after your mother's funeral. Too many bad memories. I didn't want to force her.'

'Then you'll know she would have hated this.'

'She was at that impressionable age. She didn't know what she wanted. And I was busy with you –'

'So now it's my fault!'

'I saw her come into the world. I want to see her leave it in a fitting manner.'

I'm jolted from my dreams of last summer.

No! No! I'm not ready. I'm not prepared. Please… please. Just look at me. I'm alive. Can't you see I'm alive?

Particles swirl across my vision. I'm reminded of the midges that danced above our heads as Michael and I lay on the grass. The shadow of the sycamore tree is still lengthening over my prone body.

'It's a blessing she never knew about Kiki and Keith. It would have destroyed her,' Dad murmurs.

'And she never knew her boyfriend was terminally ill. She was spared that.'

'Do you think we'll ever find out what happened to her that evening, Pauline?' Dad asks.

'I don't know, darling. We'll just have to try to learn to live with it if we don't. Perhaps there are some things we're not meant to know.'

Pauline lays Millie next to my cheek. Her head peeps above the blanket she's wrapped in. I see wisps of hair and the hint of a curl. Not straight like mine, but wavy like her father's. She begins to whimper. I'm not surprised. I must be a frightening sight, my face eroded to bone, my hair a tangle of spider webs. Even I can smell decay and brimstone in the air.

'I'll love her with all my heart, Tilda. You can trust your dad and me to do the best we can.'

I'm sorry I drove you away when I was a child. I wish you could have been my stepmother.

Pauline picks the baby up and backs away into a corner. Dad gives Oscar a shove and he walks reluctantly to the bed.

'Hello, Tilly. Sorry for all the times I took you for granted. I hope I can be a good uncle.' His voice wobbles and I feel a warm splash of tears on my arm. 'I know some of the things she'll have to go through. I'll try to do as good a job as you did with me. I've turned over a new leaf. I'm moving to Newcastle, leaving my old life in Manchester behind. I've told Dad about the problems. He's loaning me some money to get me out of the deal. Then I'm going to get a proper job. I'll make you proud of me... Oh, Tilda, what am I going to do without you?'

Pauline passes Millie to the nurse and takes Oscar in her capable arms. He's crying properly now. Sobs are shaking his body but his 'wicked stepmother' holds him steady. I know she'll love him as much as he'll let her.

'You can live at Tilda's flat, son. Adam's put it in trust for Millie, but you can look after it for her for a minimal rent... and if you look after the cat...'

'I'll take the cat,' Oscar says abruptly.

'Good. That's settled.'

Tears are rolling down Dad's cheeks. He turns to me. 'Tilda, darling. I'm here. We're all here for you, my best and most beautiful daughter. I've been so proud to be your daddy. You'll be in my heart for ever. Say hello to your mother for me.'

The chaplain clears his throat. Dr Arnold and the nurse approach my bed. The nurse gently removes the ventilator from my mouth.

Dad! Listen to me. Don't do this. I don't want to die. It's not too late to change your mind.

The nurse wheels the IV stand into the corner and begins the task of removing the sticky plasters and electrodes from my body. Lastly she removes the cannula in my hand.

Pauline brushes the hair from my forehead and gently closes my eyes with the flat of her palm. 'That's better.'

'Praise be to the God and Father of our Lord Jesus Christ!' the chaplain intones.

Oscar swears under his breath.

'In his great mercy he has given us new birth into a living hope through the resurrection of Jesus Christ from the dead, and into an inheritance that can never perish, spoil or fade. This inheritance is kept in heaven for you.'

Oscar! Help me. I'm begging you. Don't let them do this. Please. I'm sorry for all the times I've made you feel bad about yourself. I know it wasn't your fault that Mum died. I love you, really I do… You know I love you…

'In all this you greatly rejoice, though now for a little while you may have had to suffer grief in all kinds of trials. These have come so that the proven genuineness of your faith – of greater worth than gold, which perishes even though refined by fire – may result in praise, glory and honour when Jesus Christ is revealed.'

Why are you doing this? You're my family. You're supposed to watch over me. Keep me safe. I'm lost in the wood. Please come and find me. The breadcrumbs have all been eaten. The wolf has swallowed me whole, but you can still save me. I'm still alive inside. Daddy, please kiss my cheek and wake me up for school… Send for the woodcutter, Daddy. Send him quickly or you'll lose me forever… Lose myself forever… I'm sorry, Daddy. So sorry for all the trouble I've caused… I didn't mean to be naughty. Don't blame me. It was a stupid accident. Please make it better. Make it all go away. I want to live happily ever after.

'Though you have not seen him, you love him; and even though you do not see him now, you believe in him and are filled with an inexpressible and glorious joy, for you are receiving the end result of your faith, the salvation of your souls.'

The hospital chaplain begins the Lord's Prayer. The voices of my family follow the familiar pattern. 'And forgive us our trespasses as we forgive them that trespass against us. And lead us not into temptation, but deliver us from evil. For thine is the kingdom, the power, and the glory, For ever and ever. Amen.'

'It's time,' Dr Arnold says.

No! I don't want to go! I don't want to leave you all.

I'd give everything I have for one more moment with them, but I have nothing left to give. I'm trapped in the darkness behind my eyelids. I will never see them again.

A weight depresses my pillow. Dad's chin grazes my cheek. His kiss smells of soap and sorrow. A dreadful sob, wet with mucus, sounds in my ear. He pulls away. The pillow springs back into shape.

I hear a noise. It's the flick of a switch. A sudden silence, thick and empty now that the soft hum and intermittent beeps which I barely registered any more have stopped.

Suddenly my eyes are dazzled with light. For a moment I think I'm dead, but then I see my family seated around the bed with their heads bowed. The bearded doctor in the white coat has slipped through the door and is standing at the back of the room. Dad jumps up.

'Look! She's opened her eyes.'

'I've seen this before,' says the nurse who's holding the baby. 'It's as if they know. On the edge of passing to the other side, they wake up to say one last goodbye.'

Dad clasps my hand.

'Her breathing's so shallow,' Oscar whispers.

'It will be very gentle,' Dr Arnold says. 'She's in no pain.'

Pauline takes my father's other hand. Oscar walks abruptly to the window. The nurse has turned Millie away from me and is jiggling her up and down. I'm finding it difficult to focus.

What has my life been? A sliver of light in the darkness, darkness before and darkness after. Birth and death. Death and birth. The shocking, unexpected, painful bookends of life. Are they two sides of the same coin? Now I'm following in my mother's footsteps, leaving a new life behind and facing my own transition.

The student doctor approaches the bed. My vision is filled with the white of his coat. I wonder why he's come. There's something familiar about the expression in his eyes. He smiles, and the sad voices of my family fade to a murmur.

'Hello, Tilda. Do you remember me?'

'You've visited my room several times, doctor.'

'We were friends, a long time ago.'

'We've met before?'

'When you were a child.'

'Did we used to play together? I think I remember. It's a bit blurry. Are you going to help me?'

'Your injuries are self-inflicted.'

'I know it was my fault. I was stupid, careless. But I wasn't trying to kill myself, honestly. I don't want you to think that. I don't want to die. I messed up. I'm sorry, sorry for all of it. I thought I knew everything, but I understood nothing.'

'Some wounds are slow to heal, particularly the ones that are old and deep.'

'Please put me back on life support before it's too late. Tell Dr Arnold I need more time. There must be hope. I'm talking to you now, aren't I? Can't they see I'm conscious?' I look around the room in surprise but there's no one with me but the student doctor. 'Where did they go?'

'They've entrusted you to my care. Do you trust me?'

'Can you save me?'

'Time's short.'

'Please… Please help me. You're my last chance.'

'Yes… I am.'

He pours water from the jug by my bedside into a plastic cup. There's a single red rose in a vase on the cabinet. Inspector Lake left it in my room yesterday. He stood and watched me for some minutes before squeezing my hand and leaving. I know now he was saying his final goodbye.

'Would you like a drink of water?'

'I'm very thirsty.'

He smiles again. My heart jumps. With a flutter I recognise the eyes of my imaginary childhood friend in the eyes of the man.

'You remember me now?'

'Yes… I sent you away.'

'But I never stopped watching over you.'

He offers me the cup. My mouth is as dry as a sack of sand. The gap between us is only a couple of inches but it's an unbridgeable chasm. I know it's my last chance. I'm terrified I won't be able to move my hand one final time and reach the beaker. *Right hand little finger. Right hand ring finger. Right hand middle finger. Right hand index finger. Right hand thumb.* A barely perceptible twitch jerks my fingers forward. He immediately stretches down and grasps my arm with his other hand. He pulls me easily into a sitting position, as though I'm as light as a wisp of smoke, and puts his arm around my shoulders. He lifts the cup to my lips. The water slips down my throat like cool silk.

He steps back and takes a book from the pocket of his jacket. 'I've been reading an interesting story.'

I lick a drop of water from my lips. It tastes like peaches and freedom and whitest snow. I don't want to appear rude so I ask him what it's about.

'It's about the past… A history, of sorts.' He flicks to the back. 'I've reached the last page.'

'Does it have a good ending?' He runs his finger down the paper, scanning the words.

'Yes, it does. And now it's finished.'

With a jolt of surprise, I notice a trail of spindly black lines crawling from between the leaves of the book. They hesitate on the edge of the cover, then launch themselves haphazardly into the air, like a cloud of crane flies. As they float past my face, I realise they're the letters of the alphabet.

And now a larger flock is squirming free from the book. Entire words are wheeling around my bed like starlings. The white spaces between them run like rivers. Meanings wash through me, reverberating from the past. Sentences appear in a trail of black feathers, at first chaotic and random, then increasingly familiar.

Only the scientific method leads to truth… Surely it's better to keep wishing for something after death than believe in a future with no love or justice or hope… Everything on this planet was born from an exploding star… We merely return to the unchanging pot of energy that makes up our universe… And what about those parts of ourselves that aren't made up of atoms? Consciousness, soul, spirit, mind, whatever you like to call it… And how do you explain love?

Conversations circle near the ceiling, excreting random words onto the floor. Thoughts are flocking together, forming dark shadows of belief and desire. Fragments from the inner monologue of the last few months fling themselves against the window in an effort to escape, splitting apart, wheeling and dipping, reforming in an ominous cloud.

He holds up the book. The pages are clean and white. 'Are you ready to write a new chapter?'

I look down at my body. My limbs are no longer twisted with spasticity. The skin on the back of my hands is smooth and pink. I hold my fingers before my face and move them as though playing an arpeggio. I slip my legs over the edge of the bed. There's no more pain. I stand and bear my weight.

'Yes. I'm ready.'

The door of my hospital room stands open. The air dances with light. Everything is clear. Everything is seen and answered. All the love from my life is with me. I can already smell the fragrance of my mother's smile – and something greater, unbounded. A vast freedom.

He stretches out his arms. I've never seen an expression such as his before. All previous loves have been a shadow of this. 'Come. Let's walk through the door together,' he says.

And with my hand in the hand of the one who holds the key of all unknown, I do.

References

Chapter 3
'Ashes to ashes, dust to dust' is taken from the *English Burial Service*, found in the Anglican *Book of Common Prayer, 1662*.

Chapter 12
'... there are more things in heaven and earth, Tilda Moss, than are dreamt of in your philosophy' is a reference to 'There are more things in heaven and earth, Horatio, Than are dreamt of in your philosophy' by William Shakespeare, *Hamlet*, Act I, scene 5, lines 167–168.

Chapter 13
Who Moved the Stone? by Frank Morison (Authentic Media, 2006)

Chapter 23
The hospital chaplain is using The Marriage Service from *Common Worship: Pastoral Services (2000)* © The Archbishops' Council 2000.

Chapter 28
'We is born to trouble as sure as sparks fly upwards,' is a reference to 'Yet man is born to trouble as surely as sparks fly upwards.' Job chapter 5 verse 7 from the New International Version of the Bible (2011 UK).

Chapter 29

The words of the hospital chaplain are taken from 1 Peter chapter 1 verses 3–4 and verses 6–9 from the New International Version of the Bible (1984).

The extract from the Lord's Prayer is taken from the Anglican *Book of Common Prayer*, 1662

'... my hand in the hand of the one who holds the key of all unknown' is a reference to the hymn *God Holds the Key of All Unknown* written by Joseph Parker in 1887. I heard this hymn for the first time in 2016 at the funeral of a 98-year-old friend. Its opening line inspired the title of this book.

Resources

I enjoyed reading or dipping into the following books during the writing of *The Key of All Unknown*:

Andsell, Gary, *Music for Life: Aspects of Creative Music Therapy with Adult Clients* (London: Jessica Kingsley Publishers, 1995), particularly the section relating to music therapy for a patient in a coma.

Barrow, John D., *The Origin of the Universe* (London: Weidenfeld & Nicolson, 1994).

Bryson, Bill, *A Short History of Nearly Everything* (London: Transworld Publishers, 2003).

Casti, John L., *Searching for Certainty: What Science Can Know about the Future* (London: Scribners, 1991).

Dalrymple, Theodore, *Anything Goes: The Death of Honesty* (Croydon: Monday Books, 2011).

Davies, Paul, *The Last Three Minutes: Conjectures About the Ultimate Fate of the Universe* (London: Weidenfeld & Nicolson, 1994).

Lennox, John C., *God's Undertaker: Has Science Buried God?* (Oxford: Lion Hudson, 2007).

Ortberg, John, *Know Doubt: The Importance of Embracing Uncertainty in Your Faith* (Grand Rapids: Zondervan, 2008).

Ortberg, John, *When the Game is Over it All Goes Back in the Box* (Grand Rapids: Zondervan 2009)

Peterson, Eugene H., *The Message: The Bible in Contemporary Language* (Colorado Springs: NavPress, 2002), particularly the books of Job and Lamentations.

K. A. Hitchins studied English, Religious Studies and Philosophy at Lancaster University, graduating with a BA (Hons) First Class. She later obtained a Masters in Postmodern Literatures in English from Birkbeck College, London. She is married with two children.

Stay in touch with the author via her website: www.kahitchins.co.uk
Follow her on Twitter @KathrynHitchins
or connect via her Facebook page: K.A. Hitchins, author

Also by K. A. Hitchins:

Vincent's world has imploded. Only by confronting the past will he discover his future.

High-flying financier Vincent Stevens has lost everything in the economic crash – smart London flat, trophy girlfriend, champagne lifestyle – and is forced to return to the village of his birth. Dogged by family obligations and unsettling childhood memories, he wants his extravagant life in the City back at any cost. But then he meets Sarah, the enigmatic girl whose friendship will throw everything he values into question. A surprising discovery forces him to make the biggest decision of his life. Will he return to a world defined by winners and losers, or will he choose love?

'Touching, poignant, inspiring and beautifully written.'
Michele Guinness, author of Archbishop

'I can't wait to see the movie!'
Sean Paul Murphy, award-winning screenwriter, The Encounter, Sarah's Choice